SUN BROKEN

A Wild Hunt Novel, Book 11

YASMINE GALENORN

D1518522

A Nightqueen Enterprises LLC Publication

Published by Yasmine Galenorn

PO Box 2037, Kirkland WA 98083-2037

SUN BROKEN

A Wild Hunt Novel

Copyright © 2020 by Yasmine Galenorn

First Electronic Printing: 2020 Nightqueen Enterprises LLC

First Print Edition: 2020 Nightqueen Enterprises

Cover Art & Design: Ravven

Art Copyright: Yasmine Galenorn

Editor: Elizabeth Flynn

A Nightqueen Enterprises LLC Publication

Published in the United States of America

ACKNOWLEDGMENTS

Welcome back into the world of the Wild Hunt. We're at book eleven, and the start of the second story arc. The future is looming dark as Typhon rises and his emissaries begin to emerge. I love the world of the Wild Hunt, and am so grateful you do too. It's become a living, breathing entity in my thoughts and imagination.

Thanks to my usual crew: Samwise, my husband; Andria, and Jennifer—without their help, I'd be swamped. To the women who have helped me find my way in indie, you're all great, and thank you to everyone. To my wonderful cover artist, Ravven, for the beautiful work she's done.

Also, my love to my furbles, who keep me happy. My most reverent devotion to Mielikki, Tapio, Ukko, Rauni, and Brighid, my spiritual guardians and guides. My love and reverence to Herne, and Cernunnos, and to the Fae, who still rule the wild places of this world. And a nod to the Wild Hunt, which runs deep in my magick, as well as in my fiction.

You can find me through my website at Galenorn.com and be sure to sign up for my newsletter to keep updated on all my latest releases! If you liked this book, I'd be grateful if you'd leave a review—it helps more than you can think.

Brightest Blessings,
~The Painted Panther~
~Yasmine Galenorn~

WELCOME TO SUN BROKEN

Sometimes, all you can hope for is to make it through the storm intact...

Typhon, the Father of Dragons, is waking up. Amid the fallout, a serial killer with a hidden agenda emerges, targeting necromancers, psychics, and anyone who can control or deal with the dead. When the cops can't find a clue as to who's doing this, and the body count rises, the deputy mayor approaches Herne and the Wild Hunt, asking for their help.

Ember and the Wild Hunt head out on the trail of the killer, only to find themselves drawn into the dark underbelly of the Vampire Nation as they try to prevent the assassin from striking again. But the killer's far more dangerous than anyone predicted, and next in the line of danger is Raven BoneTalker. Can Ember and Herne keep her safe, or will the killer slide beneath their radar and claim Raven as their next victim?

Reading Order for the Wild Hunt Series:

CHAPTER ONE

The new moon had just passed, and the only sign of her presence was a thin crescent as she moved into her waxing cycle. I gazed up at the sliver of light as I waited beside the massive maple tree in the park. The leaves were almost full size, and they whispered lightly in the April night. We were into a warm streak, with the days running in the high sixties and the nights in the upper fifties. Beltane was nearing—a little over two weeks away—and I could feel the energy build, especially when I was around Herne. It had been a year since he had come into my world and changed everything in my life.

I turned at a low huffing sound and there he stood, my magnificent god, in his alter shape. The silver stag glimmered, brilliant and luminous, his back as tall as me, antlers rising like silver tines against the shroud of darkness that surrounded us.

He slowly approached me and I bowed my head. I always felt his divinity more when he was in his stag form. He leaned down to breathe against my cheek and

1

the scent of his musk swept over me. I threw my arms around his neck, gazing into those sloe eyes, and pressed my face against his throat.

"I love you," I whispered. "I cannot believe how much I've come to love you."

He gently stepped away from me, kneeling onto his front knees. I swung up onto his back and leaned forward, bracing myself with my hands on either side of his neck. He stood, waiting for me to give him the signal.

When I was properly situated, I said, "I'm ready," and we were off, racing through the woods under the pale moonlight. Herne wove through the trees toward a ravine, and down we went, through the undergrowth, a blur of movement. In his silver stag form, Herne could move faster than any normal stag or elk. This was his domain. The forest was his world, and as Lord of the Hunt, he ruled over it with his father, Cernunnos, the Lord of the Forest. Together, they embodied the woodlands of the world, and their presence was within every leaf of every tree, every animal that called the forest home. They embodied the wild, and ran with the Wild Hunt.

And...Herne was my boyfriend.

That last thought made me laugh. It seemed so *mortal*, but the gods shared a number of traits with mortals, with the Fae, the humans, and shifters alike. And when I had gone to work for the Wild Hunt—the agency, not the actual Hunt—a year ago, I had quickly fallen for Herne, and he had, against all odds, fallen for me.

I wasn't sure how long we had been running, it could have been five minutes or twenty, but Herne pulled to a stop next to a trickling stream. The greater Seattle area was rife with both ravines and streams, and the forest wild permeated the cities around the area with tenacious fingers, large swaths spreading between the condos and skyscrapers, shading the spacious streets of the city. The grass and weeds continuously broke through the concrete on sidewalks, jutting up through the cracks to prove that nothing manmade could keep the wild at bay for long.

Herne kneeled and I slid off his back, my thighs warm from pressing against his sides. I wandered over to the stream, kneeling beside the bank. The water played like music and I could sense there were several elementals nearby, dancing through the eddies and swirls that splashed over the stones at the bottom of the streambed.

Here in Western Washington, almost all creeks trickled over a bed of the rounded river rocks that had been left in the wake of the alluvial deposits. As I reached toward the whitecaps, a spray of water rose up, forming into a translucent being that was vaguely humanoid. It reached out and touched my fingers, and I closed my eyes as we met.

I know you. You are one of the water Fae.

The thought came unspoken, filling my mind. Only it wasn't a thought in words, but in emotions—a sense of familiarity. I smiled at the gentle mind-touch.

Like recognizes like. I am part Leannan Sidhe, I answered. *How are things here in the park? Is everything going as it should?* I patterned the thoughts into emotions and images that the water elemental would understand.

Herne and I were reconnoitering. We had heard rumors that there were unnatural forces stirring in the park. Given the current state of affairs, we had decided to

3

check it out for ourselves. There was too much at stake to just hope for the best or rely on rumor.

The elemental paused, then I felt a quiver of fear coming from it.

I have seen nothing unusual, but something is approaching. There are those who have rested in the arms of the forest for many years, deep in their death sleep, who are now slumbering uneasily. Their bodies are long gone but their spirits are approaching a wakeful state. What lures them out of their long sleep, I do not know.

And with that, the water spirit dove into the stream and flowed back into the current, and within seconds, it was gone.

"What did it say?" Herne asked from behind me.

I turned to face him. He was in his human shape now, rugged and gorgeous, with shoulder-length hair the color of wheat that was approaching his mid-back. I'd asked him to let it grow—I loved a man with long hair, and Herne wore it well. He had a five-o'clock shadow, the stubble making his jaw look even stronger, and his eyes were cornflower blue. He was wearing a pair of dark jeans and a leather jacket over a dark blue muscle shirt. His belt buckle—a silver stag—gleamed in the dim light from the sliver of moon overhead. I had given it to him on Valentine's Day, and he wore it constantly now. He was wearing motorcycle boots, with chains and studs.

"According to the elemental, the spirits who have made their rest in the park are waking up. From what I gathered, given the images it showed me, these are mostly spirits of Native Americans who died on this land before any settlers came in, though there are also some of the settlers here, and a few people who've been murdered here. They're all spirits who should have moved on, who should be long gone. As to *what's* responsible for waking them up, I have no idea and neither did the water spirit." I rubbed my chin, glancing around us.

The Seattle area had been inhabited for at least four thousand years, first by the earliest Coast Salish natives, and then, starting in the mid-1800s, by European settlers coming in. Plenty of people had lived and died in the area.

Herne regarded me gravely. "Typhon?"

I pressed my lips together, then let out a sigh. "Probably."

"Reports are coming in from Mielikki's Arrow, Odin's Chase, and all the other agencies like ours. This is happening worldwide. Typhon may still be in the process of waking, but his reach is extending out to affect all areas of the world." Herne sat down on a nearby boulder, frowning. "We knew this was coming."

"I know." I didn't want to think about it, but we had to face the fact that we were running on borrowed time. It wouldn't be long and the world would be a chaotic mess when the dead returned, in both spirit and physical form. And all we could do was wait, and take care of the collateral damage when it arose.

"Come here." He held out his arms.

I sat on his knee, leaning against him as he wrapped his arms around me. He reached up to kiss my nose, the warmth of his breath stirring my blood. I moaned gently as his tongue slid between my lips, and he shifted, lifting me into his arms as he stood. He carried me over to a mossy bank beside the stream and lay me down, kneeling beside me.

"Jeans off," he whispered.

I unbuckled my belt and unzipped, sliding my jeans down, along with my underwear. As I tugged them off over my boots, he whipped off his belt, then followed suit, his jeans down by his knees. He was facing me as I lay back on the grass, his eyes glowing in the darkness surrounding us. The fire rose inside me, and I pulled up my shirt and began to finger my nipples beneath the lace of my bra. Herne let out a wicked laugh and knelt between my thighs, his tongue searching for my center, bathing me lightly at first and then harder. I caught my breath and reached down to tangle my fingers in his hair.

He wrapped his hands around my hips, holding me firmly as the swirl of his tongue drove the fire higher. I moaned, wanting to feel him inside me, wanting him to drive the length of his shaft deep into my core.

"Fuck me," I whispered, reaching down to pull him up.

Herne's eyes glinted, shining as they began to glow. He let out a low grunt and grabbed hold of me, rolling so I was on top. I slid down on his shaft, dropping my head back as I braced myself against him, hand to hand. I laughed, feeling wanton and powerful, and as I began to ride him, he laughed again, lifting me up as he thrust to meet me.

I let go of his hands and he clasped my waist. "Touch yourself," he ordered.

I reached down with one hand to slide my fingers across my clit, and with my other, I cupped my breast, shaking my hair out to stream down my back.

I rode him hard, and as the stars began to wheel overhead, I felt dizzy with our passion. With one swift move, he smoothly rolled me over, still inside me, and began to drive himself deep into me, his chest pressed against mine.

"You're mine, love. You belong to me," he said, his voice husky. His eyes were glowing fully now and he began to thrust in earnest, driving me hard against the soft moss below us. The scent of spring soil rose to greet us, mixed with the spray of the stream. The smell of wild roses surrounded us, heady and intoxicating. I closed my eyes, merging into the energy of the Hunt. Herne was everywhere around me, and the feel of the forest called to my blood, to my heritage.

I let go, spiraling into the web we wove between us. The magic of our sex built the world anew each time we came together. As we renewed our passion and our love, I could sense the journey stretching out ahead of us. It was still new, but I had set foot on a road from which I couldn't turn away. I had made my decision, and nothing in the world would ever be the same.

"Ember, my love," he whispered as he gave one final thrust and then stiffened, pinning me to the earth below. I let go even as he did, capitulating as the waves dragged me under. As I sank into the orgasm, the world expanded, the storm shaking me to the core. I burst into tears, over-whelmed, and pulled him tightly against me.

Herne rested his head on my breast, breathing hard as the ripples of our climax began to subside. After a moment, he raised his head, his hair tickling me as it trailed down to caress my skin. "Never leave me," he whispered. "Stay with me, Ember. Please."

I gazed deep into his eyes, and right there, right then, I realized that I had everything I wanted in my life. "I don't plan on going anywhere," I whispered back, kissing him on the nose. "I don't think I could leave if I wanted to. You and I are too tightly bound for me to leave you. You've become a part of my life, a part of my world. A part of *me*."

He kissed me again, and we rested in the shade of the forest as the stars continued to wheel overhead in the darkened sky.

ON OUR WAY BACK TO HIS HOUSE, I FOUND MY THOUGHTS returning to the park. Even though I had been focused on sex, the moment we dressed I began to notice the energy that the elemental had warned us about. The forest felt uneasy, and though the magic from our union had calmed the immediate area, it didn't take long for it to begin to feel agitated again.

"Can you feel it?" I asked.

Herne gave me a solemn nod. "Actually, yes. The forest is ill at ease. I'll come out later and speak to the trees, see if they have anything to tell me." He shook his head. "I fear we haven't even begun to see the effects that Typhon will bring with him."

Typhon was the Father of Dragons, a Titan who had been cast into stasis thousands of years ago, but now had managed to shake himself out of his slumber. And as he woke, the dead would follow him, returning from the spirit world to enter ours, for he was born of Tartarus— the god who meted out punishment to the dead.

We had been preparing for Typhon's arrival for several months, ever since Cernunnos and Morgana had first warned us of his approach. While we at the Wild Hunt Agency couldn't take him on, we were assigned to take care of collateral damage while the gods worked together to find a way to drive him back into stasis. So far, they didn't have a clue on how to do that.

"Come, let's get home before sunrise," Herne said, stepping back from me. I shielded my eyes as he transformed into his stag self. The light was so bright that it almost blinded me. As he knelt for me again to straddle his back, I couldn't help but wonder how many nights we would have left to run free in the woods and make love under the stars. How long before Typhon stretched out his wings to cover the light? And how much longer before our days—and our nights—were spent chasing down the dead?

But at least, Herne would be at my side, and for that, I was ever grateful.

My name is Ember Kearney, and I'm a tralaeth. That's an ugly word that I've reclaimed. I'm half–Dark Fae and half–Light Fae, and according to the Fae Courts, never the twain should meet. But they did, in the forms of my father, who was Dark Fae, and my mother, who belonged to the Light Court. When I was fifteen, they were murdered for daring to love across borders, and as the product of their love, I was considered untouchable in the Fae Courts, a half-breed who shouldn't exist. As far as I was concerned, they could all go fuck themselves. My parents' families had been in on the double murder, and I had no use for any of them save for one uncle whom I had only recently met.

Until a year ago, I had set myself up as a freelance

investigator/bounty hunter, but then life had intervened. In the space of twenty-four hours both I and my best friend, Angel, had gone from struggling to make our way in the world to being employed by Herne, who ran the Wild Hunt Agency. My official job was to help keep peace between the Fae Courts—or, at least, helping to contain the collateral damage, which seemed terribly ironic given my heritage.

But that job had expanded, and now in addition to keeping the ever-warring factions from offing innocent people with their petty sparring, we had branched out to facing the coming darkness. And somehow, within a very short time, Herne and I had been drawn together, and I was learning what it meant to be the consort of a god.

And to complicate matters, I was pledged to his mother Morgana, a goddess of the Fae and of the sea. And my father had been pledged to Herne's father—Cernunnos. In the past year, I had seen things I never dreamed existed, and I had passed through the Cruharach—a ritual all members of Fae undergo as a rite of passage when they come of age.

A lot had changed in a single year, but even with the coming shadow, I wouldn't alter anything that had happened. For the first time in my life I belonged to something bigger than myself. I had my own home, I had friends who formed an extended family, and I had found love. And all the darkness in the world couldn't overshadow all of that.

I YAWNED AND DRAGGED MYSELF UNDER THE SHOWER. I

didn't like pulling all-nighters, but we had no other choice than to check out reports when they came in. It was seven A.M. and we needed to dress and head into work. After soaping all the grime off, I blasted myself with cold water and almost shrieked, but it shocked my system enough to drive the brain-fog away.

After toweling off and blow-drying my hair, which had grown noticeably longer over the past year, I dressed in a spare outfit I had left at Herne's—a blue corset over black jeans. I fastened a silver belt around my waist and zipped up my stiletto ankle boots. I didn't anticipate needing to go gallivanting around the forest today, and if the need did arise, I kept a spare pair of boots at work, one more suitable for tromping in the woods.

"Triple-shot mocha?" Herne asked as I entered the kitchen. While I showered and dressed, he had grilled ham and cheese sandwiches and was now pulling shots of espresso.

"Quint shot, please. I need more caffeine than that to make it through the day. All-nighters aren't that easy, even for the Fae. We don't all have the constitution of a god." I stuck out my tongue at him.

He playfully returned the gesture. "Fine. Five shots. Seriously, though, if you need a nap, you can come in late." He didn't even look winded.

"No, that wouldn't be fair to the others. I'll manage, though I may grab a few winks this afternoon, if we're not run ragged." I paused, sniffing. I could still smell his musky scent from where I was standing. "Um, not to be indelicate, but don't you need a shower before we go? I love your scent, but…"

"But I'm a little funky for the office?"

11

"I was going to use the word 'rank' but yeah, that works," I said, grinning.

He laughed and handed me my drink. "You eat and I'll have a quick rinse." He headed for the bedroom.

I slid onto a tall stool at the kitchen island, taking a long sip of the iced mocha before devouring my breakfast. I was still hungry when I finished, so I poked through the cupboards and found a box of doughnuts. Herne kept plenty of snacks around for me. The gods didn't need to eat nearly as much as the Fae or even humans, but he liked food and made sure his fridge was well stocked. I had finished my second one and was on my third when he re-entered the room, clean-shaven, tidy, and smelling like fresh rain.

"Yum, the new bath wash you bought does the trick." I polished off the rest of the doughnut. "I left your sand-wich alone."

"How generous," he said, catching me by the waist and pulling me in for a long kiss. He swatted my ass. "All right, love, let's get this show on the road."

As we gathered our things and headed out to the car, I paused, staring at the sky. It was a clear morning and the sun was shining, but there seemed to be a pall over the city. With a sinking feeling, I realized it wasn't smog. It was an energetic cloud, hanging low and ponderous. I could sense when a storm was about to break, and right now, I could sense a dark one on the horizon. Suddenly pensive, I kept my thoughts to myself as we headed downtown.

CHAPTER TWO

*D*owntown Seattle was bustling. The Seattle area only got about sixty-five cloud-free days a year, and full sunshine was so rare that almost everybody was out and about, taking advantage of the good weather. The streets were packed with early shoppers and people on their way to work. Most of the big corporations, especially the high-tech industry, allowed flextime, so the early morning crowd was sizable.

Seattle was a vibrant city, and its nickname—the Emerald City—was well deserved. The tree-lined streets were wide and spacious, although riddled with potholes. The city grew upward rather than out, due to the limited confines of the shoreline, so skyscrapers dominated the skyline, and a dizzying array of sleek new office buildings interwove with the old red brick walkups and the concrete behemoths.

Down on the docks, the ferries chugged in from across Puget Sound, ferrying in commuters. Only a block or so away from the harbor, the Viaduct Market—once known as Pike Place Market—held sway over the downtown area. Like an enclosed bazaar, hundreds of vendors set up their daily markets selling everything from flowers to food to clothing to services.

The Wild Hunt was in Old Town, which had originally been known as the Pioneer Square area. The five-story brick walkup was on First Avenue, a wide, tree-lined street that was home to a number of the *streeps*, the ever-present street people who chose, either unwillingly or willingly, to make the city itself their home. They slept in homeless shelters or crashed at the flophouses or hunkered down in the back alleys, and during the day they panhandled, offering music or dancing or other talents for their money. We knew a number of the locals by name, and they were mostly good sorts, though a few were lost in a fog, and even fewer were dangerous.

Across the street from the five-story walkup that housed the agency was an array of fetish brothels, all legal, offering all sorts of kink for a price. They were kept busy, but we never had any trouble from the sex workers or their clients. Tattoo shops, delis, and small restaurants were interspersed among the sex-for-hire shops, and a pot shop had recently joined the lineup. MJ's House brought in a lot of business for everybody, given the combinations of pot and sex, and pot and food, were irresistible.

We jogged up the concrete stairs leading to the main floor of the building. Recently the owner of the building had, by order of the city, began installing a handicapped access ramp to the side. When done, it would curve around to the left like a backward "C," starting right of the stairs. The landlord had also agreed to do more than a jury-rig fix on the elevator, which was constantly breaking down.

The first floor of the building housed an urgent care clinic focused on treating the SubCult, though humans were welcome to come in if they needed help. The second floor was home to a daycare and preschool for low-income mothers, the third floor belonged to a yoga and dance studio, and we had the fourth floor. The fifth floor had long remained empty, but someone had finally rented it out and now we had an alternative-care clinic overhead. With a chiropractor, three massage therapists, two acupuncturists, and a nutritionist, the Stone & Needle had brought in a steady stream of clients in the month since it had opened in mid-March.

Herne and I took the elevator to the fourth floor. The car opened right into our waiting room. At night we locked it to prevent anyone from accessing our floor. Only the janitor and building owner had keys to it besides us.

Angel looked up as we entered the building. She was frowning, and before we could even say good morning, she motioned for us to stop at her desk. "The deputy mayor booked an appointment this morning. She'll be here at ten and she wants the entire agency at the meeting. I told her Charlie couldn't be there, but he's going to Skype in to hear what she has to say."

Herne frowned. "Any time Maria asks to see us, it usually means trouble."

"She sounded tense. I could tell something's seriously wrong and it's going to get dumped in our laps." Angel was extremely good at reading people, just by their voice. She had never really utilized her empathic nature before, but now she was working on expanding her abilities, and she had made some remarkable strides, especially during the past month.

"All right. You say she'll be here at ten?" Herne asked.

Angel nodded. "That's what she said. I ordered some pastries and sparkling water."

"I'll be in my office, getting ready." He gave me a quick kiss before disappearing into his office.

I sat down in the chair opposite Angel's side of the desk. "I'm so tired. We didn't get home till almost dawn."

"Did you find anything?"

I shook my head. "Not exactly, but the water elementals in the park say that the spirits are waking up—spirits that should be long gone."

"Not good. But we're probably going to be in for this a lot. I assume we're going to hand the cases off to Raven?"

Raven BoneTalker didn't work for us, but we occasionally sent cases her way. She was one of the Ante-Fae, and she was a bone witch. She was also a good friend of ours.

"Yeah, and others like her, if she gets inundated. I know that Herne's looking into a few necromancers we might be able to trust." I yawned. "How's Mr. Rumblebutt?" Mr. Rumblebutt was my cat. He was a black Norwegian Forest cat, and he adored Angel, so when I stayed at Herne's, he was absolutely fine until I came home.

"Mr. Rumblebutt was purring up a storm when I left home this morning." She frowned, staring at me. "You sure you don't need a nap?"

"*Of course* I need a nap. But it wouldn't be fair to the rest of you if I took the day off."

"Not fair? Hey, you worked all night. Charlie works at night. You'll notice that he's not in here in the morning. Of course, he can't be, given he's a vampire." She pushed a file folder across her desk toward me. "Here's the breakdown of the expenses on the Quatro case. You ended up spending more on the case than you earned from it."

I sighed. Vivi Lind Quatro had hired us to do one thing: she had wanted us to eradicate a serious case of garden noles, small but dangerous creatures that liked to hang out in gardens. They had the intelligence of a toddler, the temperament of a badger, and they had *very* sharp teeth. Luckily, unlike nixienacks, they didn't travel in packs.

We had taken the case thinking it would be a simple one, but unfortunately, the noles had proven trickier than we expected. It had cost us a lot more time and manpower than we had originally quoted. Herne was always good to his word, so we ended up losing money on the case. I wasn't sure how much, but I knew it hadn't been cheap, given the tenacity of the noles.

"Thanks." I opened the file to me and scanned the figures. We had lost over two thousand on the case. Grimacing, I said, "It's not like we can't afford to do pro bono work, but seriously, that was a hot mess." I yawned again. "Excuse me. I have one hell of a headache brewing."

"Try to get some rest. Herne's a god. *He* can go for days without sleep if he needs to. You're not a goddess, and even the Fae need to sleep."

I flashed her a grin. "That's the truth. Well, I'll be home tonight. I'm not up for another night without sleep. Besides, tonight's our meeting with Marilee and she'll have our heads if we skip again."

Marilee was my magical mentor, and she had taken on Angel as well. I was learning to actually utilize my magical abilities with water, and Marilee was teaching Angel some basic magical skills. Angel was proving adept, so much so that I suspected she had some magic-born blood somewhere in her background. Mama J. had been adept with the cards, and Angel had inherited her empathic nature.

"True that." Angel held up the Quatro file. "Are you done with the case?"

"Yeah, as much as we can be. Noles always come back, but we're not going to make the same mistake twice. If we have to go out there again, we're charging more."

"I'll file it then." She tossed it in the to-file bin on her circular desk.

I yawned. "I'll be in my office until the staff meeting. See you in the break room." I wandered off down the hall, turning to the left at the end. My office was near the end of the hall, on the right. I shut the door behind me. Staff meeting was at nine-fifteen, and it was barely eight. I decided I might as well take Angel's advice so I set my phone alarm for nine, curled up on the sofa that sat under the window overlooking the alley, and promptly fell asleep.

WHEN I WOKE UP, I FELT A LITTLE BETTER. I MAY HAVE only slept an hour, but I had slept deep and the looming headache had backtracked into the distance. I stopped in the bathroom to splash some water on my face, then gathered my tablet and notes and headed for the break room.

Talia and Viktor were there, along with Yutani. Talia

had brought a container of homemade fudge. She motioned to the pan.

"I heard you and Herne were up all night, so I thought you might be dragging butt. You want a sugar jolt?" The harpy was wearing a linen pantsuit and looked as fresh as the day was young. She had sleeked her long silver hair back into a ponytail. Something looked different about her. Since we had taken out Lazerous, the liche who had stolen her powers when she was young, she had seemed more carefree. Today she was humming under her breath.

"You seem chipper today, and thanks. I'll never say no to fudge." I accepted a piece and bit into the candy, smiling as the chocolate melted against my tongue. "Mmm, good. Peppermint." The crisp mint filled my mouth. I stared at the pan, thinking I could eat the entire thing.

"I feel good." She chuckled, staring down at her tablet.

"You've got a new beau," Yutani said, snickering. "I recognize the symptoms. You're dating someone."

Talia coughed, then gave him a long look. "What are you doing, spying on me now?"

"No, but I remember the last time you smiled like that. You had started dating Gerard." Yutani swept his hair back out of his face. The son of the Great Coyote, he was also our main techie. He often left me wondering about the man behind the mask. Yutani was reserved in a way that often left me wondering.

"Oh, *Gerard*. I haven't thought of him in a long time. I hope he's doing well, wherever he is," Talia mused. "It's been a long time. And a lot of miles."

"Well, are you?" Viktor asked. The half-ogre was poring over an issue of *X-Treme*, a magazine about extreme sports. Viktor and I had shared a common interest in our love of watching all manner of snowboarding, dirt biking, street luge, and other extreme games.

"Am I what?" Talia asked, offering me more fudge. I didn't turn her down.

"Dating someone," Viktor said.

Talia threw up her hands, surrendering. "All right, I'll tell you. Yes, I just started dating someone new and it's going well. And before you ask, he's independently wealthy, he's a wolf shifter, and his father owned a multi-million-dollar company specializing in organic baby food. Tanjin inherited the company."

"*Tanjin*? That's an unusual name, even in shifter families. So he's a shifter? What's he like?" I knew full well that Yutani would be logging into the computer, doing research on the guy. We all looked after each other, and nobody wanted to see anyone get hurt.

Talia gave me a smug look. "*Before* you start snooping, yes, he's a wolf shifter. He looks about thirty, though I think he's in his sixties. He spends his days at the office, but he's set up the organization so his sister runs the day-to-day duties, since she's vice president. Tanjin is also managing his father's fortune and he organizes charity drives. His father never donated a dime to anybody, but Tanjin and his sister, Cali, are philanthropists. Tanjin's never been in trouble with the law, he's an upstanding member of the Shifter Alliance, and he's a well-respected member of the Chamber of Commerce."

Viktor laughed. "Well, he sounds nice, and the fact that you're telling us about him means it's more than a casual fling." He turned to me. "Talia never talks about her boy toys unless they're a serious item."

I was about to ask how long they'd been seeing each other when Herne entered the room, followed by Angel. They sat down and the meeting began. We covered all the usual points, including two new potential cases that had come through in the last twenty-four hours, but we all knew we were just marking time until Deputy Mayor Serenades got there.

We didn't have long to wait. Angel hustled to open the elevators when Maria texted her to say she was on the way up. She returned with two women behind her. One was a police officer, the other the deputy mayor.

Deputy Mayor Serenades was about my height, with shoulder-length blond hair pulled back in a sleek French braid. She was trim, wearing a navy blue pantsuit, and she carried a large briefcase. The look on her face was grim as she entered the room.

Herne stood, extending his hand. "Maria, I'm glad to see you."

"Thank you, Herne. This is Officer Wyles."

As the police officer took her place near the open door leading to the hall out into the waiting room, Viktor hurried to pull out a chair for the deputy mayor.

I wasn't even sure what a deputy mayor *did*. I knew she was adjunct to the mayor, but how much actual power she wielded, I wasn't sure. I didn't want to ask, though, because it seemed rude. Instead, I just murmured a hello when Herne introduced her to the rest of us, and shook her hand as she reached across the table to everyone in turn.

As soon as she was settled in a chair, she lifted her briefcase onto the table. "The mayor asked me to talk to you because we have a problem and we need your help.

We'd like you to investigate a case that's cropped up. The police department is having trouble with it, due to the delicate nature of the circumstances."

What was this? She sounded far more worried than her expression showed.

Herne frowned. "What's going on?"

"We have a serial killer on the loose, and this is one case we're trying to keep out of the papers. The police have investigated every lead they can find and come up with nothing. Somebody's going to put two and two together soon, and when they do, the media will be all over this. We don't want them to find out. Whoever the killer is, he's smart, powerful, and deadly."

That brought the mood of the room to a crashing halt.

After a moment, Herne said, "All right, I assume you need our help because you think the killer isn't human?"

"We have no clue, though I think we can assume so. We need your help because there are a lot of the magic-born in this town, and we don't want the guilds going all vigilante, which they would." She frowned. "Dealing with the magic-born can be tricky. They've been demanding a spot on the United Coalition council and I think they'll get it, which isn't exactly a problem, but they're more powerful than most of the other groups put together. Except, perhaps, the vampires."

"And just why would the guilds go into vigilante mode?" I asked.

Maria Serenades let out a long sigh. "Because the killer is targeting necromancers, psychics, and bone witches. If he—we think it's a *he*, we don't know for sure—is targeting anyone else, we have yet to see. But it's only a matter of time before the guilds notice and demand results."

I whistled. "That's specific. The psychics—?"

"They're mediums, all of whom could talk with the dead." She shook her head. "Right now, we think the killer has a very specific target range, but we could be wrong."

"Just how many victims have there been?" Herne asked.

"Too many." Maria accepted a cup of coffee from Viktor, looking glum. "Five that we know of, over the course of five weeks. With the first two, we didn't put the pieces together. But after the third murder, one of the detectives assigned to the case noticed the pattern. Of course, Chief Johalla brought it to our attention. She keeps in close contact with the mayor."

"Chief Johalla? There's a new chief of police?" Last I'd heard, the head of the department was Fae. Johalla wasn't really a Fae surname.

"Right," Maria said, fiddling with her napkin. "I suppose you've been too busy to notice, but last month Karston, the former chief of police, resigned amidst allegations of corruption. Evidence surfaced that he had been accepting bribes from a rogue vampire who was paying him to hide evidence surrounding several vampire kills. Heidi Johalla was the deputy chief and she took over the position."

Most of the Seattle police force was made up of members of the Light and Dark Fae Courts. The new chief was going to find the going a little rocky, but I doubted that the cops would deliberately botch an investigation into a serial killer, especially one preying on the magic-born. The last thing the Fae Courts would want was a war with the magical community. *Nobody* in their right mind would want that.

"All right, leave us all the information and we'll go over it. Who do we contact if we have any questions?" Herne stared at the mound of files that Serenades was pulling out of her briefcase.

Maria sighed, glancing at me before answering. "I recommend going through Abril Gonzales. I'll leave you her number. That way, there won't be any reluctance on law enforcement's side to cooperate with you." She had a sad smile on her face.

Even though she hadn't come out and explicitly said it, I knew *exactly* what she meant. The cops weren't eager to work with me, at least those of Fae blood. They didn't like having to sully their hands working alongside a *filthy* tralaeth.

"Thank you," Herne said, inclining his head to indicate he understood. "We'll get started on this. Five victims so far, you say? Do you have any hope that the killer might have moved on?"

Maria shook her head. "No. The killings are occurring at the rate of one a week. The last victim was found yesterday. Each victim has been found on a Tuesday, so there has to be some significance to the timing. But we know that most of the victims weren't killed where they were found—the ME has discovered evidence that they've mostly been killed in what we think is a rural area, judging by the residue dirt, seeds, and debris on the bodies."

"Is the murderer using the same dump site?" Viktor asked.

"No, actually. One of the victims was found in his home. They've been scattered around the city. According to the medical examiner, each of the victims died the day before they were found—they were killed on Mondays. Someone always finds them the next day; they've been placed in areas where it would be almost impossible for someone not to find them. Several of the victims were near recluses, as far as we can tell, though some had friends and family." She frowned.

"Do you think the killer wants to get caught?"

Maria shook her head. "No, or they'd leave more evidence. I think he's either sending a message or looking for notoriety."

Herne picked up the first file and glanced inside, grimacing. "Messy."

"Don't be fooled," Maria said. "Yes, the deaths are messy, but not disorganized. There's very little evidence to show that any of the victims fought back, so they either were subdued or under a charm. Or they knew the killer and didn't realize what was happening until it was too late. We thought about bringing in someone to check for magical signatures, but since we're dealing with magic-born victims, there will always magical residue because of that."

Talia shifted in her chair. "You mean none of the victims were drugged or restrained in any way? That seems unusual."

"Oh, they were restrained, but there's no evidence that they fought back. There are marks on the hands and wrists that show they may have been shackled—except for the one who was killed at home. But the tox screens showed no drugs or recognizable sedatives. We can't test for all of the herbal drugs or magical sedatives, though, so we can't rule that out."

She glanced at the calendar hanging on the wall. "We have less than a week before the killer's due to strike again. Five weeks, and not a shred of evidence that we can find to link the victims to any one thing or place in particular, except for the fact that they're all members of the magic-born. I'm afraid you're running on borrowed time if we want to prevent another murder. Somehow, I don't think this killer's going to go away all that easily."

With that, she made her good-byes, and we were left with a mess in our laps.

CHAPTER THREE

*H*erne was silent as Angel escorted Maria out to the elevator. He refilled his coffee cup and chose a chocolate doughnut from the plate on the counter. As he settled back in his chair, Angel returned from the waiting room.

After a moment, Herne set down his cup and the doughnut and picked up the first folders. The deputy mayor had left at least fifteen files, and I figured five of those were copies of the case files and the rest were general notes.

"Well, I guess we have a priority case on our hands. What do we have on the calendar for this week?" He glanced at Angel.

"We finished the Luck case, and we just have the Vine case left, but they're gone on vacation for two weeks and asked that we postpone the investigation till they get back." She paused as Herne's phone rang.

"I'll be back in a moment," he said, answering the call as he moved to the other side of the room.

I leaned forward, staring at the case files. They seemed to loom large in my sight, and I could feel the fear and worry of the officers who had prepared them. As I stared at them, the room began to spin and…

…*THE NEXT MOMENT, I WAS CROUCHING ON A BARREN SLOPE* *of a mountain, under the blazing sun.*

It blinded me, beating down relentlessly. I tried to shade my eyes, tried to see through the glare but it was so brilliant that I could barely keep it at bay. A layer of dirt and grime covered my arms, and I was holding my sword —Brighid's Flame—balancing the point on the ground. Every cell of my body felt burnt and crisped, dry like autumn leaves, and to my left, a dark army of clouds was closing in. All I could feel was an overwhelming sense of despair, as though I had lost something precious and couldn't find it.

"Where are you?" I whispered. "Where are you?"

A susurration of wind gusted by, hot and unrelenting. In its wake, I heard a faint voice answer. *I'm still alive. I can't move. Help me, Ember…I don't know where to run.*

"Run to the shadows," I said, straightening up. "Run into the darkness, where you can hide."

There are monsters in the darkness, came the whisper.

"There are monsters, yes, but your only way to safety is through the shadows. Into the shadows, now, and I will find you." I stood, knowing I had to descend into the chaos. But before I could move, a flash of sunlight hit my eyes, scorching my sight.

I jerked away and the next thing I knew…

28

I WAS BACK IN MY CHAIR ONCE AGAIN, SITTING IN THE BREAK room.

I jumped up, panicking.

"What's wrong?" Angel asked, worry clouding her face. "Where were you? It's like you checked out for a few minutes."

I tried to catch my breath. Slowly, I stopped shaking. I tried to sort out my thoughts. "I don't know what happened. I had a vision, I think." Ever since I had started working for the Wild Hunt, I'd occasionally had visions—flashes that were usually visual premonitions, though they were often more metaphor for the warning than actual depictions of events to come.

"What did you see?" Yutani asked. He motioned to Talia. "Get her some water, please."

As Talia crossed to the sink, Yutani brought up a notepad on his laptop. "Go ahead, tell me what happened and I'll write it down for you."

I stumbled over what I could remember—giving him every detail that I could think of. "I felt…like I was inches from shattering. You know how you feel when you're burned out and running on the last dregs? I felt scorched." I accepted the water from Talia. "Thank you. I have no idea what it pertains to, but I was staring at the stack of files, so it may relate to this case. Either way, I'm dreading diving into another serial killer case, although the last one ended up with us meeting Raven, so at least it had a bright spot—" I stopped as Herne returned to the table.

"What happened?" he asked. "Are you all right?"

"I had another vision." I told him what I had seen.

"Lovely. Well, keep it in mind. Meanwhile, we have yet another headache to deal with. That was my mother, Morgana. Ember, she wants to see you tonight. You're to go through the *Fantastica* again. She's expecting you around eight P.M., our time."

"But Angel and I are due at Marilee's tonight."

"Morgana knows that. She's already contacted her. Angel, you'll go alone."

I jotted the note down on my steno pad. "All right. I take it that Aoife is still the guardian of the boat?"

He nodded. "Yes, Aoife's still there."

The *Fantastica* was Morgana's houseboat. Or rather, it was a portal into Morgana's realm, and Aoife was the gatekeeper. She was an Undine, one of the Light Fae.

The trip actually sounded pleasant to me. It was a beautiful day, and a trip down to the docks would be a welcome chance to get near the water.

"What else did your mother want?" Talia asked.

"That's the headache. Saílle and Névé are up to their old tricks again." He tapped away on his tablet. "Sending you all the information now. Looks like the truce is officially over."

For a while, the two Fae Queens had called a truce when they—and we—were facing a common enemy. But the Tuathan Brotherhood had been shoved back into the gutters of the Dark Web, and now the Fae Queens were at it again. This was what I had primarily been hired by the Wild Hunt for—to help run interference between the warring courts. Both sides had been fighting since time immemorial, since they had first divided into the Light and Dark Courts. Back in Annwn, the Celtic Otherworld where Herne came from, the great kingdoms of Navane and TirNaNog fought tooth and nail, long bloody battles that never truly ended.

Here in this realm, the cities of Navane and TirNaNog that mirrored their namesakes—though on a much smaller scale—fought more underhandedly. We stepped in when their collateral damage threatened to affect innocents outside of their courts, meaning humans, shifters, and anybody else who wasn't of Fae origin.

"What the hell are those two up to now?" I asked, finishing my coffee.

"The Light Court started it, as usual. You'd think being called 'light' they might be a little less prone to incite violence, but no such luck. Anyway, it seems that Névé is out to retrieve Callan, who is still hanging out at TirNa-Nog." He grunted. "She sent a party to try to ambush him. He was with a group of guards and they were driving down I-405. This resulted in a multi-vehicle collision."

"Injuries? Fatalities?" Viktor asked.

"Seven seriously wounded shifters and five humans in critical condition. We've been charged with collecting Callan and returning him to Annwn so Morgana can deal with him. Now that the Brotherhood is no longer a factor, neither Névé nor Saílle can offer any objections when Morgana sends him back to the time period he belongs in."

"Good luck on that," Viktor said. "I don't think either one of those broads has any clue as to what constitutes a reasonable request."

"Not to mention, now that he has a taste for the modern age, is Callan even going to *want* to return to his own time?" Talia asked.

Callan was an ancient Fae warrior/hero, who had

single-handedly driven the Fomorians—a race of giants who were the Fae's mortal enemies—back into the mountains. This was in Annwn, during the beginning of the Tuathan-Fomorian Wars. Névé and Saílle had combined forces when the Brotherhood had the Fae under duress, and they had retrieved Callan's spirit, bringing a statue of him to life to act as a vessel. He was flesh and blood all right, but he wasn't supposed to be part of our timeline and the gods had been very testy over the fact that he was running around the streets of Seattle.

"Then we're going to have to kidnap his ass and drag him before Morgana. He might not like it, but that's our job and we're going to do it." Herne lightly tossed his tablet onto the table. "I've made an appointment for us to talk to Saílle and Névé tomorrow at Ginty's."

I groaned. "Another parley? I hate that shit." I mostly objected to sitting in a room with Saílle and Névé, trying to coax them into acting like adults instead of angsty teenagers. Plus, I always came away from the parleys feeling like dirt. They never *said* anything about me, and in fact, I had to admit, more than once they had been fair, but I still knew that I was dirt in their eyes.

"Well, suck it up, buttercup. You're going. So is Viktor." Herne grinned at me, ducking as I threw a wadded-up paper towel at him. "All right, let's dive into these files and see what we're up against. Angel, steel yourself. There are morgue photos in here and, given what Serenades said, they're not pretty."

Angel let out a sigh, but shrugged. "I'm starting to get used to it. I don't like it, but I can handle it." She had toughened up a lot since we started working for Herne, but she was still the most sensitive one of us, and it hurt her to see others in pain.

"All right, let's see what we have." Herne opened the files and began to sort through them.

Twenty minutes later, we were staring at a horrifying array of images and notes. The photographs were gritty, capturing detail in the extreme. Five victims, three male and two female, and all of them caught in their death throes. The murders had been brutal.

"Joy," Angel said. "There's so much joy mingling with the fear. Excitement and glee. Whoever did this got off on it, big time." She grimaced, leaning on her elbows and holding her head. "Who could possibly get such a thrill out of torturing and killing people? I mean, I know there are perverts who do, but the reality never fails to amaze me."

Herne shook his head as I moved to give her a hug. "Angel, I know it's a lot to ask, but can you pick up anything more on the killer? We can use all the information we can use."

She sniffed, then raised her head. "I'll try."

As she closed her eyes, I quietly slipped over to the counter to get the tissues. I knew how much it pained her to pick up on the gruesome details of a case.

"They knew the person. The killer was a friend, they thought."

"Can you get anything more?" Herne frowned, jotting down notes as Angel spoke.

"Yes, a little. Whoever it is, they've got...they're huge—

but not in body. In spirit? And they're not right in the head. There's something terribly wrong. The killer is far more dangerous than we think," Angel said softly, opening her eyes. "Smart, the murderer is so smart and clever and confident. The bodies are easy to find because he—she—whoever, is taunting the cops." She grimaced. "A love for torture...a love for chaos. That's all I got."

"That helps," Herne murmured. "So we're chasing someone who gets off on torture and killing, and for some reason their targets are the magic-born. You didn't by any chance get a clue of what race? Fae? Shifter? Human?"

Angel shook her head. "No, I'm sorry. That's all I got." She took one of the tissues and wiped her eyes. "I don't ever want to meet them."

"Let's hope you don't have to. Okay, let's recap what we found in the files," Herne said before swigging his coffee. "All five victims were brutally murdered—overkill, to be precise. And from what the medical examiner said, they were alive when the torture started. Toenails and fingernails were ripped off. Teeth were pulled out. Vocal chords were severed. There were burn marks in the esophagus, indicating that they were forced to drink some form of acid—the ME thinks it was some sort of clog remover. There was lye in it. And they had marks all over their bodies that looked like the killer used a cigarette to burn them. But nothing was quite enough to kill them. That came later."

I stared at him, horrified. "Good gods. This isn't just a serial killer, but a sadist, too."

"Yeah, it looks that way. The timelines are a little hazy, but the victims were still alive after all of that. Then our killer decided to go for broke and cut out their tongues. In all cases, it looks like the victims were still alive. That is, until our psycho decided to remove their hearts. Except their hearts weren't cut out. It looks like someone *smashed* through their chests and tore them out." Herne looked a little green around the gills. I had come to realize that being a god didn't guarantee an iron stomach or the ability to handle horrific events.

He laid out the photos of the victims, before and after. "Here's what we have."

There was a brief silence as we stared at the silent testament to just how far cruelty was willing to go. Finally, Viktor shifted his chair.

"What are the common links?" The half-ogre was staring at the pictures, his face bleak. I recognized the look in him by now. He was a surprisingly sensitive man, and he hated unwarranted suffering.

"They were all mediums, bone witches, or necro-mancers," Herne said. "Other than that, the police weren't able to pinpoint too many connections. Three men, two women. Four were magic-born, but one was a tiger shifter. Three necromancers, a medium—the tiger shifter—and one bone witch. Ages ranged from young—one of the necromancers—to old, again one of the necro-mancers. They all made their home in Seattle, but only one was born here. Two were married, one divorced, two were single. They didn't know each other as far as we can tell, but two were loners and the other three each had a circle of family and friends."

I frowned. That wasn't a lot to go on. "Did they frequent the same places?"

"That we don't know yet. The cops were looking into

it, but there wasn't much that they found. There was some overlap, but they didn't find any common clubs or groups."

I gathered up the photos, not wanting to look closer but realizing that we needed to examine everything we could. "It might be too late for the earlier victims, but can we get into their homes to look for evidence?"

"I'll call the families and ask. Talia and Yutani, start researching their backgrounds. See what you can dig up on the net. Yutani, if you have to, go out on the Dark Web. Necromancers often are involved in shady dealings." Herne glanced at me. "Viktor and Ember, see if you can get into their homes. Make a list of people to interview and head out this afternoon. And all of you, we don't want this information leaking out. Right now, nobody's put it together that a serial killer is running around, but it's only a matter of time."

"What about me?" Angel asked.

"Your search-engine savvy is good. While we work on this, can you see if you can find any mention of Callan and where he's hiding? We know Saílle is protecting him right now, but if we can get any clue of where he's actually hiding…"

"Will do," she said, looking grateful for the chance to research something a little less gruesome.

"Okay, then, everybody get moving." After he dismissed the meeting, I followed Angel out to her desk.

"This is a bad one," she said, shaking her head. "I can feel it, Ember. This one's a gut-wrencher." She pulled up a browser and began to type in search words to try to locate Callan. A moment later, she paused, turning to me. "I'm afraid. Not for myself, and not even for you, but this one feels like it could get personal. I don't know how or why, but it's coming close to home. Maybe it's just the energy of Typhon beginning to infiltrate the world. I find myself avoiding driving near graveyards lately, and I keep a watch on the skies, expecting to see something coming in on the horizon."

I leaned against the post behind her desk. "I understand. I have that same uneasy feeling, and after my vision today, I'm even more leery. Do you know where your fear is lodged? If it's not you or me, then…maybe just general?"

She frowned, then shrugged. "I don't know, to be honest. I can only feel it around the periphery. Do you think this has something to do with Typhon?"

I thought about it. "Maybe. But the only link I can make is the fact that all of the victims have been connected to the psychic world, and four of them specifically focused on death magic. Maybe…hey, run a check on the psychic. See if he specialized in any particular direction. He was the tiger shifter, right?"

Angel consulted the files. "Right, Mendin Casey. He was a tiger shifter and he was single. All right. I'll let you know what I find out."

"Okay." I let out a sigh. "I better get back to my desk. Viktor and I have to head out and check out the list of names. Don't forget you'll be going to Marilee's alone."

She nodded. "Yeah. But I need you to drive me home. On the way to work this morning, my car blew something, pouring smoke out from under the hood. They still haven't pinpointed the problem, so I'll have to take a taxi over to Marilee's. And before I go, I need to pick up some things from the house." She paused. "What do you think

Morgana wants to talk to you about? I don't envy you there."

"Oh, it's not so bad," I said, smiling. "She's actually pretty cool, for a goddess. Besides, I'm dating her son. She likes me...I think. Or...*I hope*."

CHAPTER FOUR

*O*ur first stop was Mendin Casey's house. Mendin had been the tiger shifter, and he lived alone in a small two-story brick house on Kinnear Place in the Queen Anne District. We parked on the street, gazing up at the house, which sat at the top of a sloping yard. A series of concrete steps—probably twenty of them—led to the bottom of the porch, where another flight led to the front door. The yard was impeccably landscaped with tidy ferns, and the lavender and juniper bushes were neatly trimmed.

As we sat in the car, I frowned. Entering a dead man's house always felt so odd. Especially when the person had lived alone. It was like there was this sudden interruption to life as we knew it. There were always reminders that the deceased had been in the middle of something, and the house always felt heavy with unfinished energy.

"I guess we should go in. The landlady said she'd be waiting for us." I glanced at my watch. We couldn't put it off much longer.

"You sure your timing is accurate? You break watches."

It was true—watches broke around me, but Marilee had taught me a dampening spell so that I didn't leak so much energy.

"No, I think we're on time. Let's go." I stepped out of the car and smoothed back my hair. I was about as presentable as I was going to look today, and that was the best I could do.

We headed up the front steps. They were steep and cracked, with moss growing between the breaks in the concrete.

"So he was renting the place. I wonder who took care of the yard, Mendin or his landlady," I said as we headed toward the porch steps. Above the porch was a balcony that opened into what probably was a master bedroom. The brick looked clean, which meant that it had been power washed during the year to blast off the ever-present mold and mildew that permeated the area.

"By the landlady's tone on the phone, my guess is that Mendin took care of it. She said that nobody has contacted her about his belongings, so I told her we'd send someone to box them up after we look through them. We can keep them while we search for any next of kin. But Mendin was a loner, so I'm not sure how much luck we'll have there."

The landlady was waiting for us. As we reached the top of the stairs, the door opened. She introduced herself as Leela, and she was younger than I had expected, though I wasn't sure why I had expected an elderly woman. But the woman standing in front of us looked to be in her forties, and she was thin, with skin that looked like she had lived a hard life. She had wrinkles around her lips in that manner that only smokers get, and she was wearing an old pair of jeans with holes in the knees, and an olive green tank top. Her hair was flame red, curling down to her shoulders.

We showed her our identification and she let us in. Mendin had died in this house, and the blood had saturated the carpet. I blinked, staring at the mess. The house needed a hazmat team. I didn't want to touch anything.

Viktor gave me a quick look and I shook my head. I wasn't about to inflict this on the team Viktor had hired to pack up Mendin's possessions. "We can't do much about his belongings until you get a cleaning team in here. You'll need people specifically trained to handle blood and any other…tissue that might be around." I turned to Leela. "We'll take a look at his computer system and try to find next of kin, but I'm not authorizing anybody coming in here until *that* is taken care of." I pointed to the carpet. "It looks like a blood bomb went off."

"That's not my fault, and I shouldn't have to pay for the cleaning." She crossed her arms, narrowing her eyes.

"You may not have to," Viktor said. "The city has a special fund you can apply to if you've been affected by a major crime, for things like this—cleaning and car rental and so forth."

"Well…" Leela gave us a resentful look, then shrugged. "Who do I call to clean up this gorefest? I doubt Milly's Maids will tackle it."

"We'll get you the number of a cleaning company specializing in hazardous waste situations like this." I looked around, trying to avoid the stained carpet. It might be dry by now, but I had no desire to walk over Mendin's grave, so to speak. It was likely he'd been killed right in that spot, given the amount of blood. After a moment, I spotted his desk and nudged Viktor with my elbow. "Over there."

"Right. Come on, if you walk across the sofa, you can avoid the carpet."

I pushed one of the recliners sitting opposite the sofa back against the wall, leaving a narrow trail around the mess. "Or we can just go this route." We neared the desk. I glanced over my shoulder at the landlady. "Did he have any pets? Any friends that you know of?"

"Nope, and not that I knew about. Mendin kept to himself and I didn't intrude. He paid his rent on time, never made any fuss to annoy the neighbors, and he was a good tenant. Steady fellow, even if he was a shifter. I rented him this house about five years ago, and he seemed to settle right in."

Leela let out a gruff sigh and dropped into one of the chairs on the opposite side of the room. She pulled out a cigarette and, without asking if we minded, lit up. As she sat there, puffing away, I had a sudden picture of her life. She seemed older than her years, hardened by life and tired of coping with everything fate threw her way. She was worn out, and it showed on her face, in her movements, in her energy.

As we approached the desk, Leela said, "I'm not much on his kind, but for someone to do this… I just don't understand the cruelty of life, you know? I don't know what the killer did to him, but there's so much blood… I already talked to the police, but there wasn't much I could tell them. I live three blocks away, and I wasn't the one who found him."

That was the second time she'd made a questionable remark about Mendin's lineage. I glanced over at her, wondering just how far her distaste extended.

"Who did find him?" Viktor asked.

"He carpooled to work. Tuesday morning, when he didn't meet them on the street, one of his coworkers came in to find out why he wasn't answering their texts. The door was unlocked and when the guy opened it, he found him." She shook her head and went back to her cigarette.

I sat down at the desk. It was one of those simple computer desks, with a hutch over the top. There was a laptop on the desk, along with a few bills, an empty coffee mug that looked like it had been used, a bowl of M&Ms, a framed picture, and not much else. The desk didn't look like it had been disturbed.

I opened the lid and pressed the power button. It came on so quickly that I realized it had been in sleep mode. And luck was on our side—it wasn't password-protected.

I glanced at the various apps. Mendin liked to play games, that much was apparent. There were at least two dozen icons for games, most of which I recognized as either role-playing games or first-person shooter games. There were a few puzzle games as well. I opened the folder leading to his documents and scanned the files. A few were labeled as correspondence, but one bore the title "Clients." I opened that one.

Viktor was watching from behind my back. "You think the killer might be one of his clients?"

I shrugged and glanced over at Leela, who was staring off into space, in her own little world. "Leela, Mendin was a psychic, as well as a computer tech. You know that, right?"

She nodded. "When he first moved in, he and I talked about that. I knew that he told fortunes on the side, or some such thing. I never put any credence in that woo-woo shit, but as long as he paid his rent and didn't mess up the house, I didn't care."

"Did he ever tell you about any of his clients? Were any particularly troublesome?"

She narrowed her eyes, then shrugged. "I have no clue. Like I said, he kept to himself, he paid his rent, and I only dropped over when there was something to fix." She paused, then added, "I'm not comfortable around Cryptos. No offense intended."

Any empathy I had for her ended with that. I glanced at Viktor, but kept my mouth shut. We both encountered plenty of prejudice in our lives, and while I'd normally call people on it, I had no stomach for a debate today.

"I see," was all I said.

"I don't mean to sound like a bigot, but…you understand."

"I'm afraid I don't, being one of those Cryptos myself. Now, if you'll excuse us, we'll get back to our work." To Viktor, I said, "I want to take his laptop with me."

"All right. You sort through his desk and I'll take a look through the rest of the house." Viktor studiously ignored Leela as he answered.

Leela grunted, then heaved herself out of the chair and headed for the door. "I'll be outside, waiting to lock up."

"Fine. We'll be out when we're done." I waited till the door shut behind her to explode. "Why do people think it's all right to say those things to our faces?"

"Because they truly *don't* get it. They don't see why we should be offended when they insult us. It's stupid, but that's the way they are. And with people like Leela, I'd like to give them the benefit of the doubt, but it seldom works out in my favor when I do." Viktor grunted, then shrugged. "Whatever. I'm going to search the rest of the house while you finish here, and then I'll be upstairs."

As he left the room, I turned my attention back to the desk. I was sorting through the shelves when I felt someone watching me. Thinking Leela was watching through the window, I turned, but no one was there.

"Hello?" I said, shivering. I waited, but there was no answer. But I could swear someone was standing nearby. "Is that you, Mendin?"

Again, there was no answer, but I felt a stirring in the air. Swallowing, I turned back to the desk. There were a stack of bills marked "Paid," along with a few cards. I looked through them. They were birthday cards to Mendin. One of them read: *I'll love you forever—Candace*.

Who was Candace? I picked up the picture and studied it. Mendin was with a girl, and his arm was draped around her. I turned the frame over and undid the back, popping the picture out. Scrawled across the back of the photo were two names: *Mendin and Candy*, and it was dated June 8, last year.

I tried to find his phone, but all I found was a spare set of car keys. I pocketed them, then crossed to the stairs and called out to Viktor.

"Did you find his phone?"

"Yes, I'm coming down," he said. For such a big man, he was surprisingly quiet.

"I think Mendin had a girlfriend named Candace. I

wanted to look in his phone to see if she's listed in his contacts. Did the police mention anything about her in their file?" We had both skimmed the file earlier, but I couldn't remember if anything about her had been noted.

"I don't remember. Well, we have his phone. I also cleared out his medicine cabinet of any prescriptions, and I found a notebook next to his bed. It looks like he recorded his dreams so we might find something of use in there."

"So we'll take his computer, phone, and a few other things. I've gathered up his correspondence and bills." I paused, then added, "Did you feel anything upstairs? Like someone watching you?"

Viktor shook his head. "No. Why?"

"Because while you were upstairs, I had the distinct sensation that someone was watching me. I asked if anybody was there, and the air seemed to stir. I'm not certain what it was, but I'm thinking it couldn't hurt to bring in Raven and see if it's Mendin's ghost. If so, he might be able to tell us something about his killer." We were relying more and more on Raven's abilities when the spirit world came up.

Raven BoneTalker had gone from being a client to being one of Angel's and my best friends over the past six months. She was a bone witch, and one of the Ante-Fae. The Ante-Fae were the predecessors of both Light and Dark Fae, and every single one had differing powers. Far more powerful than the Fae, the Ante-Fae tended to be capricious and chaotic. Some, like Raven, were good-hearted and fun to hang out with, while others were dark and dangerous. But all of them could be deadly, and few of them lived by society's rules.

"Are you sure that wouldn't trigger off bad memories, given Ulstair?" Viktor frowned.

I sighed. "You might be right. I don't know. Let me feel her out. She seems to have put his death behind her, but you never know."

Raven's boyfriend had been kidnapped by a serial killer, and in the end, we found his body in UnderLake Park, near her home. We had found the killer, but the entire journey had been dark and the end, even darker.

After a moment, I said, "I'm not thrilled about taking on another serial killer case, I can tell you that."

"Me either. We've had too many over the past year."

"Yeah, and this one looks messy." I stared at the blood on the living room floor. The carpet was saturated and stained, and there were splatters on the furniture, too, now that I looked closer. "Let's take what seems important and get the fuck out of here." I had the sudden urge to run, to get away from the house.

Viktor nodded. "Let me find a bag to carry things in." He disappeared into the kitchen and returned with a couple of large paper bags. We filled them with the laptop, the phone, as many letters and bills as I could find, and two pictures, including the one of Mendin and Candace. When we were finally ready, we headed out to the car.

Leela was waiting to lock up. I made sure she had the names of the cleaning company and the crime unit's community liaison, so she could apply for reimbursement for the hazmat team. Once we were done, Viktor and I pulled away from the curb. I glanced back at the house. It had a forlorn look to it, and I wondered if Mendin was truly there. Had he been trapped, unable to move on given the violent nature of the crime? Finally, I pushed the thought out of my mind, because there was nothing I could do about it.

By the time we got back to the office, it was nearly three. We sorted out all the things we had gathered from Mendin onto the break room table, and Talia got started cataloguing them.

"If you can find the number of a woman named Candace, we think she might be Mendin's girlfriend. I don't know if she knows he's dead, so be cautious if you call her. We don't want to just drop a bomb on her. Also, sort out the movers with the landlady—she's a bigot, by the way. 'Cryptos make me uncomfortable,' " I said, grimacing. "But she's working with us, so just…work around that. She needs to get a hazmat team in there, as soon as possible. There's blood and tissue everywhere."

"He was killed at home?" Talia asked.

I nodded. "Looks that way, unlike the rest. Okay," I turned to Victor. "What's next on the agenda?"

"We have an appointment to meet Isolde Adella, the fourth victim's wife. Chaya and Isolde were married three years ago, and from the notes in the file, delivering the news about Chaya went about as bad as you can imagine. Isolde fainted, and when she came to, she was so broken up she could barely answer any questions."

"Where are we meeting her?" I slid on my leather jacket. Even though it was sunny, I had learned the hard way to wear a protective jacket, if possible. I had been in too many unexpected fights to go in unprotected.

"Theo's Coffee Bar. It's only three blocks away, so I

thought we could walk." He picked up his messenger bag and slung it over his shoulder.

"Coffee? I'm in for that." I slid my backpack over one shoulder and we headed out, letting Angel know we were leaving.

CHAPTER FIVE

*T*he streets were bustling. A group of wolf shifters on the corner were hustling for money, playing harmonica and guitar. They were talented, and I often stopped to listen to them and give them a few bucks. Last year, we had managed to rescue three young streeps from the streets, but there were always new ones to take their place.

"Hey bruddah," one of the wolf shifters said, holding out his hand to Viktor as we passed.

Viktor high-fived him. "Yo, Pain, how you doing?"

"The usual. Looking for a flop to share. Till I find one, gotta box in the back." Pain motioned to the alley. We'd asked him once where he got his name and he showed us a ten-inch scar on his leg where he'd been caught by an illegal trap when he'd been running in wolf form out in the forest.

I sighed, glancing at the other two shifters. Shayla, the harmonica player, was Pain's pregnant girlfriend. "I take it she's sleeping in the alley, too?"

Pain's smile slipped and I could see it hurt more than his ego when he nodded. "Yeah. I make her as comfortable as I can, but you know the system. Too many in need, and not enough to go around. Until something opens up, being on a list for housing only means you're a mark on a form."

I pulled out my wallet. I was never afraid that I'd get mugged, not around the regulars who hung out on our street corner. I pulled out five twenties and motioned to Shayla, who waddled over. I pressed them into her hand. "Use this to get yourself a room over at Rayan's House for Women." I pulled out a card and gave it to her. "Call them. They'll come and get you, since men aren't allowed to know the location."

Rayan Warren, a rabbit shifter, ran a shelter for homeless women. She charged fifty a week for a cot if the woman had the money to pay. If not, she still found a way to take her in. And if Rayan didn't have room, she'd scour the town till she found someone who could foster the woman in need.

Shayla stared at the money, then smiled gratefully. "Thank you. It's getting hard to move around much and sleeping outside is even harder."

"That will cover two weeks." I turned to Pain. "She's carrying your baby. Don't try to interfere. They won't split you guys up—at least not your relationship. But Shayla's health should come before anything at this point. No taking this money and using it for booze."

Pain was an alcoholic, but he wasn't so far gone that he'd put a bottle in front of Shayla's needs. He bit his lip. "I promise she'll call them today, right after you leave.

Thank you, Ember. Shayla and my kid, they mean every-thing to me."

Viktor pulled out his wallet and he handed Pain another fifty. "She needs a place to stay and food, and so do you. Same thing—use this for a flop and food."

Pain saluted us as we took off again. I dropped a couple bucks in the guitar case for the other member of the band. I thought it might be Pain's brother, but I wasn't sure.

As we crossed the street, I glanced at the boutique shops. The lure of kink and booze ran rampant here, and while it didn't bother me, sometimes I'd see a woman posing in the window and her eyes would meet mine, and I'd see how tired she looked, or how jaded. But at least sex workers were legal now, and they made enough to keep themselves off the streets. There were agencies devoted to helping the women—and men—find other lines of work when they were ready to move on.

Theo's Coffee Bar was two and a half blocks away from the office. It was a pleasant little hole-in-the-wall, with a lot of vibrant plants vining up the walls inside, and a wide selection of sandwiches, soup, and pastries. I ordered a triple-shot mocha, and Viktor ordered a triple-shot caramel macchiato. He led the way toward a table near the window where a lone woman sat. She was tall and willowy, and had flowing blond hair tied back with a scarf.

She glanced up as we approached the table and motioned for us to sit down. After a moment, she dipped her head, then looked up. Her eyes were luminous and wet, and I could tell that she had been crying recently.

"Isolde Adella?" I held out my hand. "I'm Ember

Kearney and this is Viktor Krason. We're with the Wild Hunt."

"I talked to you on the phone," Viktor added.

She pressed her lips together, then finally sighed. "I'm not sure what help I can be, but if there's anything I can do to catch...to find..." She stopped, a stricken look on her face. "I can't say the words. I just can't say the words."

"I understand. We'll try to be as quick as we can and if you need to stop at any time, just let us know," I said, opening my pack. I pulled out my tablet, and as I noticed her reaching for her napkin to dry her eyes, I brought out a small box of tissues I carried with me. I held it out and she took one, a grateful smile on her face. I set the box down next to her and returned my attention to my tablet.

"When did you notice that Chaya was missing?" I asked.

"Two days before her body was found. So...she was found a week ago Tuesday, that would have to be the Sunday before." Isolde stopped, counting on her fingers. "That's right, it was that Sunday. She went out for a morning run—she always liked going out early. When she didn't show up for lunch, I thought maybe she had stopped somewhere on the way home for a bite to eat, or to talk to one of the neighbors. At one, I called her, but there was no answer. By three, I still couldn't get hold of her so I checked the Find Friends app and it said she was in Maritone Park—a small neighborhood park about four blocks away. I drove down there and found her phone on a bench. That's when I called the cops."

"What did they say?" Viktor asked.

"They said maybe she took a break and forgot her phone." Isolde shook her head fiercely. "I argued with them. A morning jog wouldn't last that long, and Chaya was glued to her phone. She never went anywhere without it. They took a report and said they'd keep an eye out, but to call back if she was still missing by Monday afternoon. I begged them to look for her. They suggested I call all the neighbors, but I had already done that."

I had encountered that before with the police department. The Fae did their jobs, but they were underfunded, understaffed, overworked, and tended to cut corners wherever possible.

"I did what they asked me to. I called all the neighbors again, and I walked her usual route. I didn't find any sign of her. It was like she had just vanished off the face of the earth. By Monday morning, I was frantic. I called the cops again and they stepped up the investigation. The next day they found her body. And my whole world caved in." Isolde teared up again, pressing her knuckles against her mouth.

Her pain hung heavy in the air. Love lost to murder had its own special kind of grief. I hated questioning victims of violent crimes because it felt cruel to make them relive their pain, but it was the only way we could find out anything to help.

"I'm sorry. If we could spare you this, we would. Do you want a break? Some more water?" I was ready to get her whatever she needed.

"No...I guess I have to be all right, don't I? The only other option..." Her words drifted off as she hesitated.

"No," Viktor said. "You need to be alive when we catch the bastard who did this. You need closure and justice for Chaya. And you can't let her killer have a double victory.

If *you* give up, you're giving the killer that much more satisfaction."

Isolde held his gaze for a moment, then slowly nodded. "You're right. If I give up, then he truly has won, hasn't he?"

"What would Chaya say to you, if she were here now?" I asked.

Isolde sucked in a deep breath, then let it out slowly. "She'd say *Don't let him win. Don't let my death be in vain. Find the fucker and destroy him.*" She straightened. "I'll be all right. What else do you want to know?"

"Did Chaya mention running into anybody creepy? Maybe someone who was watching her? We have five victims, and each one led vastly different lives," Viktor said.

"Five victims? Chaya's not the only one?" Isolde stared at us, wide-eyed. "So many… Chaya was always running into creeps on her runs. You know, the 'Gimme-what-you-got-baby' types. But she never mentioned anybody in particular who had been bothering her." She sounded hesitant, then said, "There was one thing. Three days before she disappeared, she mentioned that she had stopped to help someone change a tire. She did things like that. Maybe somebody asked her for help and then yanked her into a van?"

"Did she happen to mention who it was?" Viktor was recording her and we'd translate the interview back at the office. I was taking notes longhand, particularly noting changes in Isolde's demeanor—things that you couldn't pick up on a recording.

"No, but Chaya was kind. She'd help anybody who asked. Well, within reason."

"All right, so next question. The route she ran. Did she take that same route every day?"

Isolde nodded. "Yes. Chaya didn't like changing her routine. She always ran the same route, she stopped at the same espresso stand for coffee—"

"What stand?" Viktor asked.

"The Grind House, down on Spring Street across from the Spring Street Mini Park. She runs past it every day, and usually stops there for a drink." Isolde frowned. "Ran, I mean."

"Did she have any other daily habits? What was her normal route?" I brought up a map of the Seattle area. "Where did she work?"

Isolde stared at the map. "Monday through Wednesday she worked for the Community Action Center, in the domestic violence unit. She helped women who need a safe place to stay. Thursday and Friday, she taught meditation and yoga at the Spiritual Bee—a metaphysical shop in the Viaduct Market. One Saturday a month she volunteered at the Golden Lasso Women's Shelter. She manned the door."

"What do you mean?" Viktor asked.

"Most shelters work this way. Though they try to keep their addresses private, there are times when some ex-boyfriend or abusive husband finds out where his girl-friend or wife ran to. Golden Lasso is a safe place and operates under a number of Sanctuary House rules, but for women of all races, not just Cryptos. Because of the danger of an abusive asshole trying to muscle his way in, there are two women on each shift—four shifts a day, around the clock—who guard the doors. All of the guards are trained in martial arts, and all of them are more than capable of taking down a grown man. Chaya could have taken you down," she said, looking at Viktor. "She was *that* strong."

"Did she belong to a magic guild? She was a bone witch. Was that innate, or did she study for it?" I asked.

"She was born that way. Few bone witches choose to learn their craft. As to magical guilds, no. Chaya didn't like the elitist atmosphere and the snobbery so often found in the guilds. She was an outspoken advocate for revamping a lot of the rules of the local guilds and she did manage to antagonize a few of the local witches and sorcerers." Isolde paused. "Could one of them be the killer?"

I hesitated. I didn't want her to focus on an idea that might be false.

"I don't know, but we'll look into it. Right now, we're dealing with multiple victims, and we have to figure out what ties them all together." I pulled out a list of the murder victims and handed it to her. "Do any of these names ring a bell?" There was a small photograph by each name, along with a picture as they had looked when alive. She might remember a face where she wouldn't remember the name.

Isolde studied the list. "All four of these others were killed by the same person who murdered my Chaya?"

Viktor shrugged. "We think so, but we're not sure."

"I don't recognize any of them. I'm sorry, but neither the names nor faces ring a bell. I wish I could say yes." She sounded wistful, a vulnerable, haunted look on her face. She wanted to help. I could tell that much. She wanted to find the freak who had murdered her wife and it was hurting her that she couldn't do more.

I had a sudden hunch. "Isolde, did you and Chaya have an argument the morning she vanished?" I asked gently.

She froze, then her face crumbled and she began to cry. "How did you know? I'll *never* forgive myself. The last thing I said to her when she left was, 'Fine, if you're that angry then just fuck off. Don't come home till you're ready to apologize.' " She leaned her elbows on the table, shaking. "The last words I said to her were angry ones. We had a rule about never going to bed angry, but I never thought… This wasn't supposed to happen!"

And then she melted, arms folded on the table, head resting on her arms as her shoulders heaved. I swung around the table to sit next to her, gently resting my hand on her back. Giving Viktor a bleak look, I sought for something comforting to say, but there wasn't anything that I could think of to make it better. No matter what I said, unless we were ever able to contact Chaya's spirit, Isolde would carry the weight of her guilt with her.

After a few moments, she raised her head, her face red from the tears. I handed her a tissue and she dabbed at her eyes.

"I'm sorry. I didn't mean to break down like that." She paused, then asked, "How did she die? The police just told me she was murdered."

I thought of the torture that Chaya had gone through and shook my head. "Don't think about it. Please. Right now, I think you should find a therapist who can help ease you through this. You've had a tremendous shock, and it would be good if you had someone to guide you through the next few months, at least. I'm sure Angel, the receptionist at our office, can help you find someone if you don't know where to look."

Isolde leaned back, closing her eyes as she rested her head against the back of the booth. "I know you're right. I don't know how I'll manage to hold things together for a while." She paused, then said, "We're having the funeral service in a couple days. Chaya wanted to be cremated so we'll be doing that. When I was at the morgue, all they would show me was her face. She looked so calm, so still."

"The best thing you can do for your wife is to keep living," Viktor said. "Hold tight to her memory. And talk to her—tell her everything you wish you had said instead of the argument. She'll hear you. I know she will."

"Thank you for talking to us today. We'd like to follow the path she took. You said she ran the same route every-day?" I said, pulling out my tablet and bringing up the Maps app. "Can you show us on here what that route was?"

Isolde nodded, studying the map. She traced out the route that Chaya jogged and I wrote down the streets and turns. After we finished, she gave me a long look.

"Thank you for caring. Thank you for trying to find out who did this to her. I think…" She paused, then said, "If you would have your receptionist call me with a list of therapists, I'd appreciate that. I don't know where to begin."

"Angel's an empath. She'll be able to find you someone who you can work with. I'll text her to give you a call tomorrow, if that's all right?"

"That's fine. I'll be home all day. I can't handle going into work right now, and my boss gave me a month's paid leave to get everything organized." She shook her head. "I just can't believe this has happened. I can't believe our life just…shattered like this."

"Unfortunately, chaos is a part of life and sometimes it hits like a sledgehammer."

As we made our good-byes, I hated leaving her there alone at the table. She looked so lost. But there was nothing we could do to take away her pain, and all the distractions in the world wouldn't help when the night fell and she was alone in her home, with the weight of memory pressing down on her shoulders.

VIKTOR AND I DROVE CHAYA'S ROUTE, BUT SAW NOTHING unusual. I had no clue what we were looking for, but whatever it was, we didn't find it. We drove back to the office, where I picked up Angel.

On the way home, I decided to stop for fast food. Neither Angel nor I would have time to cook that night. "What do you want, pizza? Chicken? Burgers? Fish?"

Angel was in the passenger seat, staring at her phone. "Hmm? Oh, anything's fine. How about burgers? They're easier to eat and less messy than some of the others."

"Dusty Dan's okay?"

"Fine." She went back to staring at her phone.

Dusty Dan's was a small burger joint near our home. I had bought a house on 36th Avenue, across from Discovery Park. Over the past nine months since we had moved in, we had been chipping away at the list of things we wanted to change. Now, the work we had put in on the side lot—a full-sized foliage-filled lot that had come with the place—was beginning to show. Our gardens were flourishing. We had dug through the weed-covered yard and exposed good soil, along with a number of beautiful bushes that had gotten lost beneath the tangle.

I eased into the takeout window and ordered four cheeseburgers, two large fries, and two orange sherbet shakes. Another ten minutes and we pulled into our driveway. Traffic was a bitch during rush hour, which lasted from three P.M. until seven P.M. most days.

After greeting Mr. Rumblebutt, my black Norwegian Forest cat, and making sure he was fed, we carried our food out to the patio and sat at the picnic table we had bought. It was still warm, though it would cool for the night soon, and the fresh air felt good.

"So, do you think you can find Isolde a therapist?" I opened one of the bags and spread out the burgers on the table while Angel took care of the fries and shakes. "She's carrying around a lot of guilt over arguing with Chaya on the morning she disappeared."

"Sure. I know quite a few qualified doctors who could help her. I can't imagine what she's going through. I lost Mama J., of course, and you lost your parents, but somehow that doesn't quite seem the same as losing a spouse. Though I guess you can't really qualify grief—it's harsh no matter who it hits." She unwrapped one of the burgers and the smell of freshly cooked beef and onions wafted out. "I'm hungry. So, why do you think Morgana wants to see you tonight?"

I shrugged, biting into my own burger. "I have no clue," I said after swallowing. "These are good. I don't know if I remembered to eat lunch today." I paused, taking another bite, then asked, "Speaking of therapists, how's Rafé?"

Angel licked ketchup off her fingers, then took a drink

of her shake. "He's doing better. He's processing everything he went through and he's a lot calmer now. He's starting to look for work again. He made a huge decision, though." She paused, glancing over at me. "He told me he's going to stop acting. I can't believe it. I thought acting was his life, but he said that after coping with what the Tuathan Brotherhood did to him, he doesn't feel a passion for the stage anymore. He's talking about going back to school to study psychology so he can help others who have been victimized."

That was news. Rafé loved acting. And he was good at it.

"Wow. I never expected him to go that route."

"Me either, but he said it just doesn't feel like him anymore. The experience over on the peninsula changed him. Whatever the case, he seems to be a lot more centered than he was. Even before he was…" she paused, glancing down at her food.

"You have to say it sometime," I said. "Rafé was tortured. He managed to survive, and he's healed up from his physical wounds, but the ordeal isn't going to just go away. Even with the therapy, it's something he'll always remember. And events like that can alter your life. It makes the world seem like a vastly different place. I guess we shouldn't be surprised that he's changing his focus." I popped a french fry into my mouth, then said, "How are you and he doing?"

She smiled then, the glow radiating through her face. Angel was gorgeous. She could have been a model, and at five-ten, she stood three inches taller than me. Her skin was a luminous brown, her hair coiling to her shoulders in tight curls, though she almost always wore it in a high ponytail. She was lithe, with the body of a swimmer. Rafé had skin as pale as hers was dark, and his shock of red hair and trim body complemented hers. They were a striking couple together.

"We're doing better. For a while, I was ready to kick him to the curb, even though I knew it wasn't his fault, but you know what? I'm glad I didn't. He begged me not to give up on him, and he's following through. He has his anger and cynicism under control. I think we'll pull through this. I'm so grateful he's healing." She finished her dinner, leaving the extra cheeseburger for me. I had a much bigger appetite than she did.

I accepted the last sandwich. "So what's Marilee going to teach you tonight?"

"I'm learning how to ward the house this week. She's teaching me several protection rituals. I should be able to practice on our home in a couple weeks. Marilee says I have a natural gift for healing as well, and wants to teach me several spells. It feels so weird. I'm not a witch, I'm not Fae like you, but all of a sudden, here I am, learning magic." She bit her lip, then added, "Marilee says she thinks Mama J. had some form of magical ability and that I inherited it. She thinks there may be some magic-born blood in my background. I want to get tested, though it kind of scares me. Because if I have it, then DJ will likely have it, too."

I froze. "A wolf shifter using magic? That would be an unlikely scenario. I wonder how he would handle that knowledge. Wolf shifters are naturally suspicious of the magic-born, and magic. If you test true for it, how will you tell him?"

She shrugged. "I'll deal with that when and if I get

63

there. For one thing, it depends on how much. I mean, if I've only got a small percentage of magic-born in my background, then I doubt I would need to tell him. His wolf shifter nature is prominent."

"But puberty often sets off latent abilities. That's when you began noticing you were an empath, remember?" In fact, I remembered the very day when Angel told me that she had seen a dark cloud around our seventh-grade math teacher. The next day, he had died.

"I'll talk to Cooper and ask him what he thinks."

I finished the last of my meal and wiped my hands on a paper towel. "Okay, are you ready to head out? I need to get moving if I'm going to get through traffic in time to reach the marina." The *Fantastica* was located in a slip in Portage Bay over in the North Broadway District. And while traffic should have eased up by now, I still didn't want to be late. Morgana expected me to be on time and she didn't accept bad traffic as an excuse.

We carried our garbage into the house, I gave Mr. Rumblebutt a quick cuddle, and then I headed for my car while Angel called for a taxi. It had been a long day, and it was about to get longer.

CHAPTER SIX

*T*he drive to Portage Bay took me only fifteen minutes—a surprisingly short time, except that it was finally past rush hour and I wasn't driving downtown. The marina was near the Seattle Yacht Club, on a side street off of Fuhrman. Misty Lane ended in a small parking lot, with six parking slots. Two were marked "Reserved" and the others were empty. I eased my car into the slot nearest the dock and stepped out into the cooling evening.

The sky was partially cloudy, but we weren't due for rain for at least a week. I inhaled deeply, the smell of the water mingling with fresh lilacs and that slightly dusty scent that hangs heavy in the air on spring evenings. The sun was beginning to vanish below the horizon, spreading out in long crimson and yellow fingers. It was nearing eight P.M. I'd be right on time.

I headed toward the end of the dock, where a blue houseboat gently rocked on the waves. Single story, it was about the size of a school bus. Three other houseboats were moored in the slips before the *Fantastica*, two illuminated by lights from inside.

Sometimes I wondered what it would be like to live on the water. While the thought appealed to me, there was also my father's blood, the Autumn Stalker who loved the foundation of solid ground and needed the deep forests and the craggy mountains nearby. My best bet, I thought, would be to live on a lake, or near the shore between forest and ocean. But that wasn't likely to happen any time soon.

As I approached the door of the *Fantastica*, it opened before I could knock. Aoife stood there, her eyes shimmering with the same green as mine. Her waist-length blond hair was caught up in a tousled chignon, with golden strands lightly kissing her cheeks. Her eyes lit up when she saw me.

"Ember, welcome back. Morgana said you'd be coming tonight." She stood back to allow me in. As I entered the houseboat, it was exactly as I remembered it from the last time I had been here. The main cabin was long and narrow, with bunk beds buttressing the end of the room. A sofa ran the length of the starboard wall, and the bathroom door stood to the right of the beds.

Another door next to the bathroom door led to a closet. The kitchenette lined half of the port wall, and the rest was taken up by a floor-to-ceiling bay window. Everything was decorated in shades of silver and gray, and it felt very misty.

"Should I change?" I asked. Sometimes, Morgana demanded those of us in her pledge to dress up when we entered her realm. It was more a show of respect than anything else, and the first time, I had balked at the tradition but now I just accepted it as matter of course.

"Please. You'll find your dress in the closet."

I opened the closet, expecting to see the gown I'd worn the last time I'd been here, but it had been replaced with a flowing gown the color of the indigo night, beaded with crystals. The gown had tank-top straps and a sweetheart neckline. It was fitted to the waist, then flowed out in a bohemian-style skirt.

"This is beautiful. You're sure it will fit me?"

Aoife nodded. "Yes, it will fit. Go change."

I carried the gown into the bathroom and slipped out of my jeans and top, adjusting my boobs. My bra did a good job of keeping them in place, but the underwire was wearing thin and the material was beginning to stretch a bit. I needed to go shopping. I slid the dress over my head and the gown fell loosely around my legs. It was so light that I almost felt naked, though I knew that I wasn't anywhere near exposing anything except some cleavage.

I changed my boots for the slippers that went with the gown. They were better suited for walking in the sand, as I'd have to walk along the shore once I went through the portal. I stepped out of the bathroom with a smile on my face. It felt nice to be dressed up, especially after the heaviness of examining Mendin's home, and of interviewing Isolde.

"I actually need this today," I said, smiling at Aoife. "It's been a rough day and it's not likely to get any better for a week or so." I brushed my hand across my forehead, wincing. "Have you got anything for a headache?"

"Ask Morgana when you get there. She'll be able to

help you." Aoife led me to a ladder on the other side of the bathroom door that went to the roof. "Come."

I began to climb, following her up the ladder. She opened the skylight overhead but we weren't climbing onto any roof.

We climbed up onto a spit of sand next to a rolling ocean. The waves were continually singing their song as they crashed into the land and then withdrew, only to come rolling in again.

The sand spit led to a castle that was built out over the ocean. The castle was immense, rising glossy black against the setting sun, embossed with silver etchings that lined the base. There were sirens in those images, luring sailors into the ocean, and bas-reliefs of a regal people I did not recognize. The windows of the castle flickered with light from within, and a parade of battlements crowned the walls. It was still light enough to see the merlons jutting into the sky. As before when I had come here, the castle intimidated me. It seemed so heavy and oppressive for a goddess who lived on quicksilver and moonlight.

Aoife motioned to the path leading to the castle. "Do you remember the way, or do you need me to lead you again?"

"I remember the way," I said. "If you'll just wait for me so I can get back through the portal when I return." I smiled at her. "Your life must be full of waiting."

"It's not so bad. I work every other week, so I have plenty of time off. And it's not like I don't have Netflix and an e-reader! Go now, and I hope you have a good visit." She turned back to the portal and settled on a rock near the entrance.

I turned back to the castle. The path was barely twelve

inches wide, and to my left were stark cliffs towering above the castle. Beyond the edge of the cliffs, it looked like a forest took hold, but I couldn't see much of it from below. As I started walking, the sound of the ocean kept me company, the rolling waves hissing up to crash against the shore and then pull out for another assault against the land.

The water crashed around the foundation of the castle. How the structure sat atop the ocean, I didn't know, but the black of the walls melded into the dark waters that constantly churned against it. The ocean was alive, both at home and here in Annwn, and magic hung heavy in the air, coming from the land, sky, and sea. Everything had a life force, and especially here, everything kept watch.

As I approached the doors of the castle, they swung wide. I entered the hall. Instantly I could feel the Unseen —those beings who walked between worlds. They were all around me, though I couldn't see them. They seldom bothered with those on the physical planes, but now and then I knew they would come through the veils, either to help or to harm.

The hall was long and stark, illuminated by a cool, blue fire that flickered from the torches resting in wall sconces. At the end of the hall, I came to a pair of double doors. I remembered what Aoife had done the first time I arrived and placed my hand on a panel against the wall. The doors swung wide and I found myself facing a narrow path leading over the water that coiled and hissed inches below either side. The path led to a boulder the size of my house. I cautiously followed the path, placing one foot in front of the other as I navigated the narrow trail. Overhead, as when I had been here before, the clouds churned by, racing as if they were being chased by a devil. The air was thick and humid, and the smell of brine was everywhere.

I steeled myself, remembering that there were sirens in the water, and I held my breath as I passed the rocks where I knew they lurked. But this time, they were silent and didn't try to lure me in. Before long, I was standing beside the boulder. Tall timber grew straight up out of the sea—fir and cedar. Steps, shimmering mother-of-pearl, led up to a throne created of seashells. Pearls and seaweed dripped down the throne in long strands, and the entire boulder was lined with crows, all watching me closely.

Morgana sat atop the throne, in all her beauty. Here, she dressed as the goddess she was. Her skin mirrored the pale moon, her hair was long and flowing, as black as the night sky and atop her head, and she wore a crystal tiara formed of aquamarine, amethyst, and pearls. Morgana wore a dress the color of spring rain, sheer and glittering with crystal beads, and I could see every inch of her beneath the diaphanous material. Her breasts were full and round, and her waist curved into her hips in a smooth, sensuous flow.

She held out one hand as I approached, her fingers beckoning me to come forward. "Ember, well met, my pledgling."

I sank into a curtsey, feeling overwhelmed. When she came into our realm, Morgana still felt every inch the goddess, but she was more relatable, more *human*. Here, her divinity shone forth, and she felt vast as the ocean, as distant as the stars studding the sky.

"My Lady," I said, my eyes fastened on her face. She

was beauty incarnate, with a wild, feral streak that both appealed to me and terrified me.

"Rise, Ember, and be seated." She waited until I obeyed, then let out a long breath. "I assume you're wondering why I called you here."

"Yes," I stammered, sitting on a bench by the bottom of her throne. "Did I do something wrong?"

Morgana stood, descending the steps to her throne to sit beside me on the bench. And in the blink of an eye, she felt more the Morgana I knew, less terrifying and more friendly.

"Wrong? No, child, you did nothing wrong. But I wanted to talk to you about something. It's something you need to be aware of and I'm going to set you a task to correct it."

I blinked. "Correct what? Then I *have* done something wrong?"

"Not at all," she said, shaking her head. "When I talk of correction, I mean righting an imbalance that has to do with both sides of your heritage. You've been relying on your father's blood heavily and it's clogging up your magic."

I frowned. "What do you mean?"

"Think of it this way. You have two magical heritages within you. They aren't well aligned and they don't act together easily. The Cruharach allowed you to merge them enough to move into your adulthood, but you rely on your father's blood more than your mother's. Put simply, doing so bottlenecks your Leannan Sidhe abilities. If you don't start using your mother's power more, you'll find both sides weakened. You have to maintain a balance."

I stared at the ground. My mother's magic was easy to slip into, but it frightened me. The Leannan Sidhe were master manipulators and they were, in a sense, more primal and feral than my father's people. When it came to dangerous situations, I had noticed that my Leannan Sidhe side came to the surface to protect me. And yet, I didn't trust that side of myself, so I kept her under lock and key as much as I could.

"How should I do that? I can't just go all siren on people and drain them for fun." I realized I sounded churlish as the words came out. "I'm sorry. I just… That part of myself scares me and I really *don't* know how to harness it."

Morgana regarded me quietly for a moment. Then, she said, "You can never fully control it, but Ember, my son can help you, if you explain to him. He can handle that side of you."

I blinked, trying to understand what she was saying. "Are you… I don't quite… Are you saying what I *think* you're saying? Because it sounds to me like you're telling me to drain energy off Herne."

"I am. You can't harm him like you can mortals. You can let the Leannan Sidhe out to play with him. You can be the succubus with him, and not be afraid of hurting him." She paused, then leaned close, tipping my chin up so that I was staring in her eyes. "If you don't start using your powers, one day soon they'll erupt and take over, and you may find yourself doing something you regret very much."

As her words reverberated in my mind, I caught my breath and straightened. "You mean, I might go off on someone innocent and hurt them? That could happen?"

"Yes. You can't keep a tiger in a cage for long. This side of you, Ember, she's a predator. While you can channel that energy, you must give her the freedom she needs. Otherwise, she'll grow angry and pensive and the first opportunity for freedom, she'll take it, regardless of the damage it might cause."

I blushed, not certain of how to ask the next question. "So…how do I…"

"How do you free her? Let her out to play during your love play. That will be safest."

A hollow thud hit my stomach. I knew the Leannan Sidhe were intensely sexual, and their entire nature was caught up in luring men. They were muses, but dark and twisted ones. Some of the tortured geniuses from history had been caught in their guiles, sacrificing freedom—and eventually their lives—for the visions the Leannan Sidhe brought to them.

"What will he think of me, though?" I hung my head. "He loves me the way I am. What if he doesn't like that side of me when…when we're together?" I felt incredibly uncomfortable discussing my sex life with Herne's mother. Even if she was a goddess, it didn't make it any less awkward.

"You think he hasn't noticed that side of you when you turn it loose on others?" Morgana laughed, then—a gentle laugh, not derisive—and she took my hand. "Ember, my son is a *god*. A god of the Hunt, no less. He's not daunted by the wildness of your nature. He's the Lord of the Hunt, the King Stag of the Forest. Do you think that he's going to shy away from a side of you that brings even more passion into your relationship?"

Again, I blushed, but what she said made a lot of sense,

and I sucked in a deep breath and let it out slowly, trying to relax.

"When you say it, it sounds reasonable. It's just going to take me some time to get used to thinking of myself like…that."

"I know you keep your sides segregated. You think of yourself as Ember, with two other sides that play into you. But you have to merge both into yourself. You began this in the Cruharach, and you did a good job—good enough to keep you in safety for a while. But walling off the strength of your powers and relegating them to the sidelines except for the rare times you decide you need their abilities—that's not going to work in the long run."

"So, what do I do? Besides getting kinky in the bedroom?" I tried to smile, but inside, my thoughts were churning as violently as the ocean around us.

"You begin working more with water magic. You stop labeling your powers. You need to just integrate them and quit thinking of it as though you're changing clothes. You need to wear *one* outfit, not keep changing between three. I'm going to ask Marilee to start teaching you how to control and strengthen your magical abilities with water. You perform haphazard spells as it stands right now, but you need to be able to call up a storm when needed, to learn how to breathe underwater. All that will require concentrated work."

I stared at her. "You mean I can actually learn to cast spells like that? I thought my magical abilities were limited."

"They are, right now, because you keep them separate from yourself. But let your father's blood be second nature in your body when you're fighting, and let your mother's blood be second nature when magic and sex are concerned. Neither are set apart from you. Do you understand?" She shook her head, her hair flowing around her shoulders. "You are to be a priestess of mine some day, you know. You may be pledged to me now, but I'm training you to be one of my priestesses."

That was news as well.

"I didn't really know. I wasn't sure what to call myself," I said, stammering.

"Well, now you do know. So I'll be increasing your time with Marilee to twice a week, as long as you don't have any cases with the Wild Hunt taking precedence. You'll meet with her and start an intensive immersion in water magic." She stopped, then laughed. "I made a joke, didn't I?"

I laughed with her even though I felt shell-shocked. This meeting certainly hadn't gone the way I had thought it would. I wasn't sure what I had expected, but this entire line of conversation had definitely not been it.

"And once you're proficient, you'll begin training as my priestess." She frowned for a moment, then said, "I suppose that's it. Yes, I think we've covered just about everything. Oh, except this business with Callan. Herne mentioned your reaction. Please understand, when I command you to attend parley, that's final. I know you don't like interacting with Saílle and Névé, but you're going to have to get used to it. Do you understand? No more whining about it—at least not to my son and definitely not to Cernunnos and me."

Even though she was smiling, I could feel the bite behind it. Dutifully chastised, I nodded. "I understand. I'm sorry."

"We all have to deal with people we find unpleasant. Even the gods. And with Typhon bearing down, I'm certain that's going to increase, at least for Cernunnos, Herne, and me."

"He's almost awake, isn't he?" I shuddered, staring at the boiling sky. The wind had picked up and it was blowing spray from the roiling ocean across the boulder, chilling me to the core.

"Yes, he is. I predict he'll be in his full power by Litha... perhaps not till Lughnasadh if we're lucky. But even now, the dead are feeling his presence and responding. And I fear he'll be sending out emissaries soon, as his consciousness surfaces. Think of it like a great behemoth rising from the ocean depths. Even if he's still underwater, the ripples from his movements are already having an effect."

I glanced at the water, watching it foam and break against the trunks of the trees. "Are you scared?" I asked after a moment.

She paused, then lightly placed her hand on my arm. "Yes, child. I'm frightened. And so are all the others. Typhon is one of the great Titans. He's the Father of Dragons, and he is both magnificent and terrifying. He cares for nothing but his children."

"Children?" I cocked my head. "Who are his children?"

"Think for a moment. He is truly the *father* of dragons. His wife vanished into the mists—we have no idea where she is, but the pair engendered the dragons of the world. And so they lurk, living between realms, waiting for their father. When he begins to break through, the dragons will once again return to your realm."

I froze. I knew that dragons existed, but I had always thought they were few and far between, and that they abjured the mortal world. "You mean, they simply can't get into our realm unless their father is with them?"

"Exactly. Typhon's rise will open the door for the dragons to return to your world. Some are benign, even benevolent. Others are dark and vile, seeking to enslave others to do their bidding. Remember they are all shifters. And they all love the smell of gold." She paused. "There are many creatures who live outside the mortal realm, who continually seek a way in. The gods stand between them and your world, and generally, we are strong enough to prevent a clash. But Typhon...he has the key for his kind, and none of us can prevent him from using it. We're meeting daily, monitoring his progress even as we discuss ways to send him back into stasis. But...some of the gods have chosen to work with him, and so we not only have the Father of Dragons to contend with, but his servants."

God against god. The thought of that battle sent me into a cold sweat. "Are any of the gods from Annwn aligned with him?"

"A few, but more so those from the isles of Greece, and a few from the Norse and Finnish. Anywhere chaos rules, you will find servants of Typhon." She stood. "Enough now. I'm scaring you, and I don't mean to do that. While changes will happen in your world—and soon—this battle may last for centuries. Or longer. So do not trouble yourself. The world will not end tomorrow, and humanity will still continue along its path." She glanced over at the ocean. "It's time for you to return to your world, Ember. Go and be safe. The days ahead promise to be dark, but there are lights within the darkness, and there are joys within tribulations."

With that, she bade me leave. I curtseyed and said good-bye, and turned to go. Ahead, on the distant horizon, I saw lighting flare across the sky, and thunder rumbled, shaking the air and the ground. I shaded my eyes from the brilliant flash, and headed back across the narrow pathway, my thoughts so full that I barely noticed my passage back to Aoife and the portal.

CHAPTER SEVEN

*B*y the time I reached the house, Angel was already home. She had a bruise on her left cheek and was holding a wet cloth against her neck as she sat at the kitchen table, wincing. I stared at her, slowly setting down my purse.

"What happened to you? Are you all right?" I looked around, immediately scanning the room for Rafé, and immediately felt ashamed of myself.

"Yeah, it's nothing. I need to see a chiropractor, but I'll be okay. I accidentally borked a spell tonight and it backfired on me and sent me careening against a wall. I hurt my neck." She grinned, holding up a mug. "The tea will help."

"What the hell kind of spell were you casting?" I asked.

"Well, if you must know, I was trying to cast a Barricade spell—to prevent someone from attacking me. It's harder than I thought it would be and Marilee warned me not to try it, but I guess I got ahead of myself. I ended up slamming myself against the wall, face first." She gave me a rueful grin. "She laughed at me, hands on her hips, and said, 'See, I tell you these things for a reason. Now, will you listen to me?' "

I snorted. "I never would have imagined you trying to skip ahead in magic. You're always so careful."

She shrugged. "I guess. I'm getting more and more enthusiastic and I thought I'd give it a try because she showed me how to do it. I'm not sure how I bungled it, but I really did screw it up." She shifted, grimacing again. "I'll call my chiropractor tomorrow and get in, if I can. How did your evening go?"

I opened the fridge, poking around. I wanted something to take the shock off, and when I saw we had a bottle of elderberry wine, I pulled it out and poured myself a glass.

"It must have been heavy, given you're getting into the wine," she guessed.

"You might say that." I put the wine back and cut myself a slice of the chocolate cheesecake that Angel had made the day before. On second thought, I cut myself a second slice. I knew I would be going back for seconds so I might as well save time. I carried my plate and goblet over to the table and sat down opposite Angel. "Where to begin?"

"That rough?"

"She wasn't mad at me—nothing like that. But I feel as though I've just ended up with a vast data bank of information that I have to process." I licked my lips, then after a long sip of the wine, told her everything Morgana and I had discussed. After I finished, Angel sat there, looking like she had forgotten all about her pain.

"Crap. Dragons are real?" She paused, then added, "I

don't know why they wouldn't be, but…what are dragons like? I mean, I know there are Asian dragons and Western dragons, and they're different, but…*what* are they really like?"

"I suppose they're as individual as people. I do know a few things about them, other than some are bad-assed scary and others are incredibly beneficent. They're all shifters, for one thing. They can walk in human form, which makes them even more formidable. Some hate mortals, while others seem to care about us. And by mortals, I mean, most bipedals—Fae, human, ogres, all of us." I shrugged. "Anyway, I guess we'd better prepare for a host of changes over the next year or two."

"They can't stop Typhon from waking up, can they?" Angel asked, staring at the table.

I frowned. "I don't think so. To be honest, I don't think the gods have a clue of how to drive him back into stasis. So yeah, we have the Father of Dragons, his children, and the dead, all looming in our near future."

Angel let out a sigh, then said, "What about the other thing—your Leannan Sidhe side? Or should we even call it that any more, given what Morgana told you? The water witch side of yourself, maybe?"

"It's hard for me to know how to integrate the way I think about myself. I can feel each side of my heritage distinctly, yet they're both a part of me. I wonder if there's another ritual I can undergo to further merge them together." I stared at my wine, fingering the stem of the goblet. The Cruharach had been nerve-wracking enough. I couldn't imagine what it would take to further integrate the sides of myself.

"What are you going to tell Herne? I mean, I imagine

he's had some pretty wild partners over the millennia so —" She stopped, grinning. "You're about to get kinky, Ember."

"Kinky is as kinky does. I guess, part of me is worried that he'll like me better that way and that will make me wonder if he's been unsatisfied with how…tame…I've been till now. I've never been little Miss Prim, but it's not like I've been bent, you know?" I realized that was at the core of my worries. I knew logically that I couldn't hurt him. But what if he preferred the rougher side? But it wasn't like he'd be cheating on me. It would still be me, just me unfiltered. "I think I'm overthinking this."

"We both need to chill and rest, though sleep's going to be a bitch with my neck like this. Come on, finish your cheesecake and wine and let's get to bed. I fed Mr. Rumblebutt when I got home, so he's good to go for the evening." Angel's phone jangled and she glanced at the screen. "Cooper?" Worry clouding her face, she quickly answered it, letting out a groan as she shifted position. "Cooper, is something wrong?" As she tensed, waiting, I cleared our dishes off the table, but the next moment, she said, "Oh thank heavens. I was worried. So, what's up?"

Relieved that nothing appeared to have happened to her little brother, DJ—Cooper was his foster father—I rinsed the dishes and stacked them in the dishwasher, then added soap and set the cycle to going.

At that moment, Mr. Rumblebutt jumped up on the counter and rubbed against me. I swept him up into my arms and buried my face in his fur.

"Hello, rugrat. How are you doing?" I held him up over my head, my hands beneath his front legs, and then pulled him in for a long cuddle. He began to purr as he kneaded my shoulder. "Hey little dude, we have to trim your claws soon," I whispered, ignoring the sharp jabs as his paws worked their magic against my skin.

I loved Mr. Rumblebutt more than I loved myself, and I did everything I could to make him happy. There were two kitty condos in the house—one upstairs and one downstairs—and he had more toys than he knew what to do with. I also made sure that there were at least five cat beds tucked throughout the house, and I had installed a kitty hammock on one of the windows in my room. He had a view of a giant maple, where we had hung a bird feeder. Cat TV never failed to entertain.

I danced him around the kitchen—no small feat, given he weighed fifteen pounds—while waiting for Angel to get off the phone so I could find out what was going on. I was nosy, yes, but that's the way we were. Best friends since we were eight, we knew almost every secret the other possessed, and considered ourselves closer than blood kin.

She finally set her phone down. "Well, that was interesting."

"What's up?" I set Mr. Rumblebutt down. He was starting to squirm, and when I let him go, he raced over to his food dish and gave me the stink-eye. Apparently, he wasn't the waltzing type.

"Cooper had a meeting with the school today."

"DJ isn't in trouble again, is he?"

She shook her head. "He's kept his nose clean since the incident last fall. But they just finished a round of tests and DJ scored so high that they first wanted to skip him a year ahead. But he's small enough that they're leery about allowing him to enter middle school. He's already skipped one grade, and they're worried that he might get picked on if they just advance him again. So Cooper talked to the Rainier Forest Academy for the Gifted, and long story short, DJ's been accepted. He's moving over to the new school this fall. He'll be among intellectual peers, and he'll be challenged by the material in a way that just doesn't happen now. There are several shifters who go there, so he's not going to be alone in terms of coping with being a wolf shifter nearing puberty." She looked delighted. "I'm so proud of him!"

"You should be. The boy is brilliant. I've always told you that. You watch. DJ's going to grow up and cure cancer or something of the sort. I hope he enjoys the new school. Do you think he'll mind leaving his friends?"

She shook her head. "He can see them after school and on weekends. You know, I always wanted to send him to a private school, but no way could I ever afford it. I asked Cooper if it was expensive—you and I both know it is—but he just said not to worry. My little brother's going to have every opportunity Mama J. and I wanted for him, but couldn't give him." Her face was lit up like it was Yuletide morning.

I gave her a long hug. "I'm so happy for both you and DJ. Tell him I'm cheering him on, will you?" I paused. "Is the school still in Washington state?"

She nodded. "Yes, actually. It's not too far from where Cooper lives, so DJ won't have to board out. Cooper said the closer DJ gets to puberty, the more important it is that he spends time with the family pack. And DJ's integrated into their family, so they truly are his pack." She let out a sigh. "I'm happy for him, but it still feels like every day he moves a little farther from me. I'm afraid one day we'll be strangers. But if this is going to help him as much as Cooper and the school think it will, then I have to let go."

"DJ will always remember he has a sister, Angel." I slid my arm around her waist as we walked up the stairs. "Never fear that. You'll *always* be his sister, no matter what."

THE NEXT MORNING I TOOK EXTRA CARE WITH MY CLOTHES and makeup. Today was the parley and I wasn't about to walk into a room with two women who thought I was a pathetic piece of trash dressed to give them more ammo. I said I didn't care what they thought of me, but I didn't want them taking any more potshots at me than they already did.

I chose a pair of black jeans that were so new they were still stiff, then paired them with a teal corset top. The back was already laced. All I had to do was zip up the front. I put on a strapless bra, then the corset, and then wrapped a silver belt around my waist. My hair was looking good. Raven black, it coiled in long, looping waves down to my mid-back. I gathered it up into a high ponytail, smoothing it as I wrapped a silver band around the base. Then, after applying my makeup—heavy eyeliner and a smoky lid that brought out the green of my eyes—I zipped up a pair of stiletto ankle boots. I had more practical ones at the office, but I wanted those two Fae bitches to stare. Morgana's crow necklace hung around my neck, as it always did, and I added large silver hoop earrings. As I stood back, I realized I looked hot. I seldom thought of myself that way, but today I was smokin'.

As I descended the steps, the smell of bacon wafting up from the kitchen made my stomach rumble. I entered the kitchen to find Angel making bacon and eggs and toast, and she had already pulled me a quad-shot latte.

"Morning, sunshine," I said. "What do you think? Will Saílle and Névé find me acceptable?"

She grinned. "You look good enough to eat. Just make sure neither one gets any ideas and tries to nibble on you."

I snorted. "Not likely. I'm still a tralaeth in their eyes and I always will be. But I want to make their jaws drop." I held out my arms and twirled, almost twisting my ankle. "Fucking shoes. I swear, how do women wear these on a daily basis?"

"You wear platform boots and you wear heels when we go clubbing." Angel handed me a plate and my mug.

I carried them over to the table. "I know, but I usually don't go over three inches for dance shoes, and platforms and chunky heels are a lot easier to walk in."

She laughed. "Well, you could go change instead of bellyaching."

I stuck my tongue out at her. "Fine, I'll quit whining."

We finished breakfast and headed for my car. I drove Angel to the garage where she picked up her car—fixed and ready to go—and we drove the rest of the way separately.

The morning was hazy, with a thin line of clouds trailing across the sky, but it was sixty degrees already and promised to be another warm day. While waiting at a light, I asked my phone what the forecast was. The weather was shaping up to be sunny for the next three days, then a streak of rain was coming in with slightly cooler temperatures.

The warm weather had brought people out in droves, and there were bicyclists on the road. I carefully wove around them, cursing at a couple who decided they could ignore the traffic rules. But both Angel and I made it to work without hitting anybody, so I chalked it up as good enough.

The parking garage was almost full, but we lucked out and found two spaces near the front. I hated walking through the dark garage in the evenings. Even though I could easily handle a number of attackers, someone with a gun could shut me down pretty fast.

Angel and I met up at the door and headed across the street and down half a block. During inclement weather, that half a block was a long, wet, run, but today it was beautiful and lovely, and made for a nice stroll. We passed Pain, who was jiving to a beat that his buddies were playing. He was breaking a hip-hop rhythm to the upbeat blues song, and he was really quite good. We stopped to watch as he finished.

He doffed his hat and with a flourish, bowed to us. "Ladies, how you doin'?"

"We're good," I said, pulling a couple dollars out of my purse and dropping them in the open guitar case. "How's Shayla?" I looked around, but didn't see her.

"Shayla contacted Rayan's House for Women like you said and they took her in. I can't thank you enough, Ember. Shayla needs someplace safe for now. I can't know where she is, but we're texting and talking and I hope to have a place for her soon."

I paused, wondering whether to say what was running through my mind. Finally, I decided to just go ahead. "She and the baby are going to need a stable place after the child's born. Pain, what are you guys going to do? The baby can't live out here on the street, or in a flophouse."

He ducked his head, staring at his feet. Then, with a sigh, he shrugged. "I know. I'm lookin' for work. I've got a lead on a couple retail jobs. It would help if I had a reference." He gave me a winsome look, grinning.

I groaned, but pulled out my card. "Here. Use me as a reference. But don't you give that number around, you hear me?"

"Loud and clear," he said with a laugh. "Thanks, seriously. When me and Shayla have a place and are settled, I'm going to pay you back for the help you gave me the other day. I promise."

"No. Pay it forward. When you're settled and doing better, help some other kid on the street. I'd rather you do that. Okay?" I paused, then held out my hand.

He took it, shaking slowly before he let go. "Yeah, I get it. Thanks, Ember. Really."

"We've got to get to work now. You let me know when you get that job, all right?"

He waved, going back to his dancing as we dashed up the stairs to the door. I glanced back. The chances weren't great for them, but I had the feeling Pain would do what he could to ensure that Shayla and the baby were taken care of. I just hoped that fate would be kind to them.

WE WALKED INTO THE BREAK ROOM A COUPLE MOMENTS late and all eyes fastened on me. Herne slowly set his coffee cup on the table and straightened. I recognized the gleam in his eye and blew him a kiss. He very deliberately licked his lips and winked.

"You…look great," Talia said with a faint grin. "Spiffing yourself up for the Fae Queens?"

I struck a pose. "What do you think? Will they hate me less because I'm *bee-yoo-tee-ful*?"

Yutani snorted. "Somehow I doubt the only way they'd like you any better is if you appeared naked with a collar around your neck."

I choked, sputtering. "Well, *that's* not going to happen."

"Keep your fantasies to yourself," Herne muttered, but he was smiling. "You make good eye candy, love. Now get yourself some coffee and plant your butt in the chair."

Angel and I settled in with our notes, and coffee for me, and tea for her.

Herne started the meeting. "Viktor and Ember, what did you learn yesterday in your interviews?"

We filled them in on everything that had happened with Mendin's landlady and with Isolde.

"I was thinking that maybe if we asked Raven to visit Mendin's house, she might be able to pick up on something. I sensed some spirit activity there, but couldn't tell what was going on." I added, "Do you think that some disgruntled guild owner might be lashing out at members of the magic-born who refused to join one of the guilds? Even though Mendin was a tiger shifter, he worked with magic and the dead."

"That's an idea," Herne said. "Write it down. We can't afford to overlook anything. Did you and Viktor have time to trace Chaya's jogging route after your interview with Isolde?"

Viktor shook his head. "Only a cursory look. I thought Yutani could do that today while we're over at parley."

"I'm game," Yutani said. "Just give me the directions. Talia can come with me."

Herne paused, then said, "No, take Angel."

"What? Me?" Angel jerked around, staring at him, her eyes wide.

"Your empathic abilities may come in handy for this, and it's a safe-enough assignment. Talia can watch the front desk and still do her research at the same time."

"That's fine with me," Talia said. "I'm ferreting out background info on the murder victims and I'd rather not interrupt the process. I get in a rhythm and don't like to let it drop."

"Then that's set. Angel and Yutani, head out after the meeting. The streets should be less crowded before lunch."

Herne paused. "This is a good time to bring up another subject. I've decided we should have an assistant office manager, for times just like today. Angel, you do a great job, but as you progress in your magical training, we may be calling on you more. And we can always use someone to run errands and so forth. I've decided to offer Rafé the job. If that won't bother you," he said, looking directly at her. "I know it can be a strain to work with someone you're involved with."

"Gee, thanks," I said, wrinkling my nose. "I appreciate that."

"I did not mean *you* and you know it, so quit giving me grief, woman," Herne said, giving me the side-eye.

"Just checking." I pretended to study my nails, trying not to laugh.

Angel bit her lip. "Can you give me a day to think it over? I know he could use the job and it would be a good one for him, but we're just getting back on an even track. Though I suppose he might be so busy that it wouldn't matter."

"Take your time. Don't feel pressed to say yes. I truly want your input." Herne went back to his notes. "Viktor, can you contact your friend Erica and see if she can field us a list of any missing-persons reports starting from last week? If we go through them and spot any likely candidates that match our list of victims, it might help both us and the cops. I'd call Maria over at the mayor's office, but it would involve a lot more red tape than just going through our normal channels."

"Will do." Viktor made a note on his tablet. Erica was a cop in the Seattle PD, and she had been an informant for the Wild Hunt for quite a while. She and Viktor had never dated, but they were good buddies.

Herne turned to me. "How did things go with Morgana last night?"

I looked up from my notes, catching his gaze. "Well, it was informative, to say the least. By the way, I got scolded for whining about going to parley. Thanks for telling on me."

Herne snorted. "I didn't say a word. You have to know my mother keeps an eye on you since you're pledged to her."

"Gee, how lucky am I?" I said, then gave up. "Fine," I said with a laugh. "She's looking over my shoulder, then. Anyway, part of it, I'll tell you later. But we talked about Typhon and his return and there's more that I think you all should know. Unless you already know and I was just slow on the uptake."

"What?" Herne's smile faded and he straightened in his chair.

"Apparently, Typhon's return spells the return of the dragons. He holds the key to unlock the door for them, so to speak. So not only will we be dealing with the dead, but also a bunch of dragons returning. I also found out that dragons can shift into human form, so we may not necessarily know when we're talking to one."

"Crap, I hadn't even thought of that," Herne said. "I love that my mother waited so long to tell us."

"Dragons once ruled the world, long ago—or rather, they ruled parts of the world," Talia said. "They were driven out with Typhon, good and bad alike. Hopefully, the good eggs won't hold a grudge and will be willing to help us against some of their more aggressive kin."

"What are dragons like?" Angel asked. "Are there differing kinds?"

Herne frowned, tapping his pen on the table. "I hadn't even considered that the children of Typhon might return, but it makes sense. Their mother was Echidna and she was extraordinarily fond of humans, which is why some of their children and descendants like humanity and tend to be benevolent. Others, not so much. It's rumored that Typhon destroyed her before he was driven into stasis, but no one knows for sure."

"Morgana also said some of the gods are on his side," I said.

"Unfortunately, that's true." Herne shrugged. "They'll be working to undermine our attempts to drive him back. I don't think this battle's going to be wrapped up any time soon, and we—the Wild Hunt—will be dealing with the fallout for a long time to come. The gods are powerful, and we have weapons in our arsenal, but we aren't omnipotent, any of us, and we can't wave our hands and just make him go away."

Talia frowned. "I almost wish I had gotten my powers back from Lazerous. Any resources we can find to help us would be valuable."

Angel shifted in her chair. "Ask Rafé to work here. I'll focus on my training. The more I can learn, the better I can help the team." She raised her head, looking resolute.

"Are you certain?" Herne asked. "I want you to be sure."

"I'm sure. In for a penny, in for a pound." She winced. "Speaking of, I have a chiropractor appointment that I need to go to first, before Yutani and I look over Chaya's route."

"What time is your appointment?" Yutani asked.

"Eleven." She rubbed her neck. "I screwed myself over last night."

"We can stop at your chiropractor's office on the way, if that works for you."

She nodded. "That's fine."

Talia slipped out of her chair and opened the freezer over the fridge. She brought out a silicone ice pack. "Until then, try this."

Angel gratefully draped the cold pack around her neck. "Thanks. I totally didn't even think of using ice." She winced as the pack touched her skin, but then let out a soft sigh. "That feels good, actually."

"So we not only have Typhon to cope with, but his kids," Viktor said. "I'm wondering, should we talk to the

United Coalition about this? They're going to notice the rise in events concerning the dead before long."

"Let me talk to Morgana and Cernunnos about that." Herne pushed his tablet back. "All right, we need to leave now if we're going to make the parley appointment. Everybody get to work. We've got a lot of long days ahead of us, I fear."

As the others headed out of the break room, Herne caught me by the arm and, when we were alone, he shut the door and pushed me against the wall.

"You look so hot," he whispered. "You always do but right now, I wish we had the time for me to fuck your brains out." He pressed against me, his eyes luminous. I could feel his hunger and it roused my own need.

"Well, hang onto your hat, lover, because I've got a lot to talk to you about regarding that. But save it for tonight. Your mother and I had quite the discussion." I draped my arms around his neck and pulled him close, kissing him deeply, my tongue gently sliding between his lips.

He grasped my wrists, pressing my arms over my head, holding them against the wall. I could feel him through his jeans, hard against my leg, and I moaned into his mouth.

Maybe Morgana was right, I thought as I felt my mother's blood stir. Or rather, I thought, *my* blood. Maybe it was time I let my wild side out of the cage I kept her in.

CHAPTER EIGHT

*T*he drive over to the Eastside went smoothly. The traffic was light, even on the 520 floating bridge, and we made good enough time that we arrived at Ginty's a little early. As we stepped out of Herne's Expedition, I shaded my eyes as a ray of sunlight hit my face.

Ginty's Waystation Bar & Grill rested on the outskirts of Woodinville, a bedroom community of Seattle. Woodinville blended into Kirkland, which blended into Redmond, and so on. The greater Seattle metropolitan area was big, almost as large as the city of Seattle itself, and together, the area housed over three and a half million people, about half the state's population.

Ginty's was exactly halfway between TirNaNog and Navane, and there was good reason for that. While the bar was a Waystation for all races, it was primarily used when the Dark and the Light Fae Courts needed to convene talks. Waystations were also Sanctuary Houses for any member of the SubCult seeking safe haven until they could escape the city or receive a fair trial. If they were guilty of a heinous crime, they weren't eligible for protection, but if there were questions, or if they were on the run because of a bounty or something of that kind, all they had to do was ask at one of the Waystations and they would be taken in.

It was too dangerous for Saílle and Névé to meet without the rules of parley and everybody knew it, so Ginty's provided a safe haven for those meetings, and woe be to anyone who disrespected or ignored the rules. Cernunnos and Morgana made certain that the most lenient punishment for disregarding the rules of parley was still harsh, and the worst punishment was indentured servitude or death, if the infraction warranted it.

Ginty's was at the end of Way Station Lane, off Paradise Lake Road and near Bear Creek. Looking rustic and single story on the outside, with a parking lot large enough to hold a small army of cars, the bar was surrounded by empty lots filled with wildflowers, Scotch broom, and the steady drone of bees as they danced from flower to flower.

As we headed toward the door, I made sure my dagger was peace bound, as did Herne and Viktor. Without the bindings, we wouldn't be allowed in.

Waylin was at the door, a large, baldheaded bouncer who brooked no guff. He held up his hand, but we had already stopped. We knew the drill.

He ran through the spiel, his voice deep. "You are now entering Ginty's, a Waystation bar and grill. One show of magic or weapon will get you booted and banned. Do you agree to abide by the Rules of Parley, by blood and bone?"

"We do, by blood and bone," Herne said. Viktor and I murmured "By blood and bone" behind him, and Waylin nodded for us to move on into the bar.

The inside of Ginty's was far more expansive than the outer shell. For one thing, the bar wasn't one story on the inside. To the right, back of the bar, were stairs leading to an interdimensional realm that wasn't visible here in our world. The bar was mahogany, polished to a high sheen, with brass fittings and a granite countertop. Behind the bar were rows of bottles, every drink you could imagine.

Booths lined the walls and the center floor was filled with tables. A rack of antlers over the bar was so large that it made me wonder if Cernunnos himself had donated them. Paintings of the Cascade volcanoes adorned the walls. A large bay window stretched across the front of the bar, giving at least six booths a wide view of the parking lot.

We sauntered up to the bar and slid onto three open stools. The booths were mostly empty, but it was early. By lunch time, they'd all be full. I stared at the bottles. Most of the liqueurs were foreign to me, and I had the sudden desire to try something new.

"Well, if it's not the King Stag and his posse," the bartender said, wandering over to greet us. Wendy Fierce-Womyn was Ginty's right-hand woman. Once you met her, there was no chance you'd forget her. Six-two, she sported a platinum Mohawk that shimmered against her rich brown skin. She was built like a brick house, muscled and strong, and she filled in for Waylin, the bouncer, when need be.

"Hey, Wendy," Herne said, motioning to the bar. "I'll

have a glass of Blossom-Berry Mead." He glanced at me. "The best mead around, in my opinion. The Elves in Annwn make it and ship it over."

"They ask a pretty penny, too," Wendy said, pouring a glass of the shimmering honey wine. She set it in front of Herne. "What about you, Ember? And Viktor?"

Viktor shrugged. "I'll take a pint of Keros ale."

I scanned the bottles. "I want to try something new. Nothing too strong, given we're headed into parley, but something a little sweet?" I wasn't fond of alcohol that didn't have a sweet taste to it, which was one reason I avoided most red wines.

"Hmm, let me see," Wendy said, turning to stare at the shelves. "I know! Have you tried a Buckle Up?"

I frowned, shaking my head. "I've never even heard of it."

"New drink. Made with Blue Brandy, mint, and chocolate liqueur. It won't land you flat on your back, but it's a cool fire in the belly." She poured Viktor's ale and started working on my drink.

"How's it going?" I asked. I liked Wendy and wanted to get to know her better. She made me feel like a slug, fitness wise, but she was caring and a staunch defender of women. I kept thinking about asking her to one of our girls' nights.

"Not bad. I'm actually volunteering at a women's shelter. Rayan's House for Women. Have you heard of it?"

I cocked my head. "Wow, yes, actually I have. In fact, I referred a young woman there this week and it sounds like they've taken her in. Her name is Shayla. She's pregnant."

Wendy nodded. "I processed her intake. Her boyfriend couldn't come with her, of course, but he didn't have any objections and the only thing he asked was that she call him when she got settled."

"Pain is actually excited about the baby, and he's looking for a job so he can take care of her and the child. So as far as I can tell, he's a good egg." I glanced over at Viktor. "You know him better than I do. What do you think?"

"Pain's been through hell, but he's not the sort to pass on his misery. I've never once seen any indication that he's violent." Viktor sipped his ale, wiping the foam off his lips.

"Good to know," Wendy said, sliding a drink in front of me. "Taste that and tell me it's not a little bit of heaven."

I sipped the brilliant blue drink cautiously. The first taste to hit my tongue was a rich warm chocolate, followed by the hint of a smooth brandy, and finally, a kick of fresh mint. Together, the three blended into a flavor that made me want to eat it rather than drink it.

"I wonder if Angel can reproduce this in cake," I said, staring at the glass. "This is wonderful. It's a little heavy for a spring morning, but damn, it's good. I'll have to remember this. You called it a 'Buckle Up'?"

"That's the name," Wendy said. "Glad you like it." She glanced over her shoulder at the clock. "Ginty's on the way. He got slowed down by an accident, but he should be here soon."

"Are Saílle and Névé here yet?" Herne asked.

"You know I can't tell you that. I'm not allowed to tell you who's in the suites upstairs. So relax and enjoy your drinks." Wendy brought out a bowl of pretzels and a bowl of potato chips. "Here, eat something. I've got to check in the back to see if the chef's ready to take on the lunch crowd. Ring the bell, will you, if any customers show up? I'm on duty alone until eleven-thirty." She headed toward a door in back of the bar.

When she was gone, I took another sip of my drink and grabbed a handful of chips. "How long has Ginty's been here? I don't remember it from my days before the Wild Hunt. Of course, I never had the need to attend a parley, either."

"Ginty's has been around since the 1980s," Herne said. "There was another Waystation bar, but it was farther out, and a lot less accessible. Ginty's uncle owned it, and when he decided to return home, Ginty won the right to be the Waystation guard of the next bar. He had this one built and opened up in 1987, I think."

"That's the year I was born," I said.

"You're just a sprout," Viktor said with a grin.

Herne arched his eyebrows. "No, the sprout is all grown up, I guarantee you that." He leered at me, and bopped my nose.

I blushed, once again thinking of my conversation with Morgana.

"What did my mother say to you? You seem a little on edge today," Herne whispered, leaning close. His lips brushed mine as he pulled back, and I shivered. Every time he touched me, it set me off.

"I'll tell you later. I really don't want to discuss it in public," I said.

At that moment the door behind the bar opened and

Ginty strode through. "I'm here. Sorry I'm late—there was a bad crash on the freeway. We'll get things started in a moment."

Ginty McClintlock was a dwarf, around four foot five, all beefcake with ripping muscles and a braid of blond hair that fell to his waist. He was handsome and though he seemed a little gruff around the edges, he actually had a soft heart. He wore jeans and a polo shirt, along with a pair of motorcycle boots, and he drove a beat-up old pickup that was souped up like a bat out of hell.

He jerked his thumb toward the roped-off staircase and, carrying our drinks, we followed him. Turning to Wendy he said, "Hold down the fort while I'm gone."

"What do you think I've been doing, old man?" Wendy said, flourishing her bar towel as she began to polish the counter.

"Eh, woman, you'll be the death of me yet. But my Ireland would beat me senseless if I let you go." Ireland was Ginty's wife, and I got the distinct impression that while Ginty ran the bar, she ran Ginty.

Ginty led us to the velvet rope that cordoned off the staircase. He held his hand out, whispered an incantation, and the rope moved aside on its own, then neatly closed again after the four of us had passed through. I had been here often enough to know that the rope was actually a creature, summoned for protection, and it masqueraded as a velvet rope. I had asked Ginty once what would happen if someone tried to break through without permission. Apparently the rope turned into a snake with very sharp teeth, and a venom that could be lethal.

We started up the stairs. I glanced over my shoulder to

see a swirl of fog rising behind us. We had entered the interdimensional space of the Waystation.

Four steps up we came to a landing and the staircase turned to the left. The mist grew thick, shrouding our ankles as we ascended. The fog was magical, that much I knew, and it didn't feel composed of water vapor. A moment later, and the mist completely encompassed Ginty. Another moment and I entered the fog, and few seconds later, I stepped out into a long hallway. The hallway had three doors on either side, but I knew this was only a small portion of the Waystation. We were now in protected space.

Ginty led us over to the first door on the left—the room we always met the Fae Queens in. He glanced at us. Herne nodded, and we entered the room.

THE ROOM WAS LIKE ANY CONFERENCE ROOM, WITH A U-shaped table in the center and chairs around the outside perimeter. To the left, sat Saílle and her entourage. To the right, sat Névé and her attendants. Ginty, Herne, Viktor, and I took the seats at the table dividing the two.

Saílle and Névé were decked out to the nines.

Saílle was as pale as a winter's morning, with hair the color of the night sky. It tumbled down her back in a thick current of silken strands. Her eyes were piercing blue, the blue of ice floes and glaciers, and the autumn winds and winter snows trailed in her wake. She was dressed in an indigo gown, gleaming with silver beads that studded the low-cut sweetheart bodice. Her diadem was ablaze with sapphires and diamonds, and the choker around her neck consisted of five strands of amethyst, matching her earrings.

Her opposite, Névé, brought spring and summer with her. With hair the color of platinum and eyes that mirrored the rich peat of the soil when it was freshly tilled, she wore a gossamer gown that shimmered with spring green and the pink of fresh tulips. Her tiara shimmered with emeralds and diamonds. An emerald solitaire rested at her throat, set into gold, as large as a fifty-cent piece. Névé radiated the joy of flowers of spring, and the heat of summer nights.

They were beautiful, both of them, polar opposites and yet, they mirrored one another so much that it astounded me how low they could stoop in terms of battling the other. They were born to the war, though—the Fae had been in a constant state of battle since the twin courts had first evolved from the Ante-Fae.

We all knew the procedure, and no one spoke as Ginty cleared his throat and lifted a golden wand. A smoky quartz crystal glowed on the end, and as he held it up, I could feel him spinning the magic of parley around us. All oaths taken beneath the cloak of his magic were binding before the gods.

In a clear, loud voice, Ginty began to speak. "I hereby declare the Beltane Parley of the Courts of Light and Darkness, in the year 10259 CFE, open. Under this mantle, all members are bound to forswear bearing arms against any other member of this parley until the meeting is officially closed and all members are safely home. I also remind the Courts of Light and Darkness that they are forsworn by the Covenant of the Wild Hunt from inflicting injury on any and all members of the Wild Hunt team, under the sigil of Cernunnos, Lord of the Forest, and Morgana, Goddess of the Sea and the Fae. Let no one break honor, let discussions progress civilly, and remember that I—Ginty McClintlock, of the McClintlock Clan of the Cascade Dwarves—am your moderator and mediator, and my rule as such supersedes all other authority while we are in this Waystation."

We remained silent, waiting as he pulled out a long scroll. It was covered in print—all very small and looking very old. "If you stay, you agree to the rules. If you disagree, leave now, or be bound to the rules of the parley. I have spoken and so it is done."

There was a long pause, but no one moved. Ginty cleared his throat again and set down the scepter and the scroll. "Then, if you are all agreed, I shall open the parley. Herne, son of Cernunnos, you have rights of first speech." Ginty sat down next to me, giving me a look that told me he had better things to do than coddle the Fae Queens. But it was his job and he was exacting in his performance.

"Then, let me start by saying I'm here on express orders from not only Cernunnos, but also my mother, Morgana, goddess of the Fae. She and my father are deeply disturbed by the recent events in which several innocents were hurt in what can only be described as a road rage incident." He shook his head. "Queen Saílle, Queen Névé, you are to hand Callan over to me, immediately. He needs to go back to his own time. Now that the Tuathan Brotherhood has been dismantled and the Fae have been reinstated in the United Coalition, you have no more reason to keep him around. So bring him to me, and I'll take him to my father."

He sat back, crossing his arms. I knew him well

enough to know just how pissed he was at having to take time out for this. Granted, keeping peace between the two factions was our job, but sometimes it was like trying to herd cats, or rather, babysit powerful two-year-olds in the throes of a tantrum.

Saílle and Névé both stared at him, not saying a word.

"Saílle, we know you are hiding Callan," Herne said, trying again. "By order of the Covenant of the Wild Hunt, you are to turn him over to us before the end of the day."

"What makes you think he's under *my* protection?" Saílle said, inspecting her nails.

"Of course you have him," Névé said, leaning forward, her eyes flashing. "You kidnapped him as soon as the Brotherhood disbanded and now you refuse to give him back to us. Bringing him into this time was *my* idea, so you hold no claim over him and I want him back."

Saílle sputtered. "*Your* idea? *My* advisor came up with the plan to bring Callan out of the mists, so he belongs with the Dark Fae."

"You lie!" Névé jumped to her feet, leaning her hands on the table. The energy crackled off her in waves.

"Enough!" Ginty jumped up on his stepstool so he was equal to their height. "As mediator, I command silence!"

Saílle and Névé obeyed, but both looked ready to strangle the dwarf.

"You *will* behave in a civilized manner beneath the mantle of parley. Is that clear?" Ginty spread his arms out to his sides. "This entire room, *this entire Waystation*, is under my control, and you *will* behave while the Mantle of Rules holds power. Is that understood?"

I wanted to cheer, but that would just be egging them

on. Instead, I let out a satisfied sigh and waited to see what they would do next.

Saílle was the first to speak. She was tight-lipped and abrupt, but she said, "My apologies, Master McClintlock. I will refrain from interacting in a hostile manner."

Not wanting to be left the bad guy, Néve abruptly sat down and followed suit. "I, as well."

"Very well, then. Herne the Hunter, Lord of the Hunt, son of Cernunnos, has issued a proclamation from the gods. Are you stating you're going to ignore the covenant?"

Saílle looked ready to bite his head off, but said, "Of course not." She turned to Herne and in a sarcastic tone, said, "Is this your mother's *final* word?"

"It is. If you do not deliver Callan to our office by six P.M. today, you will be considered in contempt of the gods. And I would not provoke my mother's contempt, were I you. *Either* of you."

He waited, but Saílle remained silent.

"Well? Come on, I don't have all day." Herne leaned forward. "Look, both of you know you're not getting away with this one. If you want to kill each other off, feel free. I don't give a fuck, but you do *not* have the right to harm the citizens of this realm with your petty-assed bickering. *Do you get it? Do I have to spell it out for you any more than that?*"

Saílle glowered, but she kept her composure. After a moment, she said, "Tell your father we will comply. But I take no responsibility if the Light interferes. If you want Callan delivered to you safely, then you'd better send an official escort to pick him up. He'll be ready at four."

Herne rolled his eyes, but turned to Néve. "I'd better

not see *any* of your court attempting there to intervene.
Do you understand?"

Névé huffed. "You're as blustery and irritating as your
father. But the Light acknowledges Morgana's decree. We
won't interfere." She glared at Saílle. "This wouldn't have
happened if the Queen of the Dark had kept our
agreement."

"Callan asked for asylum in the Dark Court. *We* didn't
bribe him," Saílle began but Herne put his fingers in his
mouth and gave a loud, clear whistle.

"*Enough!* We'll send an official escort this afternoon at
four, with a letter bearing my father's seal. Now, go home,
both of you, and for once, try not to murder each other on
the way." Herne stood and, motioning to Viktor and me,
stomped out before Saílle and Névé had the chance to
leave. We were downstairs and out the door before either
queen could move.

As we headed to Herne's car, I glanced over my shoulder. Saílle and Névé were filing out of the bar, followed by
their retinues. As they separated toward their respective
vehicles, the two queens paused, staring at one another. I
could feel the crackle flickering between them. They
seemed to sense my scrutiny and turned toward me. I
straightened, hands on my hips, as I stared back at them. I
was everything they despised, a mix of their warring
bloodlines. They denied my right to exist even as they
sought to obliterate the other.

"I'm your balance," I whispered, so low that surely they
couldn't hear me. But they froze, still staring at me. Not
even realizing what I was doing, I said, "I'm your future,
so get used to it. You may have an eternity behind you, but
the world is changing. It's time to stop with the *us and*

them, because a *greater them* is coming and we're *all* going to be on our bellies in the trenches."

As one, they turned, exchanged glances, and disappeared into their respective vehicles.

Behind me, Herne cupped my elbow. "What was that?"

"I think, a warning." The question was, where had it come from? And who had sent it?

CHAPTER NINE

*B*ack at the office, Herne wasted no time in contacting his mother. Within an hour, two very large, beefy Elves were standing in the waiting room, along with four muscle-bound guards who might have been human. I wasn't sure, and given the dour looks on their faces, I wasn't going to inquire. I had never seen Elves look quite so buff. Their guns could put Jason Momoa to shame, and their shoulders were almost as broad as the doorframe. Their long golden hair was caught back in braids, and their eyes were the clearest blue I had ever seen, except for Herne's.

I retreated to Angel's desk, where she and Talia were ogling the men. "It looks like Cernunnos isn't joking around. He's not going to put up with any backtalk from Saílle or Névé."

Angel was practically drooling. "*I love Rafé, I love Rafé,*" she muttered. "But, oh man, those pecs…"

"And biceps," Talia added.

"Don't forget the thigh muscles. Which fill out those…

Are they wearing *leather pants*?" I licked my lips. I had a thing for men in leather and it suited them *so very well*.

"Yeah, *leather*," Talia said.

"I'd appreciate it if you'd be more discreet about drooling over my father's elite guards. Especially *you*, love, given you're taken." Herne interrupted our gawking, slipping his arm around my waist. He leaned in, nudging my ear with his nose. "I'll make you forget all about them tonight," he whispered.

I caught my breath as he kissed my neck, his hand sliding down to cup my ass. "I'm holding you to that," I muttered.

"Deal." He let go then, and headed over to where the guards were milling.

Viktor joined him, while Yutani wandered over to stand beside me.

"All right, it's going to take awhile to get there. So let's go." Herne glanced back at us. "Hold down the fort. We'll be back before closing." The elevator closed behind them, and I sighed, shaking my head to clear my thoughts.

Yutani tapped me on the shoulder. "I want your opinion on something regarding Mendin's case."

"All right, do I need to come to your office?"

He shook his head. "No, I'll email you the picture."

Sighing, I turned back to Angel and Talia. "So much for the show." But secretly, I couldn't help but think that—regardless of how good those men looked—they couldn't beat Herne in bed. There weren't many mortals, even among the long-lived, who could upstage a god. At least, not *my* god.

Back in my office, I pulled up the email that Yutani had sent. He peeked around the door. "Did you get it?"

"Yeah, just. Come on in." I motioned for him to sit down and he slid into the chair, leaning back as he propped one foot on the edge of the seat and wrapped his arms around his knee. Yutani was flexible, I'd give him that. "What am I looking for?" I opened the attachment. It was a picture of Mendin's coffee table, complete with blood spatters. "Ugh."

"Take a look on the left side of the table. There's an ashtray there. Apparently he smoked. But look near the ashtray. To one side. You might need to enlarge the photo."

I pulled the image up on my Photo-Paint program and zoomed in. *Bingo.* I saw what he was talking about. A matchbook sat there, and I could read its cover.

"*Fire & Fang?* What's that?" The words were printed across the cover, along with a bleeding heart with a dagger sticking through it.

"Haven't you heard of Fire & Fang?" Yutani waited, but I shook my head. "It's a vampire club down in the Catacombs. A kink club. If Mendin met somebody down there…"

"It could easily be a place where someone might hang out looking for victims. But we can't just assume that anybody frequenting a kink club is dangerous." The last thing I wanted to do was go on assumptions. It was a good way to veer off in a wrong direction, and it also was a good way of stigmatizing people.

"I would be the first to agree, normally, but I've *been* to Fire & Fang. It's no simple BDSM club. It's for hard-core players, of all races. And when the vampires play, they play for keeps." Yutani paused, chewing his lip. Finally, he said, "I don't discuss my personal life much, but I think you've figured out that I'm about as far from vanilla as you are from being welcomed into the Fae cities."

I almost blushed. I had realized from early on that Yutani was into kink, and he was also a top in the D&S scene. "Right."

"Well, after one visit to Fire & Fang, I knew I'd never go back. The whole consent and safe-word concept doesn't play out very often there, and that's one of the rules I do play by. I actually would have reported some of what I saw, but the vampires hold a lot of power with the judicial system, given their old-money sway over the financial district. I knew that getting on the bad side of the owners would bite me in the butt."

I chose not to remark on the fact that he went there in the first place. What Yutani did in the bedroom was his own business. "All right, so Mendin visited the club. Or he had a visitor who did and who left the matches. Why would a killer preying on those who work with death magic go there instead of a guild?"

"Several possible reasons. Guilds don't associate much with necromancers and those who do, have exacting rules. The guilds are under a lot of scrutiny, and strangers to any of the legit ones would be eyed suspiciously. It's also easier to isolate a spellcaster who *isn't* a member of a guild, one who works on their own. Mavericks tend to be loners and from what Talia has told me, Mendin didn't have a wide circle of friends."

"Okay, that makes sense. What about Chaya? Isolde's wife? Do you think she had any connection to Fire & Fang?" It seemed odd to me that someone who volunteered at a women's shelter would frequent a club like that.

"That's a good question." Yutani tapped out a note on his tablet. "We should check into the other victims, as well. Were you and Viktor going to go interview them?"

"I think so, though enough time has passed that I doubt we'll find out much that's useful. However, the cops weren't all that thorough in their investigations, so who knows?" I sat back in my chair, my alarms going off. "I have a premonition that you're onto something with this." I tapped my pen on the desk. "I don't want to wait on this. I'll call Isolde, and you call the other families. Be discreet, but see if any of the other four victims frequented that club."

Yutani nodded. "I'll check the reports and decide who to contact. Fire & Fang isn't a club name you bandy around like the Falcons Fraternity, or the Loyal Order of Lions." He stood, stretching. "Hey, thanks."

"For what?" I asked, flipping through my notes to find Isolde's phone number.

"For not being catty, or nosy, or making smart-assed comments."

I gazed up at him. His dark eyes were piercing, and I could see the Great Coyote's chaos behind them. "I've been the butt of too many jokes and nasty remarks because I am who I am. My blood makes me a target. Sexuality and what drives it…those are as much a part of you as blood. It's part of *who* you are, Yutani. I've always had a sense about you, but like my heritage, it's nobody's business but your own."

Yutani held my gaze. "You are Herne's woman, and I will forever respect that. But if you weren't…"

I finished the thought for him. "Yutani, I like you. It took me awhile to warm up to you, but I do like you. But even if I weren't with Herne, I'm not cut out to be a sub. And that's who you're looking for. I think we both know that."

He snickered then, the searching expression vanishing. "Yes, I know that. Although you'd be surprised. Some of the most powerful women I've been with have needed that release the most. Whatever the case, you and Herne are a good match, and I'm happy he's found someone who won't fuck him over like Reilly did. She was a piece of work."

Reilly was Herne's ex-girlfriend. I'd met her a couple times. She had the body of a goddess, but she wasn't cut out to be a one-man woman. "Thanks. I never expected any of this, you know. But stranger things happen." I smiled. "Now, I can't imagine life without him." Shaking my head, I waved at him as he headed back to his office, and then put in a call to Isolde.

When she came on the line I tried to figure out a good approach. Finally, I said, "Hey, I've got a delicate question, but we need to know the answer."

"Ask away. If I can help, I will."

"Do you know if Chaya ever visited a club called Fire & Fang—" No sooner were the words out of my mouth when Isolde interrupted me.

"Damn it, do they have something to do with her death?"

"You know about them?" I asked.

"Know about them? I was livid when she said she needed to visit there. I never even thought to tell you, though." She was crying again, I could hear it in her voice.

"When did she go there, and why?" I grabbed out a notepad and began to scribble notes.

"Three weeks ago. She was trying to help rescue a woman's sister who had been dragged into the sex-slave scene. There's a big difference between the sex workers at the fetish brothels, and the sex slaves at Fire & Fang. They prey on the vulnerable and needy."

I paused. The vamps were good at getting around the rules. They controlled Wall Street and had their fingers into just about every financial institution in the country. That alone bought them freedom from a number of rules, even if it was under the table.

"Did she get the woman out?"

"Yeah, though if you want to talk to her, we'll have to do a workaround. I shouldn't even tell you this, but I trust you. The shelter is hiding her until they can get her out of the area and away from any potential retaliation." Isolde paused, then added, "That club is nothing to mess around with, Ember. And it's not even the owner who's so dangerous. The clients who frequent it are more frightening than the vamp who manages it. He's just out for money for the most part. The clientele are the ones who are unhinged."

"If we wanted to talk to the woman in question, how would we go about doing so?"

Isolde thought for a moment. "Let me call the shelter and talk to them. Maybe we can set up a Zone chat, audio only. That way she can remain anonymous and yet talk to you."

"Can you get back to me ASAP? I'd really like to ask her some questions."

"I'll call down to the shelter and explain the circumstances now, and call you back."

As I set my phone on the table, Yutani peeked around from the hall. He held up his tablet.

"At least one of the other victims had a connection to Fire & Fang. The other families never heard of it, but that doesn't rule it out." He dropped into the chair next to my desk.

"Chaya had a connection, too." I told him what Isolde had said.

"That doesn't surprise me." He paused as my phone rang. It was Isolde again.

"If you want to talk to her, it has to be now. They've found a place to send her where she'll be safe, but she's leaving in an hour. I'll email you a link. Click on it and you can have a Zone conference with her, but it will be audio only. And the shelter asks you to please don't record it. We don't want her voice on record. Too many ways to trace people."

"Email it and I'll get right on it." I hung up and brought up my email. "We can talk to her now, though it's better if you just let me talk." It occurred to me she might clam up if a man came on the chat.

"Roger that." Yutani nodded. "I'll take notes. I could record it and modulate her voice so it's unrecognizable, but given you promised, I won't."

He moved off to one side. Even though we wouldn't be using a video chat, I didn't want to take any chances. Isolde's email came through and I clicked on the link, bringing up a chat window. But it was dark, with no video showing. I entered the password Isolde had sent to me and within seconds, I was in the chat room.

"Hello?" I said. "This is Ember."

A moment later, a woman's voice came on the line.

"I'm Shannon, from the shelter. Can you verify that you are not recording this conversation?"

"I promise on my word as a member of the Wild Hunt, I'm not recording our session."

"Very well. Here she is. You may call her Amy, though that's not her real name. Don't even think of asking for any identifying details. If you do, the conversation will be terminated." Shannon wasn't joking around.

"I promise."

"All right, Amy's ready. Go ahead."

"Hi, Amy, my name's Ember and I work with the Wild Hunt Agency. We need information on a few things about Fire & Fang, and I was hoping you might be able to help us."

"What do you want to know?" The voice was hesitant and fearful.

"First, did you notice anybody around there who didn't fit? Someone new to the club in the past month or so? Someone who probably wasn't a vampire, and who took an interest in any of the necromancers or psychics who might have been there?" I figured I'd jump right into the heart of the matter.

Amy paused, then said, "There were a couple people who came through. I was there for over a year, and we had a pretty steady clientele. We saw the same men—and most of the customers are men—over and over. And then there are the workers. For example, you have your blood-whores, the honey-girls, the ghosts, the ponies, the whipping boys."

"Honey-girls? Ghosts, ponies, and whipping boys?"

"Yeah. Honey-girls lure in the customers. They're the

fresh ones who haven't been beaten down yet. You know, you get more flies with honey…"

"Got it." I frowned.

"The bloodwhores are for the owners and a few vampires who don't have the funds to own a bloodwhore. The ponies are the subs and they serve as the doormats, so to speak. The whipping boys—and girls—are the ones who take abuse. Honey-girls, bloodwhores, the ponies, and whipping boys, they're all there of their own will. But the *ghosts*…I was a ghost." Her voice softened.

"What are the ghosts?"

"We were… They are…the ones brought in off the street with the promise of a warm bed and all the drugs in the world. And then we're not allowed to leave. We're the ones who would be missed the least in society. Ghosts are given to the men who want the roughest play, rougher than the whipping boys and girls will accept. Not all ghosts survive. If you get paired with a cutter or with a choker…you don't always come out the other end. And because ghosts are all streeps, most disappear without anybody ever noticing."

I closed my eyes. I didn't even need to ask what a cutter or choker was. "Is there much of a turnover with the voluntary workers? The bloodwhores, honey-girls, whipping boys, and the ponies?"

"Not really. They get plenty of medical attention when they need it, and they're fed well and kept strong because they can't do this kind of work—or for the bloodwhores, they can't give blood—if they're severely damaged."

"What about the clientele? You said they're all regulars, for the most part? We're looking for somebody who would have a focus on necromancers, bone witches, anybody who works with death." I was trying to figure out where the correlation was.

"Oh, there's more to Fire & Fang than just the kinky side. The house runs illegal gambling in the back. And as for the death cultists, well, there's also a private club who meets there once a week. We call them the Spooks."

Illegal gambling didn't surprise me in the least. "Spooks?"

"The club hosts meeting spots for several underground organizations. Even though I was a ghost, I was such a good worker they put me in charge of waiting tables for them. There's a club there for those working with death magic—we called them the Spooks. They meet every Saturday night. They're all…a little edgy and none of them belong to any regular guilds. It's amazing what people will say in front of you when you keep your mouth shut and stay in the background."

Bingo. We have contact. I glanced at Yutani, trying to think of what to ask next. He slid a note across the desk go me: ASK ABOUT ANY NEW MEMBERS.

"Did you notice anybody new at the club meetings over the past month? Of the Spooks, that is."

Amy paused. After a moment, she said, "Yeah, there were a few strangers there. Two or three. A couple of them struck me as odd because while they were new, they were *too* friendly. Striking up conversations right and left. That seemed strange, because the Spooks tend to be aloof and reticent. And as strange as that seemed, even stranger was how quickly they were welcomed in."

"Did you catch their names? Were they male or female?"

"One was a woman…the other a man. They never came in together, though."

I frowned, then looked at the functions on the chat bar. "Is there a way I can post a few pictures here, to see if you recognize any of the faces?"

Shannon came on the chat again. "Yes, see the image icon to the left? Click on that, and you can upload a picture."

"I just want to know if you saw any of these people when you were there." I quickly uploaded the "before" pictures of our five victims, including Chaya.

A moment later, Amy said, "At least three of them look familiar. I wasn't on duty all the time, so the others may have been there, as well." She identified Chaya, Mendin, and Blink. Blink was one of the other victims, and had died as horribly as the others.

"Thank you. Were any of them the man or woman you were talking about?"

"No, that I'm sure of."

"Did you see them talking to the overly friendly pair?" I knew I was hoping for too much, but if I didn't ask, I wouldn't find out.

Amy paused, then said, "I don't really remember, not all that well. I was really busy and couldn't stand around watching the group. But those three were definitely there."

I thanked her, then asked if there was anything else she might be able to add, but she had to go. As Shannon curtly wished us good luck and hung up, I leaned back, staring at the screen.

"So, Fire & Fang is sitting on a number of unsanctioned activities. *Ghosts*? Of course they're going to pick the most marginalized group, because they have no voice." I was livid. I could too easily see Pain and Shayla ending up in a place like that. "When the fuck is the city going to get it together to help the streeps?"

"Never. Because there will always be homeless people, whether by circumstance or by choice. And even though there's enough to go around, the rich keep doing whatever they can to get richer off the backs of the poor." Yutani shook his head. "It's a fact of life. Sad and heartbreaking? Yes. But with politics what they are, things aren't going to change without a drastic shakeup."

"So...I'm thinking we need to visit Fire & Fang. And we need someone who can pass for a Spook." I leaned back.

"Herne's not going to like what you're thinking," Yutani said.

"Maybe not, but you and I both know it's the best way to find out what's going on." I met his gaze. "My gut tells me that's where our killer met the victims."

We sat there in silence for a moment until we heard a commotion in the waiting room that told us Herne was back from his mission. Feeling the weight of the world on my shoulders, I motioned to Yutani. "Come on, let's go face the music and tell Herne what we're planning."

With an arch of the eyebrows, he followed me.

CHAPTER TEN

*H*erne looked exhausted and Viktor was scowling. Herne waved toward the break room. "I need coffee, and I need sugar."

Any time Herne needed a drink, whether caffeine or alcohol, I knew things had gone badly. I hustled my ass into the break room and poured him a large mug of black coffee. We had half a raspberry cheesecake in the refrigerator, but somehow, I felt that something harder was called for. I found two packages of Oreos in the cupboard and set them on the table, then decided that the cheesecake would go well with the cookies, so added it to the mix. Talia joined me, finding paper plates and silverware.

Herne and Viktor sat down. Viktor was scowling. As Herne dumped three spoons of sugar and a good third of a cup of cream in his coffee, the rest of us joined them. Angel cut the cheesecake and handed slices around.

"I hope your afternoon was better than ours," Herne said.

"Did they hand over Callan?" I asked.

He nodded. "Oh, they handed him over, but the damned fool ran. Viktor and I had to hunt him down and drag him back to Annwn by force, but not before he managed to scare the hell out of a group of elderly women who were out for a picnic in the park. One of them keeled over, so we had to call the medics."

I stifled a snort. Except for the woman fainting, it sounded like a scene out of *Benny Hill* or some idiot comedy. "Was she okay?"

"Yeah, she's fine, but no thanks to Callan. Damned fool ran through the park, waving his sword, screaming at the top of his lungs. We managed to corner him but by then, he had keyed a Bentley parked at the curb with his sword —which the Wild Hunt will have to pay for. He also tripped another woman who was trying to get her kid out of the way and broke her leg. So yet another ambulance."

"And he managed to give me a tidy gash," Viktor said, wincing. "Forty-five stitches."

I groaned. "Callen really didn't want to go home, did he?"

"Apparently not. We stopped at the urgent care clinic after we shoved Callan's ass through the portal over to Annwn, where my father's guards were waiting. They were all for cutting his damned fool head off, but I couldn't let them do that. *Unfortunately.* But Callan's finally back in his own time and my mother used a Forget spell on him. He'll have no idea of what went on here, so he won't be able to change the timeline."

"But what about the time he's been gone?" Angel asked. "Won't that play into the past somehow?"

"It already did. There was a period of time in which Callan seems to have vanished, right before he drove the

Fomorians back. He came wandering out of the mists, unable to account for where he had been. We figure that was the time he was here. So hopefully nothing will be disrupted." He sighed, shaking his head. "Fool Fae. Mucking around with time is dangerous. There are so many ways to fuck up the world by doing so. We've seen it happen."

I paused, frowning. "What do you mean, you've seen it happen?"

Herne glanced at me, shaking his head. "Let's just say, there's another parallel universe in which World War II didn't happen. Hitler never rose to power thanks to an assassin going back. However, in this realm, somebody killed that assassin before she could do her job, and… well…it was as simple as that."

I caught my breath. "I didn't know you dimension-hopped."

"I try not to. It's unsettling and even the act itself can disrupt the flow of time. However, on a few occasions, it's been necessary." He pressed his lips together, frowning.

"How are you doing?" Talia asked Viktor. "Where are your stitches?"

Viktor carefully shrugged out of his jacket. He had a bandage on his arm, covering up what I assumed were the stitches. "I've had better days. At least we took care of him." He cupped his mug, lifting his coffee to let the aroma waft over his face.

"Well, hold onto your hat. Yutani and I've made a discovery." Together, we told them about Fire & Fang. "I think we need to go undercover there," I said.

"You have got to be fucking with my head." Herne

lowered his coffee mug, turning to stare at me. "You are *not* going into Fire & Fang."

"I don't think we have much choice," I said. "We can't be sure, but it seems like the best place to start. *You* can't go. You'd be recognized in an instant. But I thought Yutani, Raven, and I could go. She can suss out magical signatures, especially when it comes to death magic."

"Have you asked her yet?" Herne rubbed his head, groaning. "Please tell me you haven't said anything yet."

"No, of course not. But it seems like our best lead at this point. And the mayor is expecting *us* to deal with this case now. They dropped the damned thing in our laps, so we're stuck with it." I tossed my notes on the table. "Fire & Fang was mentioned in three of the five cases. We can't overlook that as coincidence."

Yutani cleared his throat. "Ember can go as my woman. She'll be better off than if she goes without a man's governance. It's not fair, blah blah blah, but for Fire & Fang, it's true. They run a high male-dominance factor. Raven can get away with it, given there are both male and female members of the Spooks."

"You do realize you might as well be bait?" Herne asked. "And I may not be able to go with you, but I can sure as hell send Viktor."

I let out a sigh. "Won't work."

"And pray tell, why not?" Herne glared at me.

Yutani answered. "Ogres and similar Cryptos aren't allowed. It's vampire, human, magic-born, and Fae only. They only let shifters in if they're either magic-born or vampire, and the latter rarely happens, like with Mendin. I'm afraid it's Ember and me, boss."

Herne looked like he had swallowed a frog. "Fine. And you say Raven could infiltrate this group?"

"She stands a better chance than any of us. The Spooks meet once a week on Saturdays, so I think we should go tomorrow night." I paused, resting my hand on Herne's shoulder. "I know you're worried, but if we don't find the killer soon, there will be more victims. We can't overlook the most promising lead that we have."

Herne stared up at me and I could see the worry flickering in the depths of his eyes. "All right. But I don't like it, not at all."

"I'll go call Raven, then." I leaned down and kissed his forehead, then headed back to my office as they wrapped up the meeting.

When I explained to Raven what we were planning, I could hear the hesitation in her voice.

"I suppose I can help. I don't relish getting involved with a rogue group of necromancers, but it sounds like you don't have many options."

"No," I said. "I know it's a lot to ask, and frankly, I don't like going in there without a vampire to guide us, but I don't know any except Charlie, and he's so wet behind the ears, I wouldn't trust him down in the Catacombs. He'd probably get us killed—by accident, of course." Charlie was too newly sired to go waltzing around the Catacombs without supervision. The fact that he worked for us also made him a target.

"Hold on. I may not have a vampire who can help us, but I have a friend who's a PI and who might be able to find out some information for us. His name is Wager Chance, and he runs an investigation agency that's housed down there. He's half Dark Fae and half magic-born. Do you want me to bring him over tonight, if he can make it?"

If Raven trusted him, he'd be all right. "Call me back. If he can make it tonight, it can't hurt to ask him if he can help somehow. We'll make dinner."

Hustling back to the break room, I caught the others as they were getting ready to leave for the day. I told them what Raven had said and they all agreed it couldn't hurt to ask.

"Do you want to come over to talk to her?" I asked.

Herne and Yutani said yes, they'd be over around eight. Viktor had a date with his girlfriend, and Talia had an appointment with her hairdresser. Charlie wouldn't be in until late, given the sun was going down later every day, so Angel set out the files we needed him to enter into the computer before we left.

Angel and I stopped at the store to pick up ingredients for spaghetti and salad. We'd been so busy that neither one of us had remembered to go grocery shopping. As we were heading out of the store, Raven called to tell me that she, Wager, and Kipa would be over at around eight. By the time we got home it was nearly seven forty-five. Angel dove straight into cooking while I fed Mr. Rumblebutt and did a quick tidy-up in the living room.

I was sorting through the mail—mostly junk mail and bills—when the doorbell rang.

Raven had brought Raj, who was a gargoyle the size of a rottweiler. He kind of looked like a rottweiler, too. His wings had been cut off when he was a baby and Raven had rescued him from the demon who owned him. They were inseparable companions now.

She was decked out in a purple corset, a skirt made out of chiffon with a tulle petticoat, and a pair of platform PVC ankle boots over striped leggings. Her hair was as long as mine, though it was a dark brunette streaked with purple—a natural coloring. She was plump, curvy, and goth-beautiful.

Kipa, her boyfriend, was essentially Herne's distant cousin. Lord of the Wolves, Kipa was a wild child from Finland. He and Herne had a rocky history, but Raven was keeping him on the narrow, if not the straight, road. Swarthy with olive undertones, Kipa had long hair braided back into numerous plaits, and his beard was well trimmed but thick. He had a row of piercings in each ear, and a dolphin bite piercing on his lip.

Wager Chance, I had never met. His hair and eyes matched mine—ink black, and green as the forest, but he was tanned as though he had spent long days on the beach, and he was about average height and size. He held out his hand.

"Hello," he said. "Raven's told me a lot about you."

"Everybody take a seat. Herne and Yutani will be here soon enough." I had no sooner turned back to close the door behind them when I saw the pair walking up the sidewalk. "Speak of the devil…"

"Dinner's ready, everyone get your butts to the table," Angel called out.

ONCE WE WERE ALL SEATED AROUND THE TABLE WITH

dinner, and Raj was looking for Mr. Rumblebutt in vain—Mr. Rumblebutt was far less impressed with the gargoyle than Raj was with Mr. Rumblebutt—I cleared my throat and set down my fork.

"Here's the situation." With Herne and Yutani's help, I told Raven, Kipa, and Wager about the serial killer, the fact that the mayor had asked us to look into the matter, and what we had learned about Fire & Fang.

"So really, that's the only lead we have right now. We thought we'd go down there tomorrow night. The Spooks meet on Saturdays, and Raven's the only one of us who could possibly gain a seat in their meeting." I forked up a mouthful of noodles and sauce. Even with store-bought sauce, Angel's spaghetti tasted homemade.

"I suppose that I can't go along, either," Kipa said, scowling. "I don't like the idea of Raven going down there without me."

"I've gone down to the Catacombs on my own before. You'll just have to stay at home and wait," Raven said, bopping him on the nose.

"I've heard of Fire & Fang," Wager said. "Yutani's right. It's not a club for the faint of heart. Seriously, we're talking underground club, as in, a *lot* of questionable activities. I had a client whose husband frequented the club, and she was looking to get away before he either dragged her down there with him to sell her off, or he decided he was bored with her and killed her to avoid paying alimony. I managed to help her get away with half their assets, but she had to leave the country and go into hiding. Luckily, he was a professor at the Hexable School of Magic and he knew what would happen if I broke all the sordid details open for the board of directors to find out. He would have been out on his ass."

Wager sopped up some sauce with a chunk of French bread. "But listen, if you go down into that club, don't drink anything. Don't eat anything. Pay for a drink and play with it, but when you get the chance, dump it out. Don't go to the bathroom alone, either. Women go into that club and they don't come out. Raven can get away with going in solo because she's got an excuse—she's a necromancer. But Ember, you just don't give off the dominatrix vibe."

I caught my breath, then said, "What about if I let my Leannan Sidhe side out more? She's far from tame."

"Too risky," Herne said. "You can't always control the energy." He gave me a long look, though.

"The best bet is for me to take her in as my woman, and to say I'm looking to—" Yutani paused, glancing at Herne. "Pardon me, and you too, Ember, but the best bet is for me to say I want to watch other guys have a go at her." His expression remained impassive.

I gulped. Even the thought of that made me queasy. "I don't think I like that."

"That's partially the attraction for the men there. But I can conveniently decide no one there meets my fantasies. The fact that you'll be marked as mine should keep you safe. There's a strong hands-off policy when it comes to a top and his subs, unless permission is granted. If you go in there without being claimed by someone, I guarantee you somebody's going to try something and when you fight back, we'll all either be kicked out, or you'll be in a shitload of trouble." Yutani shook his head. "This isn't like the fetish brothels across the street from our office.

They don't use safe words down in Fire & Fang. They don't respect boundaries, except when it comes to an owner."

"I guess that's our best option," I said, grimacing. "I don't like it, but we're not letting Raven go down there alone."

"*I'm* not going down there alone," Raven said, "so no worries on that. I want you guys there. You say I can probably get in solo?"

"Yeah," Wager said. "Since you're also Ante-Fae, they'll notice right up front. They'll ask you what you want, and you can tell them you heard about the Spooks."

"How will I have heard about them, though, if they're an underground group?"

"Simple," Yutani said. "Tell them you were a friend of Mendin's. He was a loner. Nobody's going to know you didn't know him. We can give you some background on him so you can answer questions about him."

"Smart plan," I said. "I guess we have our tickets in. When we're in there, we need to be on the lookout for anybody who seems fixated on the Spooks, in particular."

Herne turned to Wager. "What kind of work do you do, mostly? And why do you have your office down in the Catacombs?"

"I have a close working relationship with the vampire community. They made room for me, and I've done a number of jobs for them. My own people—the Fae, that is —ignore me. The magic-born, well, I've never been too good at rules and regulations and my powers aren't strong enough for most of them to make a place for me in their ranks." He glanced over at me. "You understand about how tralaeths are treated."

"Yeah, I do. I'm sorry that you're on the receiving end of that, too." I frowned. Wager seemed like a nice guy.

"How did you get in with the vamps?" Kipa asked.

Wager let out a faint laugh. He tapped the corners of his lips with his napkin. "When I was younger, I used to hang out with a rough crowd. They dared me to go down into the Catacombs. Stupidly, I took the dare, and I made my way down into the underground. I got lost, and I wandered into dangerous territory. These two vamps were bearing down on me, and I thought I was done for."

"Amazing how stupid we can be when we're young," Angel said.

Wager laughed. "Right. Well, turned out the vamps worked for the bank that I cashed my checks at. I was a delivery boy. One of them recognized me because I went in there every Friday afternoon to deposit my check and get cash for the next week. He and his buddy gave me a good talking-to and escorted me out of the Catacombs. On the way, one of them asked what I was doing down there and I told them."

"I bet they liked that," Herne said, laughing.

Wager chuckled. "They scared the fuck out of me, told me to quit the gang, and right on the spot, one offered me a job as a courier for the bank. I took it, left behind BLAM —the Boys on the Lam—and my life started taking off. When I decided I wanted to become a private investigator, I talked to Ozrik—one of the two vamps who got me on my feet. He offered me low rent down in the Catacombs and promised to send business my way."

"BLAM. I've heard of that gang. Apparently, it's still around."

"Yeah, but the guys who were in it with me are all

dead. Gang violence, ODs, you name it, they died from it. I credit Ozrik and the vamps with saving my life. We get together for dinner every so often. Actually, working down in the Catacombs provides me with more jobs than I'll ever be able to handle." Wager bit into a second piece of French bread. "This is good. My kudos to the chef."

Angel brightened. "Thanks, but I just threw together a jar of sauce with the pasta."

"Don't let her kid you," I said. "She added herbs, specialty cheeses, and a smidge of her cooking magic to make this. Angel's incredible in the kitchen."

"That we can attest to," Yutani said, raising his glass. "Here's to a successful venture."

Even as we clinked out glasses together, I couldn't help but dwell on the fact that we were going in blind. We had no real idea of what to expect, or of how the killer would retaliate, if they figured out what we were doing. But I raised my glass, joining the toast, hoping that we'd find a little good luck on our side.

EVERYONE HAD LEFT EXCEPT HERNE. ANGEL WAS IN HER room, folding clothes. Herne sat on my bed with Mr. Rumblebutt snuggled against him. He absently stroked his fur, and Mr. Rumblebutt was purring loud enough to wake the dead.

"So, my mother said you were taken aback by what she asked you to do. And before you ask, she didn't tell me what that was." He lay across the bed on his side as I took off my makeup and brushed out my hair.

"Yeah," I said, setting down my brush and turning

around. "It seems that my Leannan Sidhe blood is getting...bottlenecked. I need to use those powers more frequently, and she suggested that I let them out when we're...when you and I are..." I blushed, suddenly feeling awkward, given Morgana was his mother and had been talking about our sex life.

"In bed?" Herne said.

I nodded. "Yeah, and I'm kind of freaking out about it. I know I can't hurt you—that's not the problem. But what if you like me better that way?"

"I love you no matter what. But say I do enjoy it. What would be the problem? It's not like you're a different person. You're just going to explore another side of your nature. It's not like you've got multiple personalities." He sat up, crossing his legs. "I love *you*, Ember. I love *all* of you. I love you when you're gentle, and I love you when you're a spitfire—both in bed and out. No matter what, I'm going to enjoy making love to you, regardless of whether you're climbing all over me, or whether you're curled in the nook of my arm."

I licked my lips. "Logically I know that, but—oh, I don't know why this is so hard for me!"

"I think I do," Herne said. "I think you're afraid that *you'll* like that part of yourself, and the chaos frightens you. I think you're afraid you'll become less compassionate. But that can't happen. Ember, you have so many facets to your personality. You're brave and loyal, and sometimes you're hot-headed and careless. You're loving and true to your friends. You're determined, and when someone throws down the gauntlet, you're willing to charge ahead. The Leannan Sidhe blood...it's already in play. You just haven't *fully* unleashed your abilities except for the times when they've spontaneously risen to protect you. *Why not* see what you can do with them for your pleasure as well as your protection? You might find you like that side of yourself more than you think."

He stretched out on the bed, spreading out his arms. I slowly stood, sliding out of my jeans and moving toward the bed. I had almost reached the edge when both Herne's phone and mine rang simultaneously. I was about to ignore it, but something inside said, *No, answer it.* I turned to the nightstand.

Herne was faster. He was staring at his phone, his eyes dark. "Crap. Come on, get dressed. Viktor needs us."

I grabbed my phone and brought up the group text message. Viktor had sent it to everyone. It read: SHEILA'S BEEN ATTACKED. SHE'S IN THE HOSPITAL. CAN YOU COME?

"I'll get dressed. You grab Angel and text him for directions."

All thoughts of sex out the window, I slid my jeans and bra back on, then a clean tank top. I pulled my hair back in a ponytail and shoved my feet in my boots. Within ten minutes, the three of us were heading to the hospital, praying that Sheila—Viktor's girlfriend—was all right.

CHAPTER ELEVEN

*H*erne drove, with me riding shotgun and Angel right behind me. We reached the hospital in ten minutes. He dropped Angel and me at the door while he went to find a parking space. As we rushed into the ER, we saw Viktor pacing the waiting room. He had a frantic look on his face and I could see that he had been crying.

"Viktor, what happened?" I hurried over to him, Angel following.

He gave me a frantic look. "I just want to know how she is. They won't tell me anything."

"Let me see what I can find out," Angel said, striding toward the admittance desk.

I led Viktor over to one of the sofas. "Come on, sit down. Herne will be here in a moment."

He nodded, rubbing his head. "I've never been so worried in my life. What will I do if something happens to her? I love her, Ember. I was going to propose to her on Beltane. What if—"

"No. *No what-ifs.* Put all those thoughts on hold till the doctor can talk to us." I glanced up to see Herne striding down the hallway. At that moment, Talia texted me.

I'M ON MY WAY. I STOPPED TO PICK UP YUTANI.

"Talia's on her way with Yutani. They'll be here soon." I patted his arm as Herne hurried over to Viktor's other side.

"Hey, man, what happened? Where's Angel?" Herne asked, frowning as he looked around.

"She went to find out if the doctor can tell us anything." I tapped Viktor's arm again. "Hey, big guy, tell us what went down."

Viktor wiped his eyes on his sleeve. "I was supposed to pick her up after she was done for the day. She took today off and was spending it at the library, and she had a book club meeting tonight. I was late getting there, and as I drove up, I saw the ambulance and cops. I had a feeling... I just knew, you know? You know when your gut just screams that something's wrong?"

"Yes, we know. What happened?"

"Sheila was waiting at the bus stop. I guess she thought I forgot to pick her up, and I had forgotten to text her that I was going to be late. While she was waiting, some doped-up streep pushed her against the wall and demanded her purse. There were witnesses but they weren't doing anything to stop him, because he had a knife and people are fucking afraid to get involved. She gave him the purse, but I guess she wasn't fast enough because he went nuts and slashed her throat. She collapsed, and the fucking SOB went full psycho on her, kicking her in her ribs and hips. Nobody even *tried* to stop him. There were five people at that stop and not one fucking person tried to intervene."

I wanted to say they were probably scared, but right now it wasn't a good time to take anybody else's side. "Did the cops catch him?"

Viktor shook his head. "No, but some woman got a picture of him on her phone, and she called 911 after the guy staggered off. She's in surgery now. She bled so much. There was blood everywhere, and she was lying so still." He paled, shaking. "What if she dies? I was *supposed* to be there. If I had been on time, she wouldn't be lying on a hospital bed now."

"Take it easy," Herne said. "This isn't your fault. There are always a dozen *if-onlys* for every trauma in life. You weren't the junkie who cut her."

Angel returned at that moment. "The doctor will be out in a while to talk to us. Meanwhile, does Sheila have any family in the area? They want to contact them."

Viktor closed his eyes. "Oh my gods, is it that bad? Yes, she has a sister who lives in Port Angeles, and her mother lives over on Bainbridge Island. I have Sheila's phone with me. I'll call them." He headed over to the desk, his shoulders slumped.

I let out a sigh. "Did the nurse say anything else?"

Angel shook her head. "No, though he asked me if Sheila was religious, just in case. I told them she's pagan so they're bringing in a priestess." She paused, then added, "I think it's bad. What are we going to do for him if—"

"*No*," Herne said. "I won't let Viktor go there, and we aren't going there either unless and until it happens. He needs us to be strong."

"You guys, he told me he was going to propose to her on Beltane, so…" I shrugged. "Look, Talia and Yutani are here." I nodded toward the door, where they were walking down the hallway toward us. Talia saw me and they headed over to where we were standing.

"What happened?" Yutani asked.

"A streep attacked Sheila. He robbed her, got freaked, and slashed her throat." I motioned to Viktor, who was still on the phone. "He's talking to her family now. We don't know how she's doing yet."

At that moment, a couple of cops walked in, one of them Erica, a friend of Viktor's and one of our best contacts. She zeroed in on us immediately.

"Viktor around? Oh, I see him." She glanced at the desk. "Any news?"

I shook my head. "Not yet. Viktor's talking to her family. Did you catch the guy?"

Erica shook her head. "No, but we know who he is. We got a good description from the bystanders, and one of them recognized him. I have a picture I want to show Sheila when she's able to be questioned."

"Her throat was cut. The doctor has yet to let us know how she's doing," Herne said.

"I know her throat was cut. I was there. I was one of the cops on the job. I'm the one who called Viktor. But the sooner we positively ID this guy, the sooner we can pick him up. We don't want to go after him now, because he's a lot more than just a streep."

"Oh?" Angel asked.

Erica sighed, brushing a strand of long blond hair out of her face. She was Dark Fae, but unlike most of her comrades on the force, she never turned up her nose at me. "His name is Falcon Smith, and he hangs around the streeps for a good reason, which is why people think he's one of them. In actuality, he's a crackalaine dealer. Sometimes, in between shipments, he's been known to get fucked up and go on robbery sprees. We've busted him a number of times, but he's got a sharp lawyer and he always gets off. I think he may be the front for a bigger operation run by vamps. And—"

"They own the financial district and can pay off just about anybody," Herne said, sighing. "Please do *not* tell Viktor or he's likely to hunt down Falcon and kill him. Wait until we know for sure?"

Erica nodded. "I feel bad keeping things from the big guy, but I agree." She stopped abruptly as Viktor finished talking on the phone and returned to the waiting area.

"Erica! Tell me you caught the guy?"

She shook her head. "Not yet, but we have some leads. I dropped in to check on Sheila's condition."

"We don't—" Viktor paused as a doctor in a white coat approached us. A tall black woman, she was carrying a chart and had a weary look on her face.

"I'm Dr. Fuhrman. Are you waiting for news about Sheila Masters?" the doctor asked.

"I'm her boyfriend," Viktor said. "How is she? Will she be all right?"

The doctor said nothing but opened the chart. "Have you notified her family?"

"Yes, her mother's on the way. Her father died last year." Viktor's voice was trembling. "Please tell me how she is, doctor."

"Well, she sustained a lot of damage to her throat. The

knife clipped her vocal cords and I'm not sure how much trouble she'll have speaking when they heal up. But she's in stable condition. We managed to get enough blood back in her so she's not in danger any longer. She lost a lot of blood. The assailant also stabbed her shoulder. I ended up giving her seventy-three stitches on her throat and neck, and twenty stitches on her arm. The beating left her with two broken ribs and a bruised hip, but luckily, the ribs didn't puncture a lung. She's groggy, but if you'd like to see her, I can let you talk to her for a few minutes. She won't be able to speak, and I don't want her upset, or trying to speak, do you understand?" Dr. Fuhrman gave Viktor a stern look.

"I understand. Thank you, thank you for saving her life."

"Dr. Fuhrman? I need to see her too. I have a couple questions, but she can answer yes or no with her hand. I just need her to identify a picture." Erica held up her hand as Viktor started to speak. "Don't even ask. Right now, you can help me best by keeping clear of the investigation."

"Who the hell…you have more than just a lead, don't you?" Viktor glared at Erica.

"Yes we do, but the last thing I need is for you to go running off after someone we *think* may be guilty. We don't know for sure and I don't want you mucking up the investigation, do you understand? There are…obstacles… in this case, and we need to handle it carefully." Erica turned back to the doctor. "Perhaps it's best if I see her first and then I'll be on my way. I promise you, I'll try not to agitate her."

Viktor sputtered but the doctor, taking one look at

him, agreed and escorted Erica back through the double doors leading to the ER rooms. Herne clapped Viktor on the shoulder and forcibly led him back to the sofa. Talia joined them. She could usually calm Viktor down when he was angry. Angel wandered over to the vending machines, searching through her pockets for change. Yutani and I stayed where we were. I rubbed my forehead.

"The big lug. He needs to understand there are some things he can't solve by running full tilt into the fray." Viktor was fairly level headed, but in matters of the heart, all bets were off.

"I agree, but that's not likely to happen. Erica should have waited until he went back to see Sheila before talking to the doctor. Meanwhile, this means we'll be forced to babysit him because he's not going to take this lying down. At least he doesn't know who Erica's looking for. Any dealer backed by the vamps is going to have an extensive operation. However, given the fact that this Falcon has moved on to slashing throats in his spare time, the vamps may very well consider him a liability." Yutani pulled out his tablet and began tapping away.

"What are you looking up?"

"Precursory info on Falcon Smith. I have a feeling if I go into the Dark Web I'll have better luck, though." Yutani had, a few months ago, stumbled onto a way to get into the Dark Web without being traced. He was always cautious—the Dark Web was a dangerous place in which to roam, but there was so much useful information there that he had worked on building a silent pathway into the underbelly of the internet.

"When you get a chance, do it. The moment Viktor finds out, if the cops haven't caught Falcon by then, he's going to go on a rampage." I glanced over at Viktor, who was quietly listening to Herne and Talia.

"Yeah, and that's one explosion we're not going to be able to rein in."

With that, we returned to the others.

BY THE TIME HERNE DROPPED US OFF AT OUR HOUSE, IT WAS three in the morning. I leaned against the driver's side window. "Sure you don't want to come in?"

He shook his head. "You need sleep, love. Tomorrow night you're headed down to Fire & Fang. And as much as I don't like the thought of it, I want you well rested and alert. We'll pick up where we left off soon enough." He leaned out the window and kissed me. "And quit worrying. I love you. *All of you.*"

I nodded, brushing his hair out of his face. "I can't believe how lucky I am." I paused, then added, "We need to watch Viktor. If he finds out that Falcon Smith attacked Sheila, he's going to go ballistic and hunt the creep down. If the cops don't find Falcon soon, we might have to intervene. Given the guy's connection with the vamps, it could go very bad, very quickly. Yutani's doing some sleuthing on the Dark Web. The more we know about Smith, the better. If we can hand him over to the cops, then Viktor won't have a reason to go after him. At least not until he gets out of jail."

"True that. All right, I'll do some snooping around too. You guys swinging by the office before you go to Fire & Fang? If so, I'll come in. Otherwise, I thought I'd tackle another problem—a more personal one—that my father dumped in my lap."

"No, I think we're actually going to drop in on Charlie to ask if he has any advice for us. Though honestly, as newly turned as Charlie is, I have the feeling that Yutani knows more about the vamps than our clerk."

"Just call me before you head into the Catacombs, please. Or maybe I'll drop over to talk to you before then, if I get the chance." With that, Herne kissed me again and then eased out of the driveway, back onto the road. As I watched him go, I felt suddenly lonely. I loved my own space, I liked having my own house, but the longer Herne and I were together, the harder it was getting to be apart for any length of time.

Overhead, a sudden gust of warm wind came barreling by, and I caught sight of an owl sitting in one of our trees. It stared down at me, then suddenly went gliding off the limb, sailing down to the front yard. I heard one shrill squeak, and the owl pulled up again, a mouse dangling in its feet. As the owl sailed back to its perch, I had a sudden feeling of dread and hurried inside, wanting to be away from the dark with its prying eyes.

NEXT MORNING, ANGEL AND I DRAGGED OURSELVES OUT OF bed at nine and spent a couple of hours on our weekly chores. We divided them up, and every Saturday morning, we set to, usually before breakfast, and cleaned our way through the house. Then Angel would make brunch, we'd eat, and I'd clean up the dishes.

But first, coffee. I fired up the espresso machine while

she fixed herself a cup of English breakfast tea, two bags strong. I pulled four shots and added milk, caramel, and ice to make an iced caramel latte. We sat down at the table with our to-do list, still tired from the night before.

"I should call Viktor and ask how Sheila's doing," I said, stifling a yawn.

"Text him instead. If he's still sleeping, which I would think he is, you don't want to wake him." Angel sipped her tea and glanced over the list. "Okay, this week, I have the floors, dusting, and straightening up, while you have bathrooms and laundry. We both clean the kitchen."

"Ugh. I hate doing bathrooms. But at least it doesn't take too long. I'm grateful neither one of us is a slob, though." I chugged down half my latte. "I guess we'd better get a move on."

She finished her tea and pushed back her chair. "All right. Let's get going."

Mr. Rumblebutt decided to help me with the bathrooms. He liked walking around while I worked, staring at me like some miniature micromanager. I cleaned the hall bath first, given it was the one company used. While the cleanser soaked off soap and scum from the shower walls, I cleaned the toilet, then washed the vanity and polished the mirror. I bagged the garbage, then rinsed off the shower walls and carried the rugs out to the side yard where I shook them clean. After replacing them, I moved on to Angel's bathroom, then to mine. I finished shortly before she was done vacuuming the living room. I sorted the laundry, starting a load of clothes before returning to the kitchen.

Angel finished her chores—we were both responsible

for cleaning, or not, our own bedrooms—and began making brunch. I washed my hands and set the table.

"What are we having?" I paused over the bowls. "What do we need?"

"I thought we'd have sausage cheese muffins, tomato soup, a fruit salad, and Danish pastries. That work for you?" She held up the sausage patties, waiting for my answer.

"That sounds wonderful." I pulled out two bowls, two plates, two clear ramekins for the fruit salad, and a platter for the pastries. I set the table, then arranged the Danish on the platter. After that, I fixed myself a second latte and made another cup of tea for Angel.

The sun splashed through the kitchen window, bathing us with its warmth. I sat down, turning my face toward the sun. The light soothed me at first, but then I felt an odd sting from it, and I found myself moving my chair out of the direct focus of the beam.

"It's too bright for this time of year. I'm glad to see the spring but it feels too sudden, if you know what I mean."

"What did you say?" Angel asked, carrying the soup and sandwiches to the table. She handed me the fruit salad before filling our bowls with tomato soup. It tasted like it had been simmering for hours, the flavors were so vivid and bright.

"I'm not sure—I mean…" Even though I knew precisely what I had said, I wasn't sure why I'd said it. "I feel weird. I'm not sure what's up." I paused, staring at my plate. "Maybe I'm just nervous about tonight. I wish Herne could go with us."

"You mean instead of Yutani?" Angel bit into her sandwich, then delicately wiping the corner of her mouth.

"Or along with. I like Yutani. We've been talking a lot more lately, but he's…"

"He's chaos incarnate. His father is a trickster, even if he does shift things to help rather than hurt. Yutani always has a restless feel about him. Has he said anything about wanting to take a trip or anything? Lately when I've been near him, I keep thinking he's searching for something and he doesn't know what it is."

"That's the perfect way to describe him." I shook my head. "No, he hasn't said anything. *Though*…and don't you say a word about this! He actually told me that if I wasn't with Herne…" I let the thought drift, looking over at her.

Her face was blank for a moment, then she laughed and shook her head. "No. Just no. You and Yutani would kill each other. I think you could end up good friends, but right now I can tell you that we'd have to drag the river if you two got involved."

I nodded. "I know. If Yutani and I were together, we'd either burn each other to a crisp, or we'd blow it all sky-high. He likes to control the relationship, and I won't be controlled. Not that way." I bit into my sandwich and then began spooning the soup into my mouth.

We ate in comfortable silence for a while, the only sounds those of the traffic outside, and of Mr. Rumblebutt playing with one of his squeaky toys. He brought it to me and dropped it at my feet. The toy was a stuffed squirrel that squeaked when you shook it, and I picked it up and threw it down the hallway for him. He raced to it, bringing it back again.

We played fetch while I ate. Angel and I seemed to be in a similar mood, because we ate in a comfortable silence. But the staccato *tick* of the grandfather clock

reminded me that tonight, I'd be deep into the Catacombs, looking for a murderer. Once again, the feeling of
foreboding cast a pall over my mood, but this time I let
myself drift in the sensation, not fighting, but only
observing.

CHAPTER TWELVE

I called Yutani from the grocery store. Except for the remains of last night's dinner, the cupboards were bare and I had told Angel I'd do the shopping if she would weed the raised vegetable beds we had planted.

"I'm not sure if I should dress as usual, or in some leather bondage gear, or a Love Shed nightgown with peekaboo nipple tassels." I prayed he wouldn't suggest the latter two.

"Black mini-dress, low cut. I'll bring a collar for you—don't ask, it won't hurt." He sounded like he was enjoying this a bit too much. "Wear flats. Stilettos would be more appropriate, but if we have to run, I don't want you stumbling. Also, while the dress should show off all your assets, make sure it doesn't slow you down by being too tight, and make sure your tattoo is covered."

I felt better. That Yutani was considering my safety made the whole endeavor more bearable. "Anything else? What about weapons?"

"They have a metal detector at the door. You can't bring in anything like a dagger. We're going to have to watch our step in there, and make certain we don't engage in a situation likely to blow up in our faces, because we're going in unarmed." He paused, then added, "Remember to leave the silver at home, out of courtesy to the vamps."

"Right, I hadn't thought of that."

"I'd take my whip as part of my costume, but I doubt they'd allow it in." Yutani's father—the Great Coyote—had given him a whip as a present. We weren't sure all that it was capable of, but it was woven with ilithiniam in it—a silvery blue metal that was magical in nature and difficult to find. The dwarves were able to dig deep enough to mine it, but it might as well have been a myth to most people. Great Coyote had woven the metal into thin strands, and plaited it into the braided whip as he made it.

"I wish you could. For what it's worth, Raven and I will have our magical abilities. Speaking of which, she'll be at my place at five P.M. See you then."

I hung up, mentally running over the clothes in my closet as I added various cheeses to the cart. We needed just about everything, so I made a clean sweep of the supermarket, piling the cart high. I added the frozen goods at the end—ice cream and frozen veggies and several heat-and-serve meals for when we were too tired to cook. Then, with one last stop in the cat food aisle for litter and food, I headed to the checkout stand. Three hundred and fifty dollars later, I transferred the groceries into my car and headed home.

Angel was mowing the front lawn and as I pulled into the driveway, she met me at the car, helping me carry the groceries in.

"Yutani wants me to wear a black mini-dress and flats tonight. I don't think I have a black mini-dress. I guess I have to go shopping, right? Except I really don't want to." I frowned at the bread as I handed it to Angel, who was putting the food away as I unpacked the bags.

"You should call Raven. Though she's a little curvier than you, you can still wear some of her clothes. I bet she has something like that."

"Good idea," I said, pulling out my phone. When Raven answered, I explained what I needed and she affirmed that she had a couple outfits that might work.

"I'll bring them with me when I come over. I'll come a little early so we can go shopping if what I bring isn't quite right."

"Sounds good. See you at around four-ish?"

"Let's make it three-thirty." She signed off and I went back to helping Angel put away the groceries.

RAVEN HAD LEFT RAJ AT HOME, BUT KIPA WAS WITH HER, obviously as reluctant as Herne was about us going. To my surprise, Herne showed up with Yutani.

"I managed to free some time, but I'll have to leave in half an hour," he said, looking grim.

"Come on," Raven said, motioning to the stairs. "Let's try these on you."

I followed her up the stairs, leaving Angel and the men to talk. We closed the door to my bedroom and Raven laid out the dresses on the bed. She had found three. One was a mini-dress, all right—a wiggle dress. It had a plunging square neckline and long sleeves that would cover up my tattoo. The second looked suspiciously like a chemise with spaghetti straps. And the third was a black cocktail dress that looked a little too formal.

"I think the first would be best," I said. "That way, my tattoo will be covered. Though I'm not looking forward trying to get into it."

"Good point. Here, I brought some ballet flats that have velvet ankle ribbons. These should work with the dress." She set them beside the wiggle dress and they looked like a good match. "Take off your clothes. You'll want to go commando, because anything you wear underneath will show."

I grimaced. "I don't usually go without underwear. What about my bra? Gravity isn't pretty, you know."

"Well, the dress is tight enough that it should act like a support system. It does for me. Here, strip and hold your hands up and I'll help get it over your head." She motioned for me to undress. "Hey, Wager called me this morning. He found out a few more things, but I'd rather tell you and Yutani together."

"All right, we can discuss it when we get to Charlie's." I tossed my jeans and tank on the bed. Reluctantly, I took off my underwear and bra and held my arms up. I wasn't self-conscious. Nudity among the Fae wasn't all that important.

Raven slid the dress over my head and I poked my arms through the sleeves. She scrunched the material like you do with pantyhose, and then tugged it over my boobs while I shifted them so they wouldn't be flattened against my chest. She was right—the material held them in place, though I could clearly see my nipples. Finally, the dress was down to my waist and while she tugged on the back, I tugged on the front. It barely reached my upper thighs, but I wasn't worried about it riding up. Even my corsets didn't feel this snug. I might as well be wearing a body-length girdle.

"Crap, this dress is making me claustrophobic." I glanced in the mirror. Every curve of my body was accentuated beneath the side ruching. "I feel more naked than I did without my clothes."

She bit her lip, staring at me for a moment. "You look more naked, to be honest. It works on you, though, and it's perfect for where we're going." She walked me over to the mirror.

The dress was low cut, the wide square neck barely skimming my nipples. The sleeves came down to my wrists, and the material clung to my hips. I was aware of every single inch of my body, especially the fact that I wasn't wearing underwear. The dress was sex on a hanger.

"Wow." I stared at myself, unable to pry my gaze away from my reflection. "I'm…"

"Hot. Sizzling. Here, sit down."

"I don't know if I can."

"Just keep your legs together when you do." She guided me onto my vanity bench and I pressed my knees together. Raven undid my ponytail, brushing my long locks and using a curling iron to give the waves even more curl. They fell around my shoulders, cascading down my back. Raven pinned one side back with a red rose barrette.

"You should do your makeup. Lay it on a little thick."

She joined me on the bench, leaning forward to check her own face. Raven was wearing a purple PVC corset, a black multilayered skirt with petticoat, a low-slung black belt, and a pair of gold hoop earrings.

"You look great."

"Let's hope I can worm my way into the Spooks, or the evening might be a complete bust." She touched up her eyeliner, which was thick and cat-winged to the sides. As she brushed her hair, the purple highlights shimmered under the light.

I tucked my phone, one credit card, and fifty bucks in cash into a small clutch and slipped into the flats, struggling to place my foot on the edge of the bed in order to tie them up. Raven had me sit down again and she knelt, wrapping the ribbons around my ankles and tying them securely for me.

"Ready?" I asked Raven.

She nodded. "Not really, but let's go. Oh, you aren't carrying silver on you, are you?"

"No, why?" Then I stopped. "Oh, right. The vamps."

HERNE TOOK ONE LOOK AT ME AND TRIED TO VETO THE mission, but with all of us arguing against him, he finally caved.

Yutani fastened a leather collar around my throat. It was studded with stainless steel spikes and a gold O-ring at the throat. I cringed, but it identified me as having an owner.

Finally, we made it out the door and on the way to Charlie's apartment. It was nearly six P.M., so we had plenty of time. According to Amy's information, the Spooks met around nine, and we didn't want to arrive early in case something gave us away.

WE HAD FIRST MET CHARLIE DARREN ON A CASE. HERNE had hired him out of pity, I had the feeling, but it had turned out to be a good thing. Charlie was brilliant with numbers.

His sire had been killed by the vamps themselves due to his rogue nature, so Charlie was left adrift without a sponsor in the Vampire Nation, which was pretty much akin to being an orphan in a college frat house that only accepted legacies.

Charlie hadn't embraced his vampire lifestyle, but his parents had disowned him, his girlfriend had left him, and he had agonized over having to drop out of college.

He had wanted to be an accountant. Now that he worked for the Wild Hunt, Herne had decided to pay his way through night school, so he was training to become a CPA. Once he graduated, he would take over the business end of things as a way of repaying Herne. Charlie came into the office during the evenings, since vamps couldn't walk out under the daylight, and he often showed up at our parties. He and Viktor were friendly and they hung out together.

"At least he lives in a better place than that rat-infested slum we first found him in," I muttered.

"That he does," Yutani said. "And he now has the most important thing he could have."

"What's that?" asked Raven, from the back seat.

"*Hope*. I think that if more vampires didn't feel so hopeless, they'd be less dangerous and more capable of keeping themselves in check. Look how well most of the bankers do."

"Yeah," I said, "but you forget one thing. A lot of those bankers can easily hire somebody to take care of their enemies. They can exact all the revenge they want and get away with it."

"Say what you will, I maintain that's different than a vampire who destroys out of despair." Yutani turned into a parking garage on 27th Place West. The Invest, a five-story building, was gated, with a doorman in front, and a pair of guards who met the elevators coming up from the garage. Residents and visitors had to transfer to an internal elevator system at the main lobby. The building was high security and high tech—the first of its kind in Seattle, built specifically for vampires.

The windows were all tinted and each apartment sported blackout curtains that completely prevented the light from entering. The windows were also barred, though the bars were like shutters that could be opened only from inside. Each apartment contained a reinforced safe room, without windows, that could be locked from inside. Charlie hadn't been able to afford much beyond a dive until he came to work for us, but now he had managed to secure one of the apartments at the Invest. Most vampires preferred to live down in the Catacombs, but some, like Charlie who wasn't deeply rooted in the vampire community, still preferred to be aboveground.

Yutani pulled into the visitor parking section and we headed over to the elevator. The ride was smooth—

whoever had built the apartment building had made certain it was comfortable from the elevators on up. As the doors opened, a security guard gave us the once-over. He was human, pure brawn, and he carried an all too lethal-looking gun. He was wearing a security uniform, and he held up his hand as we stepped into the lobby.

"What business do you have here?" His gaze slid over both Raven and me before moving suspiciously to Yutani.

"A coworker and friend lives here. He's expecting us. Charlie Darren." I straightened, meeting his gaze. "My name is Ember, this is Raven, and Yutani. Please let him know we're here."

"Take a seat over there." The guard pointed to a low banquette against the wall beside the elevator. We waited there while he pulled out his cell phone and made a call. A moment later, he jerked his thumb toward an elevator on the opposite wall. "Go ahead. He's waiting for you." He still looked dour, but that wasn't our problem.

We filed into the elevator and I punched the button for the third floor. As we began to ascend, I relaxed. "I'm glad Charlie found a good place, but honestly, the guard gave me the creeps."

"That's what he's supposed to do—intimidate. Anyway, we won't be here long." Yutani glanced at his phone. "It's quarter of seven. We'll leave by eight, because it will take us awhile to make it through the Catacombs to Fire & Fang."

Charlie was waiting for us at the door. He was not your typical vamp, at least in looks. Charlie's hair skimmed the top of his shoulders, and he was lanky and lean. He had learned to dress better—instead of an old polo shirt and torn jeans that rode too low on his hips, he was wearing a V-neck sweater and a pair of crisp jeans that fit him perfectly. He had gotten rid of the glasses, which had been purely for show after he was turned, and he looked more comfortable in his skin.

He was holding a bottle of blood and he swung the door wide as we approached. "Come in. I just made a batch of homemade bread, since I knew you'd be coming."

Vampires could eat, if they wanted to, but most lost their taste for food as it did nothing for them physically. They needed blood to survive, and Charlie preferred to buy bottled blood rather than get it fresh from the vein. He really didn't have the stomach to be a vampire, though he did feel the urge to feed, but he was so angsty over it that I doubt if he had ever fed off anybody.

We sat around the table, accepting warm fresh bread and ice-cold milk. It made for a surprisingly good snack. I didn't eat or drink much, though. My dress was so tight that I worried about getting it back down over my hips if I had to use the bathroom.

"So, have you had the chance to find out anything about Fire & Fang?" Yutani said.

"How could he—" I started, but Yutani shook his head.

"I called him last night and told him what we were planning."

"Before you start," Raven said, "Wager called me with some more info this morning. He had to do some digging, but he found out that Fire & Fang is owned by a company known as KL-Type A Enterprises. It's a vamp organization. They have their hands on a number of businesses worldwide. Not just nightclubs, but brothels, sex shops, taverns, restaurants, and hotels."

"Basically, the entertainment world," I said, thinking. "Are all of their businesses legit?"

"Wager said no, though it would take awhile to figure out which ones aren't. But Dion Von Strand, one of the veeps, has ties to some known sex traffickers throughout Southeast Asia." Raven frowned, tugging on the ankle strap to her chunky-heel Mary Janes. "He's been known to hang out with Marl Renault, a Frenchman who has been linked with poaching safaris and child sex-slave rings. Authorities have tried to catch the pair, but they always manage to slip through the loopholes."

I let out a slow breath. "We have to watch our step then. But the fact that the club lures in streeps—ghosts— tells me that the apple doesn't fall far from the tree."

"The apple hasn't even fallen off the branch," Charlie said, leaning back in his chair and crossing his legs. "I have a few friends who live down in the Catacombs— more than I did when I first went to work for you, thanks to Herne. They looked into Fire & Fang for me. What they found out made them back out of our agreement real fast. They wouldn't even take the money I offered them for information. Be on the lookout for a vamp named Eldris, he's the manager of the club. And I did get you these." He tossed what looked like two gold coins on the table. "These are your tickets in. One for Yutani and Ember, one for Raven."

I picked up one of the coins, examining it. On one side, it had the logo of Fire & Fang, the name inscribed over a bleeding heart with a dagger through it, and the other side had two words printed on it: Member-Guest.

"What are these?"

"Tokens. One of my informants stole them off of a

member some time back. They aren't tied to any particular member, so you can bluff your way in. I did find out that Mendin was officially a member, so you can use his name. They can't very well check up on you, since he's dead." Charlie smiled, the tips of his fangs showing. He still hadn't learned how to control them. They were recessive—descending when a vampire was hungry, or when they were new. And Charlie was still considered very new at this.

"So, we show these at the door?" Yutani asked.

"Yes. You tell them that you were invited as a guest and when they ask, tell them Mendin gave you the tokens. They shouldn't question you further. Those beauties are rare and only are given out a few at a time to established members. They have a magical signature that's tricky and can't be easily imitated, so the doorkeeper will be able to tell you aren't trying to get in with a fake ID, so to speak." Charlie shook his head, toying with one of the coins. "You need to be careful. If my informants were scared enough to back off from accepting a hefty bribe, you know there's danger there."

"Heard loud and clear," Raven said. She thought for a moment. "They didn't happen to mention anything about the Spooks, did they?"

Charlie shook his head. "I asked, but the only thing they know is that the necromancers who come looking for the group tend to be chaotic and most consider themselves anarchists."

That seemed to be about right. "Okay, then, I guess we're done here. We'd better be on our way. Charlie, thanks. Wish us luck." I stood, tugging on the bottom of my dress, trying to make it stretch a little longer.

Charlie somberly escorted us to the door. "Be careful. The Catacombs are dangerous for those who haven't had much experience down there. Don't forget the tokens." As we headed toward the elevator I glanced back and smiled, but he just nodded, his expression serious.

CHAPTER THIRTEEN

There were a number of entrances to the Catacombs. Viktor and I had gone through one in the Viaduct Market on a search shortly after I had begun working for the Wild Hunt, but Raven offered to take us through one of her routes, which would arouse less interest and seem more natural for someone looking to hang out at Fire & Fang.

"I know where all of the entrances are—at least, most of them," she said. "Over the years, I've picked up quite a bit of information about them."

The Catacombs had begun life in two separate sections. One was known as Underground Seattle, and it had been born through a fire that destroyed a great deal of the city back when Seattle was new. On rebuilding, the planners raised the street level in order to avoid the continual flooding from Puget Sound. The burned-out areas were still open, with a number of businesses still functioning, and entrance down into the lower level was provided by a series of ladders. But as the businesses relocated, the streets were built over the underground areas until the lower level was abandoned to the homeless. A few underground nightclubs operated down in the Underground, until the city flushed them out.

Meanwhile, the vampires had been living in the Catacombs, a series of tunnels originating from long before Seattle began to flourish. Eventually, the vamps broke into the lower levels of Seattle and absorbed them. Now the entire network of tunnels was known as the Catacombs, and through use of sealants and retrofitting, they were no longer victim to the tidal vagaries of the Sound, and they were shored up with enough load-bearing walls and beams to prevent the weight of the city from caving in.

The Catacombs went down at least four or five levels —I wasn't sure how many, to be honest, and I doubted anyone except the vampires actually knew. The lower the level, the more dangerous for those still breathing. There were other creatures in the Catacombs besides vampires, ones far more deadly.

The vamps had agreed to forbid entrance to minors, so the city officials turned the other way when it came to questionable activity. There were warning signs posted at the official entrances, warning that anyone entering the Catacombs was knowingly taking a risk and wouldn't have any legal backing if they wanted to press charges for something that happened down there.

Raven led us to a back alley entrance near the Viaduct Market. The place looked grungy, dank and a little dangerous. There were at least a dozen streeps camped out in the alleyway, their cardboard homes made out of old appliance boxes and plastic tarps. We skirted around one man, an elderly gentleman with white hair and a long stringy beard. He coughed, then gave us a foggy glance. I saw a bottle of Nite-Ease in his hand, a cough suppressant, and my heart sank. I turned to Raven.

"Do you have a few bucks? I just have my credit card."

Without a word, she opened her purse and handed me a ten-dollar bill.

I knelt beside the old-timer. "Here. Take this and get something to eat."

He stared at the money, then gave me a toothless smile. "You have a good heart. So does your friend."

"Be safe, and put that where nobody can steal it."

As we walked off, I thought that at least it was warm. I glanced back to see the old guy shuffling toward the back door of a convenience store. Whether he bought food or booze, at least he'd have some comfort for the night.

There were a lot of homeless around—mostly human, though also some shifters. The Fae who were homeless tended to head out in the forests or they crossed over to Annwn.

Tent cities stretched along the freeways, and although the United Coalition was working on the issue, they weren't working fast enough. Though the poor might always be with us, there were things that could be done to mitigate some of the harsh conditions, but that cost money. And the arguments about how to raise that money, and who was responsible, usually axed any actions that might be forthcoming.

"Here we are." Raven glanced around.

Though the alley was lined with streeps, most of them paid no attention to us. Two buildings down, a small group of younger kids in their late teens were gathered around a burning barrel, warming their hands.

The building Raven had stopped in back of was a tall brick walkup. There were steps leading down below street level to a door. A bouncer leaned against the door, wearing no shirt, a pair of black tuxedo pants with red suspenders that stretched over his mammoth chest, a bowler hat, and he carried a very large cane that looked wicked enough to beat up a giant.

"Here we go. When we enter, just follow my lead." She motioned for us to follow her down the steps to the bouncer, who held up one hand.

"They're with me." Raven produced a golden key from her purse. The bouncer motioned for her to move to the door, and she unlocked it. He stepped back, allowing the three of us to enter.

The club was dimly lit, and it took over the entire bottom floor of the building. There was a stage off to one side, with a couple strippers performing under one spotlight. Over beneath another light a blond woman was spanking a very large man who was crouched over her knee. He was wearing a ball-gag, a chest harness, no pants or underwear, and he was blindfolded. The blonde seemed to be enjoying her job. She was dressed in what reminded me of a baby-doll nightgown.

The bar itself was crowded. As my eyes adjusted to the dim lighting—provided mostly by battery-operated candles—I could see the leather and lace–clad patrons lining the polished mahogany counter, drinking and talking, some leisurely watching the strippers, while a few others had their eyes on the man being spanked.

I cleared my throat and gave Raven an inquisitive look.

She just chuckled. "Hey, Kipa and I like to mix it up. This is tame compared to some clubs." Before I could answer, she led us to a curtained doorway, pushing aside the velvet drapes as she ducked behind it. We followed and found ourselves in a harshly lit room with four unmarked doors. The sudden change made me squint as the brash light assaulted my eyes.

"This way," she said, leading us over to the second door. She inserted her golden key in the lock, turned the knob, and opened the door. We found ourselves staring into a long hallway that ended at a double escalator. "This leads down to Level Three, Sector Seven, where Fire & Fang is located. Be on guard, keep together, and don't be flippant. But I'm sure you know how to behave in the Catacombs."

As the heavy door closed behind us with a thud, I wondered what we were getting ourselves into.

WE TRANSFERRED ESCALATORS ON EACH LEVEL. THE HALLS of the Catacombs were busy, with a hustle that felt like it belonged on the streets of a film noir version of New York. But there was a shadow that loomed over the crowds, a darkness permeating the air. It wasn't *evil*, but it reminded me of the feel of powerful old-money magnates, of gangsters and players, of too much power concentrated in too small of an area. Most vampires were silent figures in the dark corners of the exclusive country clubs, who with one nod could signal someone's demise. They could ruin careers, destroy families, make people disappear, all without a flicker of guilt.

I slid closer to Yutani, all too aware of my skimpy dress and all my bare skin. Yutani seemed to sense my discomfort, for he wordlessly reached out, taking my hand in his. In the shadows he seemed to glimmer with a power of his own. He was growing into his position as the Great Coyote's son, and the magic of being the son of a god was beginning to manifest in his aura.

Raven, too, walked with confidence, her fire flickering in her eyes. She had let loose her glamour, which was far more powerful than that of any Fae. The Ante-Fae were otherworldly, and even when they appeared as human, there was an energy that warned people to beware. I had my own glamour, but it paled next to hers.

To either side were shops and businesses, including restaurants for the living, blood salons for the vampires, boutiques with expensive clothes and even more expensive jewelry, souvenir shops, and just about everything you could want.

As figures glided by they glanced at us, and the gleam of the vampires' eyes shimmered in the darkness. We were being assessed and measured, weighed as to whether we were easy marks. We were in their territory and had left our protection at the door.

"Ante-Fae," one of them whispered as she paused with her companion. They pulled back, and I caught the faintest hint of uncertainty. Raven straightened and the next moment her glamour grew, an edgy dance of death and fire, and the two vampires hurried off.

Yutani continued to hold tight to my hand—for which I was grateful—and we followed Raven through the bustle of the Catacombs.

Up ahead, as the hallway curved, I caught sight of a large neon sign that read "Fire & Fang." Loud music echoed into the halls as the double doors opened and a man—a vampire—exited the club, two women clinging to his arms.

Yutani glanced over at Raven. "We should get our tokens out."

She nodded. When they had their tokens in hand, we approached the doors. The guard at the entrance to the club was a tall black man, a vamp, who must have been six foot five and at least one-ninety in weight. He was wearing a black turtleneck, gray slacks, and sunglasses, and he had a large diamond stud in one ear. He crossed his arms, staring down at us.

"Passes?" His voice was surprisingly soft, like smooth silk.

Yutani held up his token and the guard took it, barely glancing at it as he ran it under some sort of UV light. He handed it back to Yutani, nodded, and opened the door.

"She belongs to me," Yutani said, pointing to my collar as he walked through the metal detector and entered the club.

I held my breath but the guard merely nodded me through. The metal detector beeped, but within seconds they had ascertained that the metal was the gold necklace I was wearing. The next moment, Raven joined us, and we were in Fire & Fang.

The club looked just about as I had pictured it.

Multiple booths lined the walls, each shadowed in privacy, with candles burning on the table. A few couples were dancing, while several seating areas were full of customers. The din echoed through the club, a hundred voices all talking at once. A spiral staircase on one side led up to a door. The bar itself was made of polished marble, and almost every bar stool was taken. Yutani spied a couple of empty stools and, with a look at Raven, he and I moved toward them.

Raven barely acknowledged us, but instead made a beeline for one of the seating areas. There were approximately twenty people there, and the energy emanating from that corner made my stomach knot. *Magic, heavy magic.* That had to be the Spooks.

Yutani and I reached the bar and settled ourselves on the stools.

"What'll you have?" The barkeep was a tall, thin woman, who looked like she had eaten too little for too long. But her arms looked compact, and I had the feeling she had more muscle than she knew what to do with.

"Whiskey for me. A cognac for my pet." Yutani tossed a bill on the table and the bartender nodded, moving away to pour our drinks.

Remembering Wager's advice, I played with my drink after the bartender slid it in front of me. Yutani took one small sip and then set his drink down.

"Pardon me," a soft voice came from behind us. We turned to find a long-haired blond vamp standing there. His eyes were piercing blue, but they were beginning to haze over with red, and he licked his lips, not bothering to hide the tips of his fangs. He was wearing leather pants, no shirt, and had at least four gold chains draped around his neck. He was gorgeous, and his vampiric glamour was hitting me full force. He meant business.

I forced myself to remain silent. As Yutani's pet, it wasn't my place to speak.

Yutani gave the vamp a slow once-over, a sly smile crooking his lips. "Yes? What can I do for you?"

The vamp held his gaze for a moment, still smiling.

Then, he turned to me. "Is she available? I'll pay you well and I promise to leave her unmarked."

I suddenly realized I was getting wet. Feeling confused and then frightened, I tried to force myself to look away from him, but I couldn't seem to lower my gaze. He promised passion and sex and nights unending, and all of the allure hit me like a rolling wave, stirring my Leannan Sidhe blood into full force. I tried to rein myself in. It wasn't safe to let that side of myself out. Not here, not with so much raw sex and lust running through the club.

Yutani took one look at me and slowly stepped between the vampire and me. "I'm sorry, but I'm not ready to accept offers yet. Come back later, friend."

The vampire looked frustrated and his eyes were fully crimson now, but he pulled his glamour back and stiffened. "I *will* return. My name is Eldris, if you change your mind. And I *do* pay very well." He abruptly turned and slid through the crowds, looking for other marks.

Yutani leaned in as if he were going to kiss my neck, but he lingered over my ear. "That was dangerous. I can feel your energy from here. You have to rein yourself in or you're going to attract more than we can handle."

"It's not my fault," I whispered back. "If I stood up right now, my stool would be sopping wet and so would the back of my dress. I've never been around a vampire that strong. Hell, I've hardly ever been around *any* vampires and I didn't expect to respond to him that way."

"He's old. Very old, to have as much power as he does." Yutani pulled away.

The bartender returned to where we were sitting. "You've stirred some powerful interest, friend. You'd best watch your footing. Eldris is the manager of the club, and he gets what he wants." She eyed me, biting her lip, then turned back to Yutani. "If you don't want to rent her out, I advise you to leave the club *now* to avoid a confrontation. The first time, Eldris asks. The second time, he takes."

I tried to catch her gaze. She was human, and I could work my own fair share of glamour. It occurred to me she might answer some questions, if I could charm her. And then, I felt the urge rising. My mother's blood, already triggered, sprang to life and without thinking, I reached out and stroked my hand down the bartender's face.

"What's your name?"

She hesitated, almost pulling away, before catching her breath. "Aida." She stared at me for another moment, then whispered, "You're so beautiful."

"That's right," I whispered, letting my fingers drift down her cheek. "And so are you. Aida, we need a few answers, and we're really hoping you might be able to help us."

She was lost now, caught in the waves of my glamour. I poured it on full strength, my gaze holding hers, my fingers lightly stroking her face, promising pleasure if she would only cooperate. I leaned closer, my lips close to her own.

"What do you want?" she asked, lost in my thrall.

"We need to know about the Spooks. I want you to look at a couple of pictures and tell us if you recognize them." I glanced at Yutani and mouthed, "The victims... the ones we aren't sure of."

He looked like he wanted to kill me, but instead, he brought out his phone and tapped away, bringing up the pictures of Patrick and Dorian, the two Amy hadn't been able to place at Fire & Fang. He showed them to Aida.

"Do you recognize them? Did they come in here? Were they members of the Spooks?" I asked, licking my upper lip ever so slightly as I remained face to face with the barkeep.

She was breathing heavily now. She glanced at the pictures. "Yes, I do recognize them. They used to come in here, but I haven't seen them the past few weeks."

I glanced around. Nobody was watching us that I could tell, and I couldn't see Eldris around. Leaning forward, I placed my lips against Aida's and gave her a long, deep kiss, breathing energy from her, drinking in her life force. Yutani forcefully grabbed my arm after a moment, and I almost backhanded him, but caught myself. I broke away from the bartender, doing my best to rein in my thirst.

"Please…more…" Aida whispered, looking glassy eyed.

I forced down the desire to siphon off more energy and managed to shake myself free from the urge. After a moment, I said, "You need to lie down and rest. Ask someone to take over your shift. As you sleep, you won't really remember what happened."

She nodded, shaking, and turned away.

"What the hell was that?" Yutani asked, keeping his voice low. But he looked fit to be tied. "That *wasn't* keeping a low profile. What if Eldris had seen you?"

"I don't think he did, and what it was, was me gathering information. Otherwise, we're just sitting here, waiting for Raven. Now we know that all five victims belonged to the Spooks." I glared at him, feeling testy, then with a shrug, turned back to the bar. I wanted to go home, grab Herne, and work off the energy that had built up in me. I was so horny I could barely stand it.

"Come on, let's wander over toward the Spooks and see how Raven's doing," Yutani said, still looking pissed.

I followed him, keeping a step behind, as we approached the seating area where Raven was talking to a group of what I could only assume were fellow bone witches, necromancers, and other members of the magic-born who used death magic.

As I tried to maneuver around a couple who were dancing, I jolted into someone. I turned to apologize and found myself staring at one of the Ante-Fae. I wasn't sure whether they were a woman or man, but they snorted, graciously stepping out of my way and motioning for me to proceed. I tried not to look back as I passed by, but I couldn't help but wonder what business the Ante-Fae had here.

The pall around the Spooks was heavy, looming like a cloud. Most of them were men, but there were a few women. One in particular caught my attention, but I couldn't figure out why. She was gorgeous, with long blond hair, an athletic, lithe figure, and ruby lips. Her eyes sparkled but in the dim light, it was hard to tell what color they were. She was wearing leather pants, a black V-neck sweater, and a pair of black stiletto ankle boots. And she was talking to Raven.

Raven caught a glimpse of us out of the corner of her eye and very softly inclined her head, then turned away, ignoring us. After a moment, she excused herself and headed for the sign indicating the restrooms. I waited for a beat, then followed her, with Yutani behind me. He stood outside the door, keeping watch, as I entered.

The women's bathroom was luxurious, with a leather sofa in one corner, stools in front of a vanity, and high-end fixtures everywhere. Raven sat down on one of the stools and began to touch up her makeup. She said nothing as I sat beside her, staring into the mirror, but she pulled out her phone and mine suddenly vibrated with a text message. I glanced at it.

I DON'T WANT TO TALK IN HERE. CHANCES ARE THEY HAVE THE ROOM BUGGED. BUT I'VE FOUND OUT QUITE A BIT. I THINK WE SHOULD LEAVE SOON, THOUGH, BECAUSE THE LONGER WE STAY, THE MORE CHANCE WE HAVE OF BRINGING UNDUE ATTENTION TO OURSELVES.

I AGREE, I texted back. I ALREADY HAVE THE MANAGER OF THE CLUB ON MY BACK, WANTING TO RENT ME FROM YUTANI. I FOUND OUT A FEW THINGS TOO, SO LET'S GET OUT OF HERE BEFORE THINGS GO SOUTH.

Without saying a word, I stood, put my phone back in my clutch, and headed out the door. Yutani and I began heading toward the front of the club. I glanced over my shoulder just in time to see Raven following us.

"Leaving so soon?" The voice was unmistakable. Eldris stepped out of the crowd, in front of Yutani. "I was hoping we'd have a chance to discuss my proposition."

Yutani paused, motioning for me to stand behind him. "She's not feeling well. I'm taking her home."

I immediately adopted a stricken look, placing on hand on my stomach.

Eldris crowded in closer. He lowered his voice. "Some-how, I don't think that's the truth, Yutani. Herne sent you, and I want to know what you're doing in my club."

CHAPTER FOURTEEN

I caught my breath as Yutani glanced at me, then turned back to Eldris.

"Is there somewhere we can talk?"

Eldris let out a slow laugh. "I thought you might change your mind. Follow me." He turned and began walking briskly through the crowd. They parted for him as though he were royalty.

Yutani and I followed. I wondered what Raven would do—she had already exited the club. But I didn't want to give her away. We followed Eldris to the spiral staircase. He lightly took the steps two at a time and Yutani and I followed. At the top, Eldris opened the door into a long hallway.

"Shut the door behind you," he said.

I obeyed. The hall looked utilitarian, the walls were painted a light cream, and the bulbs along the way were fluorescent. Eldris marched down the hall, all business now, until he was halfway to the end. He stopped in front of an office door that had his name stenciled on the frosted glass pane. He opened it, ushering us in, then shut the door and flipped on the lights.

A large oak desk sat toward the back, with two computer monitors, a desk blotter, what looked like a planner, and a large accessories tray. It was the desk of someone who actually got things done. Behind it sat a leather chair. On the opposite side, toward us, were two leather wing chairs. To the left of the door was a loveseat covered in a blue microsuede along with a matching oak table. To the right were a series of filing cabinets and a smaller desk with a laptop on it.

"Sit." Eldris motioned toward the wing chairs. He positioned himself behind the desk and adjusted the mouse, staring at the screens. I wanted to peek over the top to see what he was looking at but decided that wouldn't be the best idea.

"So you know who we are?" Yutani asked.

"Of course. I make it my business to know who walks through the doors of this club. We'll wait for a moment while Larry brings up your companion."

Uh-oh. I glanced at Yutani. That must mean they knew about Raven.

Sure enough, not five minutes later, someone tapped on the door. The front door bouncer was standing there with Raven and the other Ante-Fae I had seen. Raven looked irritated as hell. The other Ante-Fae looked bored. The bouncer motioned for them to enter and then closed the door as he left, all without a word.

"Raven BoneTalker, welcome to my humble abode." Eldris's tone was a combination of suave and sarcastic. It reeked of arrogance. "And Trinity, as well. Wait for a moment and I'll get you another chair." He stood, brushing past them to the desk with the laptop. He pulled the chair over beside me, then motioned for Raven to sit down. With a sigh, she did as he asked.

"I'm afraid, Master Trinity, you will have to stand."

Trinity shrugged, remaining silent.

I glanced at Raven, then at Trinity with a questioning look. Raven shook her head.

"Since we're all here, let's begin. I'm Eldris, and I'm the manager of Fire & Fang. You are Yutani, once known as Yutani the Fire Walker, but you left that last name behind." He turned to me. "Ember Kearney, I believe, the consort of Herne? Raven BoneTalker, the Daughter of Bones. And Master Trinity, Lord of Persuasion. So why are the Wild Hunt and the Ante-Fae prowling through a vampire sex club? What are you looking for?"

He was polite, I'd have to give him that.

I let out a sigh. "We have no clue what…Trinity, is it?… is doing here. But how did you know about us?"

"How *wouldn't* I know? You come in, bearing talismans that we phased out last year. My guards who are monitoring the surveillance cams run everyone who isn't a vampire through a facial recognition program. Ember and Yutani, you're well known in this city to those who have the right information." Eldris leaned back in his chair, crossing one leg over another. "I approached you earlier, hoping that you would reveal yourself, but you chose to play it close to the bone, so to speak."

Leave it to the vamps to be as high tech as they could get. I glanced at Yutani, wondering just how much we should tell him, at least in front of Trinity. I had no clue who he was or what he wanted.

"Herne sent me to watch over her," Trinity said, pointing at me. "I suppose you know about that, as well?"

Crap. *Of course* he did, because it was like Herne to do that. I grumbled under my breath but stopped when Raven touched my knee.

As I fumed, it suddenly occurred to me that the vamps wouldn't want to be associated with a serial killer, even if it was just by a way of them entering his club. It would bring scrutiny onto Fire & Fang, which Eldris was unlikely to welcome.

"All right. If we tell you, will you help us?"

Yutani glanced at me. "You aren't…"

"I am. I believe that if Eldris knows the score, he's likely to cooperate with us. And having his cooperation would make life a whole lot easier." I cleared my throat. "We believe that a serial killer may be operating through your club, using it to find his victims."

Eldris shifted. Only slightly, but enough to tell me that I was right. He tilted his head, his long hair skimming his shoulders, a golden halo around his head. Even without using his vampiric glamour, he was absolutely gorgeous. His eyes, which had still been bordering on crimson, were back to their piercing blue.

"Are you serious?"

"As serious as I can get. We have reason to believe that someone's preying on members of the Spooks. Five victims so far. And all of them have two things in common. They all work with death magic and they all belonged to the Spooks." I leaned forward. "You wouldn't want that getting out, would you? I somehow think that the cops would stop looking the other way at some of your more questionable activities if they thought a killer was connected to your club."

Eldris narrowed his eyes. "I see your point. So that's why you charmed my bartender. You wanted information." He ran his gaze over me again. "Leannan Sidhe. I should have known. And yet, you're not full-blood. Tell me, what other blood do you possess?"

I hesitated, then shrugged. "Autumn's Bane. My father belonged to the Autumn Stalkers."

Eldris chuffed like a tiger. "Really? Then Herne must have himself quite a playmate. And an efficient huntress. All right, tell me more. Are you positive that the killer has been operating out of my club?"

Yutani frowned. "Not one hundred percent, but it's the only connection we can find. The killer has a thirst for pain. I don't suppose you have a list of regulars here?"

"Of course we do, but you're not getting it. I somehow think you'd be dismayed by the names you'd recognize on it." Eldris paused. "And you, Raven. You were scoping out the Spooks, were you not? I can smell death on you like a perfume, clinging to your body and soul."

Her eyes were dark. "Yes, I managed to convince them that I was lonely for company who understood me. Although my being Ante-Fae put some of them off at first, and scared the hell out of a few others. But I secured an invitation to return."

"If you need to, the four of you may return then. I'll give you complimentary memberships for a month and I'll alert the guards that you're to be allowed unfettered access. But do *not* mistake my cooperation for friendship. I simply have no desire for my club to go public as the home of a serial killer. In exchange, you will keep all mention of Fire & Fang out of the news." He leaned forward, his eyes once again clouding crimson. "Do you understand?"

I nodded. "We'll keep the club off the official record. We have to move quickly. The killer's been striking once a week, and right now, one of the Spooks down there could be lined up as the next victim. We'd like to keep the official number at five instead of letting it grow to six." I glanced at Raven. "Did you find out anything tonight?"

"I met several people who might be nursing a grudge. But honestly, I couldn't pick out any one in particular. Truth be told, they all seemed pleasant enough."

"Sociopaths usually are," Eldris said. "I know that from my days when I walked among the living." He paused, then added, "Give me names, and I'll have my guards shadow them if they come in during the week."

Right then, I realized just how anxious he was to keep this out of the news. If he worked for KL-Type A, his job would be on the line if the news hit the streets. Perhaps, his life.

"I only know them by their first names, though I did manage to take pictures of them on my phone. I'm good at hiding what I'm doing."

Eldris reluctantly gave us his phone number, and Raven texted three pictures to all of us. The men were dour looking, and one made me nervous by just looking at his eyes. They were dead. Flat, devoid of emotion. That was an alarm trigger right there.

"Who's that?" I asked, pointing to the picture.

"His name's Michael. He's a necromancer, and he has a huge chip on his shoulder. He was bitching about one of the local guilds and how they turned him away twice because he was unfit for membership. He even said he wanted revenge."

"But…the victims are—*were*—members of the Spooks. Why would he target members of a group that accepts him?" Yutani asked.

Raven paused. "I don't know. Maybe the victims told him to shut up. Most of the Spooks tensed up when he started ranting. One of them, I think her name was Pam or something, told him to shut the fuck up, that they'd heard it before and he needed to get over it."

"That could trigger someone," Eldris said. He folded his arms. "Scorn from those who supposedly accept you has tarnished many a friendship. If I were you, I'd look into his background more. Hold on a moment and I'll give you his full name."

"You really do know the background of every single person who walks through those doors, don't you?" I asked as he swiveled his chair and began typing away on his keyboard.

Without looking up, Eldris said, "I told you, we use facial recognition software. And when it doesn't come up with a name, I have my own investigators. Every person who comes into this club is logged and filed."

Raven snorted. "Blackmail. You use the information against them, don't you?"

"I wouldn't necessarily call it blackmail, just…persuasion." He snapped his fingers. "Here we go. Michael Gould. By day, he works as a…a janitor? Well, that just goes to show that being a powerful spellcaster doesn't guarantee riches. Michael worked for a tech company until he was fired for leaking secrets. He was blacklisted. After that, he couldn't find a job in his field anywhere, so he took a job as a janitor in… How interesting." Eldris looked up. "He works in the same building where his former tech company—Hi Rez—is located. I wonder if they know he has access to their offices at night. They close down at seven-thirty each day and he works the night shift. So he has keys to his old company, even though they unceremoniously showed him the door. How fascinating."

"Wow. He could be stealing secrets from them still," I said. "Do you think he's capable of murder?"

"Well, he's into rough sex play. He was a member here before he joined the Spooks, and one of our girls refused to be in the same room with him," Eldris said. "She agreed to rough play, so we had to let her go for refusing to entertain our clients."

I glanced at Raven, who winced right along with me. "Seriously? You let them rough up the girls? What kind of fucked-up joint are you running?"

Eldris paused, looking up from his screen to stare at me. "Do I come into your place of business and ask what kind of half-assed work you're doing? No, I do not. You're allowed to have an opinion, but that doesn't mean you're allowed to share it with me."

Yutani glanced my way, just enough to tell me it was time to shut up. "We wouldn't think of questioning your operations. We're just grateful you're willing to help us."

Eldris snorted. "Yes, I'm sure. Is there anyone else you need information on?"

"Do you have any background information on our victims that we should be aware of, that might not make it into the official reports?" Raven leaned forward. "You know what I mean."

Yutani fed him the names and Eldris typed them in. "Most are clean, given what I usually see come through here. There might be a few tidbits, but I doubt it." He printed out a couple pages of information and handed them to Yutani. "Now, you do realize you owe me a favor."

"A favor done never goes unrewarded," Raven said. "Old vampire saying."

"Exactly. I'll call you when I need you. I know where you work. Now, if you'll excuse me, I need to make my rounds again." He followed us to the door, stopping me with a cold hand on my elbow. "I know you aren't his pet, but are you sure you wouldn't be interested in a little fantasy?"

I stared at his fingers, resisting the urge to slap them away. "No, thank you. Not unless you want Herne to pay you a visit, because he would. And he's not always the best-tempered god around."

With that, Eldris gave me a genteel nod and led us out of his office to a side door where we found ourselves on a balcony overlooking the alley. "There are the fire ladders. You may exit this way, so as to not draw any undue attention to yourself."

I stared at the iron bars of the balcony. Iron and the Fae got along just dandy, if you didn't mind welts, burns, and—with prolonged exposure—death. "If I touch those, it's going to hurt like hell. I need some gloves." I spoke to Yutani, not Eldris.

"I didn't bring any," Yutani said, a worried look on his face.

I glanced at Eldris, who seemed to almost be enjoying my predicament. But Trinity saved the day. He reached in his pocket and brought out a pair of black evening gloves, handing them to me without a word.

"Thank you," I said, and he nodded at me, still looking disinterested in anything that had happened.

Yutani studied Eldris for a moment, who was just watching as he leaned against the doorframe, an amused look on his face. "You're doing this on purpose, aren't you?"

I stopped him. "Never mind, it doesn't matter." I gauged the drop to the ground. It was about twenty-five to thirty feet down. Once I reached the midpoint on the rungs, I could drop down and do little more than scrape my knees. I swung over the edge, making sure the satin of the gloves were firmly swaddling my hands, and began the slow descent down the rungs.

I could feel the energy of the iron through the material, and through the soles of my ballet flats. It pulsed, aching bone-deep, but at least it wasn't burning me. Once, I slipped and my elbow hit the ladder. I caught my breath, but managed to stifle my shout. I didn't want to give Eldris anything to crow over. A few moments later, I reached the two-thirds point.

I glanced down at the ground. There, under the dim light of a back alley lamp attached to the building, I could see nothing to impede me, so I exhaled and jumped, landing in a crouching position. The gloves cushioned my hands from the pavement. Shaking, I stood, steadying myself on the nearby brick wall.

Raven hustled down the ladder next, grimacing. The iron hurt her, too, but not as much as it did me, and she was quicker than I expected her to be. The Ante-Fae were less prone to iron burns than the Fae were, though it still stung. They were our forebears, and apparently, the Fae race had weakened as it had evolved from the ancient stock. Trinity followed, and then Yutani.

I handed Trinity his gloves, ready to ask him a million questions, but he just took them, winked, and before we could say a word, he was gone in a blur of movement so fast that I could barely follow him.

"Well...that was interesting," Yutani said. He linked arms with Raven and me and we headed toward the street where we started the uphill trek toward the car.

Thirty minutes later we slid into Yutani's car with a sigh of relief. The streets of Seattle were steep, and my feet hurt. I wondered how Raven was faring, but she seemed fine.

"So...that didn't go exactly like we planned," I said. "Who the hell is Trinity? And could this Michael Gould be the killer?" I leaned my head back against the seat, sighing.

"This is the first time I've met Trinity," Raven said. "I have no clue who he is. As for Gould, I'd bet money on him, given what I saw tonight."

"Could be," Yutani said. "I'll do some more research tomorrow. Eldris was full of himself and no doubt he has a really good spy network, so to speak, but frankly, I'm not going to trust a vamp to tell me everything."

I nodded. Eldris troubled me. For one thing, I was embarrassed that I had responded to him, but then again, vampire glamour being what it was, I tried to tell myself that it was all par for the course. They had a seductive charm and even the Fae weren't immune. But aside from that, he bothered me. He was a puppeteer, a master of manipulation. As I thought it over, a little part of me inside whispered, *You don't like him because he reminds you of yourself. You're just as much of a vampire as he is. You just drink life force rather than blood.*

I texted Herne that we were all right, and that we were onto his spy, Trinity. Then, trying to push the evening out of my head, I stared out the window as Yutani drove back to my house.

CHAPTER FIFTEEN

*T*he next morning, I woke up feeling slightly hung over, even though I hadn't had anything to drink. Raven had gone directly home when we arrived back at my house.

Angel had plied me with hot cocoa and chocolate chip macadamia nut cookies, and I finally relaxed enough to go to bed, where I fell into a deep sleep. But my dreams were restless, and I found myself wandering under a dark sky.

THE CLOUDS ROLLED BY OVERHEAD, THREATENING A thunderstorm, and I was standing on top of a mountain, staring up at the roiling sky. I was carrying my sword and I hunkered down, squatting on my heels as I closed my eyes, trying to catch…trying to catch…

There it was. Faint at first, then it raced past, blurred and yet I could hear the words. *Help me…I can't take this…help me…*

I looked around, but there was no one there. "Where are you? Tell me where you are!"

But the voice just echoed around me, then fell silent. The skies broke open and lightning forked across the horizon, a vivid spiderweb, and raindrops splattered on my cheeks as thunder rumbled behind. But when I brushed the drops off my face and tasted them, I realized they were salty. They were tears. Awash in a sea of despair, I slowly stood, raising my face to the sky.

As quickly as they had come, the clouds passed and the sun broke through, blazing white. I squinted against the sudden light, feeling helpless. All around me were rocks and boulders, and I realized I was standing in an ancient caldera. The wind was blowing up another storm and as I steadied myself against it, I tried to focus on the voice—tried to remember who I had lost, but the brilliance of the day blinded me.

"I'm so tired," I whispered as I began sinking into the earth. I struggled to get free, but she kept sucking me down and I began to panic. But the wind kept blowing and soon, I was neck-deep in the sand, with no one to save me.

"EMBER, WAKE UP! EMBER?" ANGEL SHOOK MY SHOULDER.

I struggled to pull out of the mire, and finally opened my eyes. I was in bed, fighting against my covers, and Angel was standing over me, wearing loose pajamas.

"What? Where…" I bolted to a sitting position and glanced over at the clock. It was six in the morning. "Angel?"

"You were having a nightmare. I woke up when you started shouting. What on earth were you dreaming?" She sat on the edge of my bed as I pulled the covers up around my chin. I leaned back against the headboard.

"It felt like the one I had the other day. Like all of those I've had before we've gone into a bad situation. I wish I knew who I was looking for."

"Was it a male or female voice?" Angel brushed my hair out of my face. Her voice was soothing and I had a sudden glimpse of her in the future, tending to her children with the same care and concern.

I tried to recall, but finally shook my head. "I don't know. I really don't."

"It's okay. Everything will be all right. Just breathe." She glanced at the clock. "Do you want to go back to sleep?"

Truth was, I wanted to fall into a dreamless sleep and sleep the day away, but the nightmare loomed too close. "I think I'll get up. What about you?"

"I'll get up with you. Want to go out to breakfast? Or should I make something?" She yawned. "We have some blueberry muffins. I can make eggs and bacon."

"That's perfect." I slid out from under the covers. "I'm going to take a quick shower. I still feel grimy from last night, though I think it's more psychological than anything." I hadn't told her everything that had happened. We had gotten home late and Angel had been dozing off on the sofa, waiting up for me.

"I'll meet you downstairs." She grabbed my covers and yanked them away. "Come on, sleepyhead. Get up and get your pale-assed self into the shower!"

That got a laugh out of me. I jumped out of bed. It was

a little chilly, but I padded over to the window and opened it, letting the fresh air stream in. The screen was tight, to keep Mr. Rumblebutt from escaping, and I leaned on the sill, staring out.

"The warm weather is holding." I closed my eyes. The dream began to loosen its hold on me, slipping away as a light breeze played over my body, waking me up.

"You're probably giving someone a good show, you know," Angel said with a laugh.

I shook my head. "Nope. There's a couple tall trees full of leaves and needles between us and the nearest neighbor. Besides, serves 'em right if they're gawking." Feeling revived, I turned toward my bathroom. "Okay, I'm going to shower. I'll meet you in the kitchen."

Angel closed the door behind her as I headed into my bathroom.

As I stepped under the warm spray of water, I realized I was on edge. Not just from the dream, but I was horny as hell. I wanted relief, but I wouldn't see Herne until later. I paused, slipping out of the shower to open one of my vanity drawers where I pulled out my favorite toy.

Returning to the shower, I closed my eyes, leaning back against the wall, thinking of Herne as my hand drifted lower on my body, sliding down my stomach. I caught my breath, spreading my legs as my hand traveled over the neatly trimmed hair. I slipped my fingers between my lower lips. My nipples stiffened as I began to lightly caress myself, focusing on the pure sensation of arousal. The water spraying on my body took on a heightened sensuality, streaming down my body. I set the showerhead to pulse, and then lowered the handheld set to beat a staccato tattoo against me.

The drive and force of the water sent me reeling, and I slid back on the bench, raggedly panting. The continual pulse of the water against my clit hit hard, and I picked up the ribbed, pink dildo and slid it deep inside me, letting out a moan as it stretched me wide.

All I could see was Herne's face. The onslaught of imagery—Herne sliding into me, his hair draping down to tickle my shoulders, his mouth on my breast, his eyes gleaming as he held my gaze, his hands holding my wrists against the bed—all coalesced into one wracking orgasm.

Moaning as the ripples echoed through my body, then slowly began to subside, I let the showerhead fall against the floor of the shower. When I was breathing normally again, I washed off my toy, lathered up and soaped myself all over, then rinsed off.

I wrapped my towel around me as I headed back into my bedroom. Feeling relaxed and ready for the day, I slid into a pair of black jeans, then decided to wear my green corset top. It was already laced, so all I had to do was slip it on and zip up the front. I preferred zipper corsets to busks—they were quicker and sturdier, in my opinion. The steel bones of the corset felt secure, and I shifted my boobs to where they were peeking over the top but still contained. I added a silver belt, then slid on a pair of green sandals to match. Once my hair was brushed back into a high ponytail and I had applied my makeup, I headed downstairs.

Mr. Rumblebutt was chowing down on his breakfast, and Angel was behind the counter, whipping eggs for the scramble. I could smell the bacon cooking in the oven.

"Want me to set the table?" I asked.

"You look nice, and yes, thank you." Angel paused,

then added, "DJ called me this morning. He's excited about the new school. He's invited me down to see the campus this summer. He won't start till September, but he wants to show me the science labs." She went back to cooking, but I could feel her excitement. Her brother hadn't forgotten her.

"You're happy," I said, grinning at her.

"I have to admit, the fact that he wants me to come spend a weekend with him and he wants to show me where he'll be going...yeah, I'm happy. I feel so left out of his life. I know this is best for him, but I still struggle with it. I wonder what Mama J. would have said about me letting him go." She didn't look as morose as she usually did when she was talking about DJ.

I had the feeling that Angel was slowly coming to grips with the fact that her brother was better off where he was. And that he had specifically asked her to come down and see his new school would go a long way in making her still feel part of his life.

She poured the eggs into a pan and began scrambling them. I finished setting the table, then began fixing my mocha. I had just taken the first sip when my phone rang. It was Kipa.

"Hey, what's up?" I glanced at the clock. It was still only seven A.M., so I was surprised to find him calling.

"Did Raven spend the night at your house?" He sounded concerned.

I frowned. "No, we got back here around one and she headed home without stopping in. We were all exhausted. Why?"

"Because she hasn't come home yet. I waited up half the night, then figured she probably crashed over there. I didn't want to call, because I thought you were all probably exhausted. I fell asleep on the sofa. I just woke up to take a leak and I glanced in her room. She's not there. I checked for her car and it's not out front." He paused, then —voice shaking, asked, "Do you think she got into an accident?"

"I don't know." I stared at the wall, thinking furiously. What could have kept her? "Are you sure she didn't wake up early and decide to go get breakfast before waking you up?"

"No. I called her phone and it went to voice mail. Ember, I used the Find Friend app and it pinpointed her phone in UnderLake Park. I went looking for it, and I found it. I also found her purse, but nothing else. Her credit cards were still in her purse, along with some cash and jewelry. I was hoping that you'd say somebody stole her phone and she spent the night with you, though I knew it was a long shot."

Crap. That was exactly what had happened with Chaya's phone. It had been found on a bench. "Stay there. We'll come over." I hung up and turned to Angel. "Belay breakfast. Raven's missing. We need to call Herne and head over to her house."

I called the Herne and he said he'd call everybody else and meet us there.

By the time Angel and I arrived at Raven's, all sorts of scenarios were playing over and over in my mind and none of them were comforting. I kept telling myself that it was all a misunderstanding. That she went out to buy breakfast for them and had lost her purse. That she had gone out for an early morning walk and lost her purse. Oh, so many things to try to keep my mind from going to the one place I really didn't want it to go.

Kipa was pacing, frantic. Raj looked terrified. Angel immediately knelt beside him and gave him a hug, and he leaned into her with a grunt. Kipa made a beeline for me. "Tell me what happened last night. When did she leave your place?"

I braced my hands on his shoulders and backed him over to the sofa. "Dude, sit down. Breathe."

He paused, staring at me with those deep brown eyes, then slumped on the sofa. "I'm sorry. I'm just worried sick. Raven's the responsible one. She always calls."

"I know, I know…" I sat down beside him as Angel and Raj wandered over.

"Ember, I know something's wrong. I just…do."

Raj tilted his head up toward Kipa. Then, blindsiding me, the gargoyle said, "Raven not here. Raven okay? Raj scared."

I blinked. In all the months I had known Raven and Raj, I had *no clue* he could talk. I glanced over at Angel, who looked as startled as I felt.

But Kipa simply reached out to pat Raj on the head.

"You talked," I said, staring at Raj.

"You're the only other people who know that he can talk," Kipa said. "Raj remains silent until he feels the need. But he and Raven chat it up all the time."

I let out a soft breath. The gargoyle had taken me by complete surprise. "I'm honored," I said. "Please trust us to keep your secret."

Raj stared at me, his eyes solemn and wide. "Raj likes

Ember and Angel. Ember and Angel help find Raven? Raj is scared."

"Of course we're going to find her. Don't be scared," Angel said, not missing a beat. "We'll make sure that she comes home safe."

At that moment, the doorbell rang. I motioned for Kipa to stay put while I went to answer the door. It was Herne, and he had Yutani with him. They pushed through into the living room.

Herne glanced at me. "Viktor and Talia are on the way. What happened?"

As we entered the living room, I told them about Raven not making it home, and about her phone being found in UnderLake Park. "I suppose we should search the park. I hate to think that she disappeared where Ulstair vanished. It would be a horrible coincidence. But at least we know that Ulstair's killer is dead."

"Could she have simply hurt herself? Raven isn't exactly the most graceful person," Herne said.

"I suppose. We have to hope for that," I said.

Kipa looked up at Herne. "I know how much trouble I've caused you in the past. But help me? Help find Raven?"

Herne nodded, sitting on the edge of the loveseat. "Of course. Her car is gone, you say?"

"That's the odd thing. Her car's gone, but you can't drive into the park from here, and she always takes the trailhead when she takes Raj for a walk. It would make no sense for her to leave her car elsewhere." Kipa frowned, shaking his head. "I don't understand what's going on.

"I wonder if it broke down on the way home. Maybe she took a taxi home or maybe she called a LUD? And when she got home she could have gone for a walk in the park. I know that's stretching it, but we should call the LUD headquarters to find out if they logged a trip here last night." I turned to Angel. "Can you do that?"

"On it," Angel said, pulling out her phone and moving over toward the dining area.

LUD — or Let Us Drive — was a rideshare agency. They had practically replaced taxis, although there were a few independent contractors still around.

"Kipa, Yutani, and I will search the park. I wish we had a scent dog." Herne frowned, glancing at Yutani. "Can you pick up scents in your coyote form?"

Yutani shook his head. "To some degree, but I don't have as keen of an ability as a dog." He glanced at Kipa. "Or a wolf."

"I'll call my wolves to help us. They can try scenting her out." Kipa jumped up, looking relieved to have something to do.

"Angel and Ember, stay here and wait for Talia and Viktor." Herne paused as Angel returned. "What did LUD say?"

"No one with her description, name, or address called for a LUD last night."

"We need information on her car—her license plate for one thing, and the make and model. Kipa, do you remember?" Herne asked.

Kipa snapped his fingers. "She got her insurance bill just the other day and I know she hasn't paid it yet. Let me go get it. It will have her license plate and the make and model on it." He vanished down the hall toward Raven's office.

"Viktor can ask Erica to put out an APB. If we can find

the car, maybe we can find Raven." Herne paused, looking at me. "Yutani filled me in on what happened last night. Do you think anything there might have precipitated this?"

I shrugged. "I doubt if Eldris is behind this. He seemed as eager to find out who the killer is as we are. I don't think he wants any prying eyes on his club. Raven did mention that there was a rather obnoxious man in the Spooks—a Michael Gould. We were actually speculating on whether he might be the murderer." I paused. "By the way, sending another Ante-Fae to watch over me? That's tacky…but sweet."

"Trinity's okay. He's an oddball, but I knew he could get in there without a fuss." Herne gnawed on his lip, then said, "All right. When Talia and Viktor get here, have Viktor call Erica about this Michael Gould. We have to check out everything we can."

As the three men headed toward the door, I sat down beside Raj and draped my arm around his shoulders. He looked up at me, and I could see the worry in his eyes.

"Try not to worry," I said softly. "We're going to do our best to find her."

Raj leaned his head against my knee, and we sat like that until the men had left the house.

BY THE TIME VIKTOR AND TALIA GOT THERE I HAD GONE through Raven's phone, looking for anything that might give us a clue. There were no calls since before we went to the club. There was one text that had come through shortly before we left Fire & Fang, after our meeting in the bathroom. But the only identifier was a *P* for the name. It said, HERE'S MY NUMBER. And Raven had texted back, GOT IT.

"This wouldn't be Gould, unless he has a weird nickname." I frowned, chewing on my lip as I tried to figure out who it was. I thought about calling them, but that seemed a little premature. And what would I say? *I found your phone number in Raven's phone and we're looking for her, have you seen her?*

Viktor immediately called Erica, who said she would put out an APB on Raven's car, and one on Raven, as well.

"I should call some of her friends. I know a few of them," I said. "Maybe someone had an emergency and she drove over there."

"But why would her phone be out in the park?" Angel said.

I shook my head. "I have no clue. But it's worth a shot." I pulled up Raven's list of contacts. The first person I would call would be Llew. He was a good friend of hers and he owned the apothecary shop where Raven read tarot cards.

"Yes?" The voice on the other end sounded groggy, and not at all happy to be woken up at seven in the morning.

"Llew, this is Ember, Raven's friend. I was wondering if she contacted you this morning? Is she by any chance over at your house?"

His grumpiness changed to curiosity. "No, should she be?"

"She seems to have disappeared. We're trying to locate her. We found her phone, which is why I'm calling you, but her car is missing and so is she. Have you talked to her since last night?"

"No, I haven't. She's supposed to come down to the shop today, though. She has a couple of appointments in the afternoon. She didn't call me to cancel." He sounded genuinely concerned now. "Would you like me to come over? I might be able to do a Location spell to see if I can figure out anything."

"If you wouldn't mind, that might be helpful. We're at her house. Kipa, Herne, and Yutani are out searching for her in the park."

"I'll see you in about half an hour. Have you eaten breakfast?"

Surprised by the question, I said, "No. We haven't had a chance. Angel and I were about to eat when we got the call from Kipa."

"I'll stop by my husband's coffee shop. He makes the best pastries in town. I'll bring over something to eat. I'll be there in twenty minutes."

As he hung up, I glanced at Angel. "Her friend Llew works with magic and he might be able to help us. I suppose I should call a few of the Ante-Fae who she hangs out with." I paused, thinking of Trinity, but he seemed to have been on our side. I scrolled through Raven's contacts.

My gaze fell on Raj. I looked over at Viktor and Talia. "Why don't you to check on her ferrets? I doubt if they've been fed today unless Kipa remembered. And they need their cages cleaned. She does that first thing every morning."

"I'm not sure why you want us out of the room," Talia said, "but we'll take care of the ferrets. Where are they?"

"In the room at the end of the hall." As soon as they were out of sight I turned back to Raj. "Raj, do you know the names of Raven's friends from the Burlesque A Go-Go club?"

"Raj knows some of her friends. Raj doesn't like all of them, but some are nice." The gargoyle gave me a winsome look. "Raj hungry."

"I'll get you something to eat," Angel said. "Meanwhile, you help Ember."

"Raj help Ember. Ember and Angel are nice. Raj likes Ember and Angel."

"And we like Raj."

"Raven has some friends. There's Apollo. Apollo is a pretty boy. Raven also likes Vixen. Vixen owns the club. Raj likes Apollo and Vixen. Raj does *not* like the Vulture Sisters. They're scary."

"Thank you. Does Raven have any other friends not from the club?"

"Wager. He likes Raven but she doesn't like him the same way he likes her. And Wendy. Wendy's funny. Wendy could break Ember's neck without even thinking about it."

I remembered Vixen and Apollo from a trip to the club with Raven. But *Wendy*... I frowned, wondering if that was the same Wendy I knew from Ginty's bar. I scrolled through the contacts. There was a phone number for Apollo, as well as one for Vixen. And I found numbers for Wager, and one for Wendy Fierce-Womyn. Yep, the bartender at Ginty's, all right. I decided to start with Wager, since we had talked recently. As I waited for him to come on the line, I glanced over at Angel who was carrying a dish full of something that smelled like tuna.

"Does Raj like tuna? It's all Angel could find," Angel

said to the gargoyle. "I mixed it up with some leftover macaroni and cheese."

Raj's ears perked up. "Raj loves tuna. Raj loves mac and cheese. Raj thanks Angel." He followed her over to the corner where she set his plate down and he began to eat, devouring the makeshift tuna casserole.

Finally, Wager came on the phone. He sounded as groggy as Llew had.

I filled him in on what was going on. "Did she call you after she left my house?"

"No. That's not like her at all. Give me the name of the troublemaker at the club and I'll see what I can find. Also, who did you say the club owner was?"

"Michael Gould. And the owner is a vampire named Eldris. He's trouble, I can tell you. I don't trust him in any way, shape, or form."

"Give me your number so I have it. I'll call you as soon as I find out anything."

I gave Wager my cell number, and then called Apollo. All I got was an answering machine, so I left a message and my personal number. Next, I called Vixen, but the number went directly to the Burlesque A Go-Go and I got a recording saying they would be open at eight P.M.

Finally, I put in a call to Wendy. She answered on the first ring.

"Hey, Raven...what's up so early?"

"Actually, this is Ember Kearney. You remember—from the Wild Hunt?"

"Right. What are you doing with Raven's phone?"

"We have a problem. Raven's missing." I gave her the rundown. "Did she by any chance contact you since midnight last night?"

"No, she hasn't. I'll let you know if she does, though. Do you think she's okay?" Wendy asked.

"I hope so. I don't know what I think right now, but I need to hope that she's okay. The odd thing is that her car is missing and yet her phone was found in UnderLake Park."

"That is odd. She lives right at the trailhead of the park, I know. We went walking there last week. Keep me informed, would you? Raven and I've become closer over the past month or so."

"Of course. Do you mind if I add your number to my contacts? And I'll text you so you have my number, just in case she shows up at Ginty's."

"Of course. That's fine."

"Well, I've contacted everyone I can think of." I set Raven's phone back on the table, staring at it. "It just doesn't add up." I headed toward the ferrets' room. "Viktor! Talia! Come on out." I hadn't wanted for them to see me talking to Raj, given he kept the fact he could talk a secret. A really good secret, in fact. We had known Raven and Raj since September, and not once did I have a clue that Raj could speak.

Talia came out, followed by Viktor. "We fed the ferrets and played with them. There's something odd about them," Talia said. "I can't put my finger on it, but they don't feel like ferrets to me. Not entirely."

"What do you mean?"

"You know how it feels when you're interacting with someone who's putting up a mask? It feels like that. They *look* like ferrets and they *act* like ferrets, but there's something more to them. I just can't figure it out."

"She's right," Viktor said. "Did you have any luck?"

"Her friend Llew is on the way over, with breakfast. He works magic so he might be able to cast a Location spell."

"Any other leads?"

"I called everyone I could think of," I said. "But nobody had any leads." At that moment the doorbell rang and Angel went to answer it.

CHAPTER SIXTEEN

*W*hen she came back she was followed by Llew. I had met Llewellyn Roberts a couple times at Raven's house, and I thought I had been in his shop once or twice in the past few years. He ran an apothecary, and his husband ran a nearby coffee shop and bakery.

Llew was carrying a large pastry box, which he handed to Angel, and a large messenger bag over his shoulder. He glanced at me and crooked his finger. "I have a question. I noticed something outside."

I followed him out to the driveway.

Llew knelt by the side of the drive. "There's a strong magical signature here. I don't know whose it is, but it's neither Raven's nor Kipa's. That much I can tell you."

I knelt beside him. "What are you getting at?"

"She would park her car here, right? I can feel her signature all over this area. But there's *another* magical signature mixed in there. It had to have come from someone different. They're both just about the same half-life level, which tells me that Raven was standing here at the same time this other person was."

I frowned, thinking. "Can you tell *when* they were here? Could this be residue from a few days ago?"

Llew shook his head. "No, magical signatures fade after twelve hours or so, unless some form of spell is actually cast. So, I'd say that the latest they were here was…" He glanced at his watch. "You said she left your place past midnight?"

"It was probably more like one or two in the morning."

"Then I'd say it had to be after that. She left here around seven the night before, you said?"

"She was at my house by four P.M."

"Okay, then this definitely happened after she returned. The signatures couldn't last longer than twelve hours, not and be this distinctive." Llew straightened up. "There's something more."

"What?" I tensed at the tone in his voice.

"The strange signature? It's not human. And it's not shifter or magic-born or anything I recognize, but it's most definitely steeped in magical energy." He shook his head. "I have no clue *what* was here, but whatever it was, it's a lot stronger than Raven is."

I shivered. "A goose just walked over my grave," I said, staring at him. "Do you have *any* clue what it might be?"

"No, and *that* scares the fuck out of me. I've felt a lot of magical signatures in my life, and I've met a lot of magical people, but…there's something chaotic about this—wildly chaotic."

I moved closer to him and he draped his arm around my shoulder. "I'm sorry, Ember, but this isn't good news. I think that somebody swept Raven away."

"How do you explain her phone in the park?" I asked, my voice tight.

"I don't. Decoy, maybe? To throw you off guard? The same with her car vanishing. Or maybe they knocked her out and took her away in her own car?"

As we stood there, I began to shiver. A moment later, there were shouts as Kipa and Herne came jogging up with Yutani behind them.

"Did you find anything?" I asked.

Yutani shook his head before the others could answer. "No, we didn't."

Llew quickly told them what he had discovered. We were gathered in the driveway when a man and woman crossed the street from the house opposite of Raven's. I knew that Kipa had bought the house to free Raven from an unending series of rotten neighbors, and that he had rented it out to an Irish sister and brother.

Twins, Meadow and Trefoil were magic-born, and they were members of LOCK, an organization originally founded by Taliesin—the son of the goddess Cerridwen. LOCK was some sort of record-keeping organization, though it had a paramilitary branch as well. Since they had moved in, she hadn't had a problem with any neighbors since.

Meadow was short and sturdy, and she had long red hair that was swept up in a messy chignon. She was lovely, in a sturdy, rosy-cheeked sort of way. Trefoil was tall and lanky, pale-skinned with hair as long as his sister's. He had a swimmer's build and hazel eyes that were so magnetic I felt like I might fall into them and not come up for air. They were both dressed in khaki cargo pants. Meadow wore a green tank that curved nicely over her bust, and Trefoil was wearing a black mesh tank that showed off his abs. Neither looked easy to tangle with.

"Is something wrong?" Trefoil asked.

Kipa turned to him. "Raven's missing."

Meadow knelt beside Llew, frowning. "What the hell? Tref—feel this." Her accent was strong but understandable.

Trefoil joined his sister. He held his hand out over the space where Llew had found the magical signature, then quickly pulled it away. "You've got trouble, for sure. This is no member of the magic-born."

"I know, but I can't pinpoint who it belongs to. Can you?" Llew asked.

Trefoil and Meadow stood up. Trefoil turned to Herne. "Lord Herne, this feels like divine energy."

Herne and Kipa exchanged glances, then Herne cleared his throat. "Let me summon my mother. If anyone would know, she would." He pulled out his phone and moved off to the side to call Morgana.

Meanwhile, Kipa stared at the patch of ground that was keeping us all so captivated.

"I'm not that good with magical signatures," Kipa said. He raised his head, a stricken look on his face. "But would a god just drive off in her car?"

"You and Herne drive," Yutani said. He turned to Llew. "How strong of a signature is it?"

"Very strong," Llew said. "That's why it confused me so much. While most members of the magic-born are powerful, this goes beyond anything I've ever felt. Trefoil's right, that's the only thing this can be." He held out his hand. "I don't believe we've met. My name is

Llewellyn Roberts, and I'm a friend of Raven's. I own the Sun & Moon Apothecary in downtown Redmond."

Trefoil shook his hand, and then Meadow followed suit. "I'm Meadow O'Ceallaigh, and this is my brother Trefoil. We work for LOCK. We're also members of the magic-born."

Herne returned then, looking grim. "My mother's on the way. Let's go inside until she gets here. It won't take her long."

We filed back inside, where we found that Talia and Angel had raided Raven's refrigerator and made sandwiches to go with the pastries that Llewellyn had brought. As we settled around the table, they poured coffee for us, and I noticed that Raj was working on a second breakfast. He was very much a hobbit when it came to food.

None of us were in a particularly chatty mood, and we silently finished our lunch until the doorbell rang. Angel went to answer and returned with Morgana behind her.

Herne's mother was a stunning beauty, although most of the gods commanded a regal presence, whether or not they were beautiful or ugly or terrifying. Morgana was in one of her particularly commanding moods. I could tell because she was taller than she usually presented herself. She was standing about six-five, today wearing a black linen pantsuit with a brilliant blue tank beneath the jacket. A silver belt encircled her waist, and her long flowing hair had been gathered up into a sleek ponytail.

"Mother," Herne said, standing. "You know everyone here except for Trefoil and Meadow. And this is Llewellyn, one of Raven's friends."

She graciously nodded at the three, then took a seat at the end of the table. "I stopped out front to examine the driveway. You're right. There is a strong signature there and it *is* of divine nature. It's terribly chaotic and there's a malevolence about it that leads me to think we're dealing with one of the gods of chaos."

I paled. "It can't be Typhon, can it?"

Morgana shook her head. "If Typhon landed in Raven's front yard, there wouldn't be anything left of the neighborhood. No, but there is that malign element to it." She paused, then sighed. "I found out some particularly disturbing information this morning. The case you're on? The serial killer case?"

"Yes?" Herne asked, looking like he didn't want to hear the answer. I knew exactly how he felt. Events felt like they had just gone into a freefall, and one of our friends was caught up in the vortex.

With a grave look, she said, "It isn't just happening here. I'm getting reports from all over the world that necromancers and bone witches are being targeted. It seems there is a systematic attack on those working with the dead. At the same time, reports of the dead rising are increasing. It occurs to me that since bone witches and necromancers can control the dead, and they're being targeted, then someone's trying to remove impediments to controlling spirits and…well…corpses, for what you will."

"Typhon," Angel whispered. "You said that he would bring the dead with him. Could he be sending out…I don't know…*scouts* to pave the way?"

"More along the lines of emissaries. We told you that some of the gods are aligning themselves with him. Especially the gods of chaos."

"Excuse me?" Llewellyn looked like he was about to faint. "Who's Typhon? And what the hell is going on?"

"I'm afraid you're about to be let in on a secret you really *don't* want to know," Morgana said. "Trefoil and Meadow, how much do you know about this?"

Trefoil looked at Meadow, then said, "Some. LOCK knows about Typhon. While some of the researchers haven't been notified, some have. I think you should know what we do for the organization."

Meadow nodded. "I think you're right, Tref, considering what's happening. We belong to the paramilitary side of LOCK. We answer to the Force Majeure and they occasionally send us out on missions when there's a grave danger that cannot be controlled on local levels. We were sent here to keep an eye on activities surrounding the dead and we report directly back to the Council. LOCK, as you know, was created by Taliesin, who belongs to the Force Majeure. Therefore we are directly under their control."

"My father is the current leader of the Force Majeure," Morgana said. "He's Merlin."

Meadow blushed. "I didn't make the connection," she said. "Forgive me, my lady."

"Nothing to forgive," Morgana said. "I didn't even think about my father being part of this. I haven't heard from him in a while. That was shortsighted of me. So the Force Majeure sent you here to keep an eye on the signs that Typhon is nearing?"

Trefoil nodded. "Yes, we're advanced scouts, you might say. And it seemed handy being across the street from a born bone witch. Since Raven was born a bone witch, and her mother is one of the Bean Sidhe, we thought she might notice some of the increased activity and be able to help us if need be."

"No wonder you jumped on the house so quickly when I put it up for rent," Kipa said.

"We had been looking for a place near her for a while." Meadow bit her lip. "So what is this about a targeted attack on necromancers?"

Morgana sighed, pulling out her phone. She checked her notes and said, "I'm afraid it's true. We're getting reports from all over the world that necromancers, bone witches, and mediums who specialize in talking to spirits are being killed. Most just outright, not in as horrific a way as your victims here have been. We think that Typhon has sent emissaries into the world to destroy the opposition, so to speak."

"Crap. Then our killer is just one of many," I said.

"Right. The gods had decided to enlist all of those working with the dead in our fight against him. We're scrambling to enact safety measures for those still alive. We've had reports of more than two hundred deaths so far and it's just increasing." She shook her head. "This is a blow we didn't expect."

"What are you doing to keep them safe?" Llew asked.

"We've put out the word through some of the magical guilds that they're to allow the necromancers and bone witches access, so we can keep an eye on them. We've been getting some resistance, but the guilds won't fight the gods for long, not when my father steps in. All the other agencies of the hunt—Mielikki's Arrow, Odin's Chase, and Diana's Hounds—are sending their agents into the guilds to discuss matters. In fact, I was about to call a meeting with the Wild Hunt for just that reason."

"What are we going to do about Raven?" Kipa asked, his face ashen. "Do you think that the killer has her? Do you think it's truly one of Typhon's emissaries?"

I glanced at Herne. I had the feeling we were both thinking the same thing, given the revelations that Morgana had dumped on our shoulders. "We need to speak with Eldris again. I'm pretty sure that whoever Typhon's emissary for this area is, is working through the Spooks. That's the only place in Seattle that most of the necromancers and bone witches gather."

"One thing," Trefoil said. "That signature out there? It's definitely feminine, and I'd say someone who's batshit crazy."

"Let me call my father." Morgana abruptly stood and headed toward the hallway, pulling out her phone.

I was trying to take everything in that it happened. All of the sudden, we had gone from a simple serial killer to an emissary from Typhon, who—along with others—was sweeping through the world attempting to kill off anybody who could deal with the dead. And that meant that Typhon's emissaries were *everywhere*.

"If they're killing off those who deal with the dead, what else are they going to do?" Talia murmured.

"I wonder if Raven's still alive," I whispered.

"The killer usually dumps the bodies on Monday, so I think we can assume that Raven is still alive. Unfortunately, *our* serial killer, or emissary if you like, has a thirst for pain." Yutani stopped, as if suddenly realizing what he had just said. "I'm sorry, I didn't mean to…"

"No, we know you didn't. It's just—it's Raven out there. Viktor," I said. "Can you call Erica and see if she's heard anything about the APBs?"

"I'll do that right now," Viktor said, pushing back his chair and pulling out his phone. "While I'm at it, I can get an update on Sheila's attacker."

While he called Erica, I stared at my plate, moving the food around. I had lost every ounce of my appetite. Herne, who was sitting next to me, reached out and took my hand. I looked at him, needing the reassurance in his eyes, but I was surprised to see that even he looked shaken.

Viktor returned, shaking his head. "They found Raven's car. It was ditched on a side street near the entrance to the 520 floating bridge. Erica'll let me know if they find any prints. But given what Morgana said, somehow I doubt they're going to be able to place any fingerprints they might find."

"How's the search for Sheila's attacker, and how is she?"

"The hospital called me this morning with an update. She's going to be all right, but she still can't even attempt to talk. As far as the freak who slashed her, Erica said they're on his tail." Viktor pressed his lips together, remaining surprisingly calm.

Morgana returned at that moment. "My father will be here shortly. Herne, he wants you to pick him up a list of supplies." She handed him a paper.

"Grandpa is coming here?"

Trefoil almost choked on his coffee. "*Grandpa*? You call Merlin *Grandpa*? One of the most powerful magicians ever?"

"Well, he *is* my grandfather." Herne glanced over the paper. "What's he planning?"

"Don't ask, just follow directions. Meanwhile, Ember?"

"Yes, Morgana?" I stood, ready to do whatever she needed.

"We need to go into Raven's ritual room." She glanced at the others around the table. "Angel, I need you, too."

Angel blinked. "Me?"

"Yes, I need two of Raven's friends who are close to her. But Kipa's too emotionally involved. Meanwhile, Llewellyn, you and Trefoil cordon off the energy signature. We don't want anybody disrupting it. Kipa, go with Herne. It will keep you occupied. Meadow, my father asks that you go print off any information that you received from the Force Majeure."

"What should we do?" Yutani asked. He motioned to Viktor, Talia, and himself.

"Call Eldris," I interjected. "Tell him we need the fucking truth. We need to know *anything* about a woman who joined the Spooks within the past few weeks." I paused. "Last night, I saw Raven talking to a woman. She seemed deep in conversation." I thought back to the evening before. "She was beautiful with a capital B. She had long blond hair, she looked highly toned, and she was wearing leather pants and a black sweater. I remember her because she was so stunning." I shook my head, suddenly realizing I had fallen into a reverie just thinking about her.

"What the hell?" Herne asked." You just flickered in and out. Not physically, but I could feel you slipping away."

"He's right," Morgana said. "Yutani, make the call now. I want to hear what this vampire has to say, and if he tries to blow you off, give me the phone."

Yutani brought out his phone and punched in a

number. "I need to talk to Eldris. Please tell him this is Yutani from last night." He paused for a moment then added, "Call him to the phone. It's an emergency." Another pause. "He's going to want to talk to me—"

Morgana yanked the phone out of his hand. "Listen to me," she said, her voice echoing, a steel will behind it. "Call your master to the phone or I will personally come down there and tear your club apart. And you'd better believe that I can do it."

I found myself terrified. And then I realized she had forced magic into her voice, magic that could travel through the phone lines.

A moment later, she spoke again. "Is this Eldris the vampire? Owner of Fire & Fang?" It was her turn to pause, and then she said, "I want to know whatever you can dredge up about a woman involved in your necromancers' group, the Spooks. You either tell me what I want to know, or I destroy your club… This is Morgana, goddess of the Fae and the Sea. I would highly recommend that you not question my authority or authenticity… Good, very good. She was there last night, talking to Raven BoneTalker. She wore black leather pants, a black sweater, had long golden hair, and apparently was about as hot as you can get."

By now we were all watching her, transfixed on her side of the conversation. I could just imagine Eldris squirming in his seat and it made me smile, despite all the strain we were under.

"You don't say? Do you know anything else about her? You'd better tell me." Morgana paused once more, then finally said, "All right. But if I call you back, you answer. Give me your personal number. *Now*." She motioned to me and I found her a pen and notepad. She scribbled something on it, then said, "I trust you will cooperate with my son Herne, and all members of the Wild Hunt from now on. In fact, you and I might want to have a conversation sometime soon. I'm sure you would make a most helpful informant. And I wouldn't spread that around." Laughing gently, she finished the call and handed the phone back to Yutani. But there was no mirth in her eyes.

"Did you find out anything?" Herne asked.

"I found out too much. You and Kipa go get the things on that list. Get back here as soon as you can. Llew, you and Trefoil get out there and preserve the magical signature. Everybody scramble." She motioned for me to lead her toward Raven's ritual room. Angel followed, looking apprehensive.

Once we were in the room, Morgana shut the door, then turned to us. "I know who your killer is. And she's definitely one of Typhon's emissaries. I had a suspicion when you described her, but I was hoping I was wrong."

"Are you going to keep us in suspense?" I asked.

"You're going to wish I would, but no. You have to know. I'm afraid were going to have to conscript Llew into working with us. He can't find out about all of this and just go off on his merry way. At least Trefoil and Meadow are already on our side." She paused, shaking her head.

"Who are we up against?" I asked.

"Remember I told you how some of the gods have taken Typhon's side? Some of them are greater gods and some are lesser. And it appears he has taken some of the lesser gods and appointed them as emissaries. The person who stole Raven away is none other than Pandora."

I stared at her, unable to say a word.

"You mean Pandora as in Pandora's box?" Angel whispered.

"None other. And Pandora is as dangerous, chaotic, and crazy as they come."

CHAPTER SEVENTEEN

andora. Surely, someone had made a mistake. But as I gazed into Morgana's brilliant eyes, I realized that she wasn't joking. There was no smile behind her words, no hint of levity. I sat down on the floor near Raven's main altar, gazing at a massive crystal ball that was set on a pedestal next to the altar table.

"Surely you're not talking about…" I paused, knowing the question was futile. "Why would she work with Typhon?"

"He's the father of chaos, even more so than Loki or a number of the other ancient gods. Pandora loves tormenting humans. Although your myths about her are off track as to her origins, the fact remains that she carries the world's ills in her bag and lets them loose whenever she feels like it. Down through time, Pandora has found one way after another to plague the human race. She considers humanity her play toys. It doesn't surprise me to find her mucking about with ways of destroying this world."

"Why does she hate humanity so much?" Angel asked. "I thought she *was* human."

"Common misconception. Pandora's original name was Anesidora. She's one of Zeus's daughters. He sent her to Earth because of Prometheus's love for humanity, as an antithesis."

"And she's here, now."

"Pandora is beauty incarnate, but beneath that beauty lurks a heart of stone. From the time she was born, Zeus trained her to be his weapon. He nicknamed her Pandora so that the humans wouldn't know who she was, and he gave her the gifts of chaos and destruction. You'll notice she carries a bag with her. You'll never be able to get it away from her. In that bag are some of the worst glitches and misunderstandings the world has ever seen."

"Does Zeus know she's working for Typhon?" I asked.

Morgana frowned. "That's hard to say, but it makes sense. She has neither conscience nor compassion."

"Can she be killed?" I was afraid I knew the answer to that, but I needed to ask anyway.

"No," Morgana said. "The best you can hope for is to temporarily banish her. But it won't hold forever, and Pandora has a long memory."

Feeling thoroughly defeated, I slumped back against the wall and rested my head, closing my eyes. "How do we chase her out?"

Morgana shrugged. "That's what we're going to ask my father about. Along with several other things. He has faced most of the gods at least once."

"So what do we do now?" I asked.

"Llew had the idea to do a Location spell. I am much better equipped for that, and I can call upon Arawn and

Cerridwen for help. I wanted you two here because, even though Kipa's her boyfriend, I consider that you and Angel have the strongest connection to Raven."

"What about Raj?" I asked.

"I don't want to frighten him. And I don't think he would be able to focus the way I need him to. Ember, you and Angel join hands with me." Morgana placed the statues of Arawn and Cerridwen on the floor in the center, before taking her place. Angel and I formed the other two points of the triangle around the statues.

"Why don't you just go see them in Annwn?" Angel asked.

"I could, but that would take longer than this. And I would have to take both of you with me. You're going to be the anchors, connecting Raven's energy to me. I want you to both think about her. See her in your mind's eye, visualize her as clearly as you can. Don't let go of my hand for any reason unless I tell you to."

She took my hand, my fingers began vibrating as her energy flowed through me, through my other arm and into Angel's hand. I heard Angel gasp, but brought my focus back to the image of Raven. I tried to block out everything I could except for her form, for the sound of her voice. Even as Morgana began to speak I held tight to the thought of Raven.

"Oh most gracious Arawn, Lord of the Dead. Cerridwen, Keeper of the Cauldron, I summon thee. I, Morgana, goddess of Fae, goddess of the sea, stand before you. I need your help, and I don't have time to come visit you in person. Please, appear to me. Be here now."

Her voice thundered and it felt like it shook the very walls. I braced myself, continuing to hold tight to her hand and to Angel's. I couldn't help but open my eyes as the flow of heavy magic swept around us.

I stiffened, every hair on my arm standing at attention. As I looked around, I saw a mist rising from the statues, forming what looked like a mirror. At that moment, Angel opened her eyes and she trembled, but said nothing.

Overhead, within the border of the portal, a figure appeared.

A black skeletal king, massive, he had red eyes and wore a long silver cloak. As he stepped through the portal I saw that he was almost transparent, and I wasn't sure whether he was really here.

Before I could even take him in, a majestic woman appeared. She, too, came through the portal, and moved to the other side. Her hair was caught into braids that hung down the front of her dress, and she wore an elegant rust-colored gown with a hunter green apron over the top. Around her head was a golden circlet of Celtic knot-work. I struggled to keep Raven in mind as I watched Arawn and Cerridwen appear.

Morgana gazed up at them, then inclined her head slightly. "Lady Cerridwen, Lord Arawn, welcome and thank you for hearing my plea."

"Why did you summon us?" Arawn asked, and his voice sounded like the thunder of a thousand horses galloping across the plain.

"Your priestess, Raven, has been kidnapped. We believe the kidnapper is Pandora, sent by Typhon to destroy his enemies. Raven is one of the Ante-Fae, a bone witch, and —"

"We have heard that Pandora was set to enter the

world." Cerridwen glanced at Angel and me, a curious look on her face. "And who are these women?"

"This is Ember Kearney, my pledgling, and this is Angel, her friend. I am using them as a conduit to Raven's energy since they are two of her best friends."

Arawn tilted his head. His features were barely discernible on that skeletal face. "What do you seek?"

"Help in casting a Location spell. We need to find and rescue Raven before Pandora kills her." Morgana dipped her head.

Cerridwen's smile faded away. "That little bitch has my priestess? Hold tight."

Morgana glanced back at Angel and me. "Focus on Raven."

I close my eyes, focusing on everything I could remember about Raven. From the gentle way she interacted with Raj, to the almost willy-nilly chaos that she embodied. I tried to remember everything about Raven's cadence and her looks.

As we sat there, holding hands, a jolt of energy entered the circle. Cerridwen had placed her hands on Morgana's shoulders, and the energy running through the circle skyrocketed, amplified beyond measure. Angel let out a little cry but she held tight.

I felt like the wind had been knocked out of me. The jolt sent me backward, but I held tight to their hands, trying not to pull away. I caught my breath as the room began to swirl, and the next moment…

...I FOUND MYSELF LYING ON MY BACK, STARING UP AT THE blazing sun.

I shaded my eyes as I rolled up, frantically looking for Morgana and Angel. They weren't with me, and neither were Arawn and Cerridwen. Instead, I found myself sitting on a plateau overlooking a deep valley in the middle of a bowl-shaped meadow. Overhead, the sun glared down, and I began to sweat. I stood, swaying as a deep drumbeat reverberated beneath my feet, as though the heart of the mountain was pulsing.

There was something in the middle of the caldera and I frowned, trying to make it out. Whatever it was, I had no clue, but it looked long and silver from here, raised on a dais. I squinted, trying to make out what it was, but I was too far away.

Frowning, I began to descend the walls of the ravine into the center of the valley. As I approached the center, the object came into focus. It was a long hospital counter —metal, with a catch tray around the sides of it, and the tray was filled with blood.

I stood there, trying to figure out what it was doing out in the middle of the mountains, when two figures approached. One was the blonde I had seen with Raven, and she was dressed in shiny pleather. *Pandora.* Behind her walked Raven, a dazed look on her face. I started to call out but realized neither could hear me. They walked over to the table and Pandora motioned to it with a flourish, like a magician. Raven lay down, eyes still ahead, totally compliant.

Pandora stood back, looking delighted. Then she squatted and set down her messenger bag and opened it up. A moment later she stood, and I saw a pair of pliers in her hand. Her eyes gleamed as she said something. Raven opened her mouth and Pandora leaned over here and—

With a scream, I tried to lunge forward, to stop her. I leapt toward Pandora and...

"EMBER! EMBER, SNAP OUT OF IT." MORGANA'S VOICE echoed through my head and I opened my eyes. I was still holding her hand, still holding Angel's, but I was flat on the floor, staring at the ceiling. I blinked as they helped me sit up.

"I seem to have taken a little trip," I murmured, looking around for Arawn and Cerridwen. They were nowhere to be seen. "Did I scare them off?"

Morgana snorted. "Not likely. No, they gave their answer and vanished and then you started… I don't know what you were doing." She let go of my hand, turning to me with concern.

"Remember I told you about the visions I get? I just had one." I paused, realizing what she had just said. "Did you say they told you where to find Raven?"

"Not as specific as I would have liked, but they gave me a general area." Morgana frowned, giving me the once-over like she expected me to faint or collapse. "Tell me what you saw."

I told her. "I've been in that area before, at least in visions. I've had several recently and each time, I knew I was searching for someone but I didn't know who. I heard someone screaming for help but I couldn't find out who. Today I saw Raven. Pandora was getting ready to…" I paused, unable to finish my sentence.

"Raven acted as though she were under a spell or drugged."

"Chances are good she is. Pandora has many gifts, and one of those is the gift for charming others. Classic gift of a sociopath, and truly, when you break it down, that's what she is." Morgana paused, then quietly added, "Make no mistake. Pandora has no conscience. She has no remorse. To her, torturing others is child's play, like making a puppet move on a string. She's quite detached from any emotions except her own warped sense of happiness."

I bit my lip. "Zeus really did a number when he raised her, didn't he?"

"You have no idea. She's dangerous because she doesn't care. She finds her joy in others' pain. It pains me to see Zeus's daughter take Typhon's side. Zeus isn't the most friendly of gods, and he's well known for manipulating others for his own amusement, but I doubt that even he would be happy to know what's going on." Morgana motioned for us to follow her toward the door. "But now we have a place to look for your friend. And Arawn and Cerridwen also gave me an idea of how to perhaps banish Pandora, at least long enough to rescue Raven."

WE GATHERED BACK IN RAVEN'S KITCHEN. RAJ HUNKERED in the corner, a worried look in his eyes, and I knelt beside him to give him a hug.

"We'll find her," I whispered to him. "We'll do everything we can to bring her home safe. No matter what, don't you worry. You'll be taken care of. We'll never let anything happen to you."

Raj leaned his head against my shoulder and, in the faintest of whispers, said, "Raj misses Raven. Ember makes Raj feel better. Raj glad he talked to Ember."

I began to get the hang of his cadence. "Ember really thinks Raj is special. Ember is honored Raj is talking to her and Angel."

At that moment, Herne and Kipa reappeared, several shopping bags in hand. They were all marked Taco Grande. That's what Merlin had requested? A major taco splurge. Morgana caught my gaze and shrugged, then motioned for them to set the bags on the table. She looked around at the crowded room. "Herne, a word, please?"

"Yes, Mother." Herne followed her to the kitchen.

The rest of us gathered around the table. There weren't enough chairs for everyone, so Kipa, Viktor, Trefoil, and Yutani stood back. Herne and Morgana reappeared.

"Too many people are going to muddle the energy," Herne said. "Talia, Angel, and Yutani, please go back to the office and just…carry on."

"Llewellyn, Trefoil, and Meadow," Morgana said, "I'd like you to wait across the street. We may need your help but as Herne said, too many magical signatures confuse the energy and will make it harder to pinpoint Raven when we go after her."

Nobody really wanted to leave, but they obeyed her. Talia patted me on the arm as she and Yutani headed for the door. "She'll be okay. You'll find her," she said.

I nodded, although I didn't feel as confident as I wanted to be.

Once they were all gone, Herne, Viktor, and Kipa moved into the living room. Morgana and I sat at the table, waiting for Merlin.

"Who was your mother?" I asked her. I vaguely remembered being told who Morgana's mother was, but right now my thoughts were on Raven and if I didn't take my mind off of her, I'd be imagining all sorts of horrible possibilities.

"Viviane, the Lady of the Lake." She paused, then said, "Most people think she was water Fae in nature. They picture her as a siren or something."

I frowned, nibbling on one of the pastries Llewellyn had brought. The raspberry flavor was bright and tangy. "So, she *wasn't* water Fae?"

"No," Morgana said. "My mother was actually one of the Ante-Fae, as close to a water elemental as you can get without actually being one."

That made a lot of sense. After a moment, I asked, "How did you meet Cernunnos?"

"I was out on a berry-picking trip. My father was off on one of his many missions, and my mother had asked me to spend a few days picking berries so we could make jam against the winter months. She lives in a small cottage on the side of Lake Avalon, in between the worlds. My father lived there with her for a long time, but he gets wanderlust and by the time I was...well...if I were human I would have been in my late teens, he had left again. I stayed home and helped Mother tend the garden and guard our forest retreat."

"It sounds idyllic."

She smiled. "Well, idyll is in the eye of the beholder. I was lonely, a lot. So I went on a three-day journey to pick berries. I had a small sledge with me so I could carry the buckets, and one of our goats was pulling it. I was deep in the forest when a massive bear lumbered out. He was hungry, and he must have smelled my berries because he charged me. I backed away, hoping he would go for the fruit and leave me alone. But then I saw he was wounded, and that had turned him mean. He ignored the berries and charged me. I tried to climb a nearby willow, but the bear was almost on me. At that moment, a horn echoed through the forest. The bear stopped, and even my goat stood at attention. I scrambled up into the tree. The horn sounded again, closer, and then Cernunnos stepped out into the clearing. He was massive, and his antlers rose so majestically. I was caught in the lock of his gaze and lost my heart."

I remembered seeing Herne in the woods for the first time, before I knew it was him. He was so regal, in his stag form. He had saved my ass, and Angel's little brother. When he showed up at my door, there had been an instant connection.

With a gentle smile, I said, "I understand."

Morgana reached out to stroke my cheek. "I know you do. Cernunnos sent the bear off after healing him, and then he invited me to eat dinner with him. I did, right there in the forest. He provided bread and honey, and a roast chicken, and we had some of the berries I had gathered. I couldn't seem to remember that I was sitting with a god, I had already tumbled head over heels for him. When evening came, he took me back to his palace. I wanted him, but he wouldn't sleep with me. I didn't want to leave, but he made me return home the next morning. He told me that he would come by every so often. I grew up, and eventually my father came home. Merlin taught me to use my magic. And several times a year I met privately with Cernunnos."

"Did he ask you to marry him?" I found myself pulled into her story. It was like a fairytale, only this time, it was real.

"One night, about eight years after I first met him, he took me for a midnight ride. The moon was bright, and we sat on the edge of the lake. He asked me if I would be willing to leave my world and join him in Annwn. He said that if I were to marry him, I'd be given an elixir and it would change me into a goddess, to rule by his side. I'd be leaving everything in the outside world for him. I didn't even have to think. I said yes. I wanted to be with him always.

"My mother reluctantly let me go. My father was angry. He had expected me to join the Force Majeure one day. He had also developed a fondness for Arthur and wanted me to marry him. I refused. We fought and I ran away, leaving everyone behind. When I had Herne, some years later, my mother got my father to relent. We met and made up, and we've been on good terms since then."

I thought over what she said. What would happen when…if…Herne and I made it to the altar? I was wearing his promise ring. That didn't mean we'd end up married, but it was a step along that direction. I wanted to ask more but the doorbell rang.

Morgana paused. "That must be my father. Herne," she called over to where the men were sitting. "Please let your grandfather in."

Herne jumped up and ran to the door. I stood, uncer-

tain as to what to say or do. Morgana flashed me a reas-
suring smile.

"It will be all right. My father likes the Fae—both
sides." She cleared her throat as Herne returned. Behind
him was a man of medium height, who was wearing a
long gray cloak over a pair of jeans and a pale blue shirt.
Merlin's hair was silver, down to his waist and caught
back in a ponytail. His eyes glittered with the same blue as
Morgana's, and I could see the family resemblance.

He spotted her, and the sober expression on his face
gave way and he opened his arms. "My daughter, well
met." As she moved forward for a three-way hug with
Merlin and Herne, I glanced over at Viktor, who gave me
a thumbs-up.

"Now," Merlin said, pulling back. "Tell me what's going
on and why you called me. I know Typhon is coming, but
what weighs so heavily that you need my immediate
help?"

Morgana motioned to me. "This is Ember Kearney.
She's Herne's consort. One of her friends has been
kidnapped by Pandora and we need your help in getting
the girl back."

The smile vanished and Merlin turned to me, his
expression grave. "Oh, my dear. If Pandora has her, we
may already be too late." And just like that, he swept to the
table and we gathered around to make plans.

CHAPTER EIGHTEEN

I kept stealing surreptitious glances at Merlin as we laid out everything we knew. He would give his utmost attention to whomever was speaking at the time, totally focused on what they were saying. When I told him about our visit to Fire & Fang, I found it almost unnerving to be under his scrutiny.

Morgana said, "When I talked to Arawn and Cerridwen, they showed me a nearby mountain that Pandora appears to be using for her hideout. Raven's there. For some reason, she's chosen a different location than usual. Cerridwen was able to tell me that."

My ears perked up. "Mountain? Like the mountain I saw?"

"I think so. It's a barren place, with scrub brush growing on it but few trees. It's actually a hill, although in some places it would be called a mountain. Mount Bracken. It's up on Highway 2, near the Skykomish River. Have you heard of it?" Morgana leaned back, frowning. "I don't know the topography of the area here, so I'm not exactly sure how far that is."

Herne pulled out his phone and began tapping away. "Give me a moment. All right, here it is. It's somewhere near Lake Serene, and the Bridal Veil Falls Trailhead. It would take us about two hours to get up there, if we start now. Perhaps less, depending on traffic." He looked up at me. "How much time do you think we have?"

Taken aback by the question, I shrugged. "I don't know. Morgana?"

She, too, gave a shrug. "It would be helpful if there's a portal in the area. It would cut a great deal of time off your travel and it would make it easier to get her back here, in case Pandora has already roughed her up."

"Let me give a call. I know exactly the person who would have that information." Herne moved away from the table.

I noticed Merlin watching him. "Have you had much time to spend with your grandson over the years?" I ventured. I wasn't certain whether it was an appropriate question, but I was curious. How much time had Herne spent with his grandfather?

Merlin shook his head. "It would be nice to spend time with Herne. But I'm always on the go, it seems. I was on the go when his mother was young, too. That's one of the few things I regret in my life." He looked over at Morgana, who shrugged.

"I knew that you were a busy man. There were always so many things that required your attendance. And when you took over the Force Majeure, I knew better than to expect you home for dinner. I would like for you to spend more time with my son, though. I'd like him to know you better."

"I'll try," Merlin said.

I had the feeling that his promise was more for appearance's sake rather than being true. I didn't pursue the subject, but turned to Morgana. "If Pandora is a goddess, how are we going to get Raven away from her?"

"Wait till Herne comes back. My father can tell us how to best approach her."

There was a studied nuance running between Morgana and her father. It wasn't exactly *tension*, but a formality that I hadn't expected. I sensed that Merlin might be one of those parents who always promised more than he came through with. A promise of time together, a promise to help out, a promise that he was listening…

"I hate sitting here," I said. "Pandora could be torturing Raven right now." I was rapidly losing all patience and my frantic feelings were bubbling to the surface. We knew where she was. I wanted to go get her.

"She could be," Merlin said.

"That's not helpful," Morgana said, glaring at him. She turned to me. "We'll get underway as soon as we can. There's nothing I can say to make it easier, but I promise, we'll do our best to get her back."

I turned to Morgana with a grateful smile. "Thank you. I'm so worried."

Viktor reached over and took my hand, giving it a tight squeeze. "Herne and Morgana won't let us down."

I nodded, pushing away from the table and walking over to stare outside. The weather was holding steady. At least we had that in our favor. At that moment, Kipa came up behind me. He gave me a sideways glance and lowered his voice.

"I don't like him much either," he said.

I couldn't help but grin. "Great minds think alike. I have the feeling Herne isn't that fond of his grandfather, either."

"Those who work with magic at his level… There's something less than human about them. A detached nature, and it can come through as cold and calculating. Remember Louhia? From Pohjola?"

I rolled my eyes. "How can I forget her? She was fucking scary. But you're right. She had a ruthlessness to her that made my skin crawl. The gods don't have it, though, not like that. At least not the ones we've met."

"I think the humans are closer to us in nature then the magic-born. At least the greatest among the magic-born. It seems an odd thing to say, but I've met quite a few higher-level witches and magicians and sorcerers. They all have that streak of callousness to them."

"Kipa, Ember? Come back to the table, please." Herne shoved his phone in his pocket. "I found a portal we can go through. It's actually a local portal."

"What do you mean, 'local portal'?" I asked.

"The native people of this area created it. They also have portals throughout the state. We very seldom use them because we don't like abusing our welcome. But I just called Quest Realto and she has contacts. There is a portal in Issaquah that leads to the Skykomish River. Very close to where we're going. She also has friends who live up there—the portal keepers there. She called them and they'll wait for us and provide us with a vehicle."

I breathed a sigh of relief. "Thank the gods. That's such good news. When do we leave?"

"I don't want to go back to the office to pick up supplies. So I asked Quest if her friends could gather some things for me. You don't have any of your weapons on you, do you?"

"No, and I want my sword. I saw myself in one of the visions carrying it. Actually in *most* of the visions. There's some reason I need to take Brighid's Flame with me."

"All right. I'll call Yutani and ask him to gather our weaponry and bring it to us. Quest said her friends can supply a tent and some gear for climbing, in case we need it." Herne jumped up again, taking off to call Yutani. I glanced over at Raj. He looked lonely and frightened.

I knelt beside him and once again put my arms around his shoulders. "Would you like Angel to stay with you while we're gone? We're going to go find Raven now."

Raj let out a little gulp. "Raj likes Angel. Raj lonely, so Angel will stay with Raj?"

"Angel will stay with Raj, yes." I called Angel and asked her to come over to stay with Raj. "We'll be gone, but Kipa will leave his key under the mat." I glanced over to where Kipa was standing. I walked over to his side. "Leave your key under the mat for Angel. She'll come stay with Raj. You certainly kept Raven and Raj's secret."

"Of course I did. That he can speak wasn't my secret to tell." He paused, and I could see the fear in his eyes. "I think I love her. I mean, I *know* I do. It's still hard to say and to be honest, neither one of us has said the words to each other. But…"

"But the fact is, you have fallen in love with Raven?"

He nodded. "I don't think she's ready to hear it yet.

And that's fine, I can wait. But I can't stand to think of someone out there hurting her. She never wants me to interfere, at least not without her instigating it, so I stood back when she went to the club with you. It wasn't my place to stop her, but I wish I had. I wish I had argued with her, even made her angry. Just…something, anything so she wouldn't have become a target. I feel like my heart is a second away from shattering."

I rested my hand on his arm. "We'll get her back. We have to get her back. She's our Raven. Raj can't make it without her."

Herne interrupted. "Yutani and Angel are on the way with our weapons and some prepacked camping gear that we always keep ready. Grandfather, it's time to tell us what we need to know about Pandora. How do we defeat her? How do we get Raven away from her?"

MOUNT BRACKEN WAS LOCATED A FEW MILES FROM THE trailhead leading into Lake Serene. The portal that would lead us to the area was located in the yard of one of the portal keepers named Gatsby. He had been named after the literary character by his bibliophile mother. Quest told Herne that Gatsby was half dwarf, half human. While his people would accept him better than the Fae would accept a half-breed, he preferred to live on his own, away from his father's people. She didn't tell Herne why, and he wasn't about to ask.

Yutani and Angel made it over to Raven's house in record time, and they had brought my sword and several weapons for Herne and Viktor. Yutani had obviously wanted to go along, but Herne told him no.

"If you go, the chaos from your heritage combined with the chaos from Pandora could wreak havoc. I can't take the chance that she might be able to use you as conduit. She's a goddess, remember."

"I may have only found out about it, but I'm the *son* of a god." Yutani stared at Herne, and I almost thought he was challenging him, but then he shrugged and looked away. "I'll take care of the office with Talia. The three of you be careful."

"We will," I said, clapping him on the shoulder as I walked past, following Herne out to his Expedition. I turned to Llewellyn, who had crossed the street when he saw us exiting the house. "Watch over Raj for now. Angel's here and she'll keep you company. I'm hoping we'll be home by tonight, but there's no way of telling."

"Let's get moving," Morgana said. She climbed in the second row of seats, and Merlin gingerly sat next to her. Viktor and Kipa sat in the back. I rode shotgun.

As we took off, I glanced over the back seat at Merlin. "It just occurred to me, you were around long before cars were ever dreamt of. What did you think when you saw technology emerging?"

He stared at me for a moment. "Quite honestly, it just seemed like a different form of magic. Magic for the non-magical. And though technology did push those of us who work with magical energy into a corner, it also gave us room to regroup and plan out how much we wanted to be involved in the new emerging societies. I will say that modern medicine is a whole lot better than relying on leeches and amputations." As abruptly as he spoke, he stopped, looking back out the window to indicate the conversation was over. I glanced at Morgana and she shrugged, rolling her eyes. Oh yes, there were definitely family issues at play here.

The road to Issaquah was packed, I-405 was a tangle of cars, but we made it through after passing several accidents. I remembered that there was a Mariners game today over in Seattle, and southbound to I-90 was a mess with people heading across the bridge to the stadium.

Once we cleared I-90, we continued until the exit to Issaquah. Issaquah was a smallish city, but it ran right into Renton and Redmond, and like all the bedroom communities on the Eastside, it was an unending stretch of city interspersed with large patches of trees and greenery. It was kind of an old-fashioned town with a rustic feel downtown, but beneath that studied rustic demeanor lie the heart of a trendy hipster community.

Gatsby Jones lived up in the Issaquah Highlands, on Harrison Drive NE. His house was a small ranch on a large lot, in sharp contradiction to the McMansions that crowded together on a sprawling development.

We pulled into the driveway, and I saw the requisite twin oaks in the backyard. Actually, a portal could be between other trees than oak trees, but they were the most common. As we tumbled out of Herne's car, a sturdy man about five-five stepped out onto the porch of the house. It was neatly kept, small but tidy, and it looked as though he had put a lot of work into the upkeep. The yard was meticulous, which surprised me given he was half dwarf. Dwarves weren't known for their gardening skills.

Herne strode forward, holding out his hand. "Gatsby, I presume?"

"Aye, that's my name. Quest said you'd be on the way. I've got the portal ready for you. You'll come out in the yard of the portal keepers who own the lot next to the trailhead. They keep watch over it year-round. They'll have a vehicle gassed up and ready to go for you."

He didn't ask what we wanted, but that was no surprise. The portal keepers were there to serve, not to enquire beyond making sure of who was using the portal.

"Thank you kindly," Herne said. "We appreciate this. What are the names of your friends who will be waiting for us?"

"Niles and Leila Greentree. They're part of the Elemental Fae—forest dryads."

"I thought that dryads couldn't touch any form of metal, at least not easily," I said. I held up my hand. "Ember Kearney, at your service."

Gatsby grinned as he shook my hand with a firm, seasoned grip. "Nay, lass. I can tell why you might think that, but you're water Fae yourself, at least part of you. I can smell the ocean on you. You should know more about the Elemental Fae."

I shrugged, blushing. "Let's just say I'm not up on all of my kin."

"Well then, you have a thing or two to learn. Anyway, they'll have whatever equipment they could pull together. I see you've brought some of your own."

Viktor had been unloading the car, and I turned to see a pile of gear on the ground. Viktor began hoisting packs over his shoulder, and he handed me Serafina, my bow, and quiver of arrows, and my sword. I slung my bow and quiver over my shoulder and fastened the sheath for my sword around my waist on my belt. Herne fastened his sword around his waist, and he slung his own bow over his shoulder. Morgana and Merlin held out their hands and staves appeared, shimmering into their palms. Kipa picked up a large hammer from the pile and tested it against a rock, cracking it with one solid blow. He closed his eyes, and suddenly four wolves appeared, massive creatures that padded over to his side.

"You look ready to me," Gatsby said. "I wish you luck on your quest. I'll be here when you return and I'll take care of your car until then. You'd better keep the key, but if you have a spare one I can move it into the garage."

Herne unfastened a spare key from his keychain and tossed it to the half dwarf. "Thank you, Gatsby. We're ready."

I glanced overhead. "What time is it, before we go?"

"It's going on two, Ms. Kearney." And with that Gatsby held his hands out to the trees and between the oaks a large vortex appeared, crackling with brilliant blue energy. It sizzled and sputtered around us, and if I hadn't known what to expect I would have been afraid that I would be electrocuted. Instead, though, I had become an old hand at this. With Herne and me leading the way, we headed through the portal, followed by the others.

CHAPTER NINETEEN

I wasn't sure what to expect, but we came through onto a rough-and-tumble looking lot. As we stood there, sorting ourselves, a couple hurried to meet us. They weren't regular Fae. They reminded me of the Elves in Annwn. Niles and Leila Greentree were as ethereal as Gatsby had been solid and sturdy. But someone was waiting with them, and I immediately recognized Trinity.

"Welcome," Leila said, staring at me with wide eyes. But there was no judgment in her expression, simply surprise. "Gatsby said you'd need an SUV and some supplies. We have one ready for you. I hope that will work."

"As long as it can make it up Mount Bracken, we're good," Herne said. "Hey, Trinity."

I glanced at Herne, a question on my lips.

He glanced at Viktor, Kipa, and me. "Trinity knows the countryside all around here. I asked him to come with us. He's an excellent scout."

"And spy," I said, a faint smile on my lips. "At least this time we know why he's here."

Herne sighed. "I am not letting you run off to places like Fire & Fang without sending someone along I can trust."

"I was with Yutani," I said, narrowing my eyes.

"And I love Yutani, but he does carry chaos on his shoulders. He can't help his lineage, but the more it comes out, the more cautious we're going to have to be until he settles into his birthright. The Great Coyote doesn't deliberately trip up most people—well, some he does, but not most. But his presence alone brings havoc down on the shoulders of those he's around."

"Pardon me for interrupting, but Ms. Kearney, Trinity definitely knows the lay of the land around here. You're lucky he's with you," Niles said.

Trinity caught my gaze and flashed me a subtle grin. His long dark hair was caught back in a braid and I realized his heavily lined eyes were just normal—it wasn't eyeliner after all. He was wearing a pair of black and olive zebra–striped stretch pants, a black leather jacket that was fully zipped, and a pair of heavy steel-toed boots.

"You, I know." Trinity gave Viktor a nod. "How do you do?"

Viktor held out a meaty hand. "How do."

Trinity shook it, then said, "I'm Trinity. He/him, if you're wondering." He paused, glancing at Niles. "I'm ready."

"Do we really need a guide?" I asked Herne. It wasn't that I didn't want Trinity along, it was that Herne was… I paused in my thoughts. *Herne's doing what he feels is best as leader of the group.* It was too late to pull back my question, but I resolved to be a little less ready to jump on my boyfriend's back.

"Yes, you *do* need a guide," Trinity interrupted. "Trust me. Mount Bracken is haunted, for one thing, and for another, there are dangers there that you won't be likely to spot until it's too late. I can see the signs because I've traversed these mountains for hundreds of years. There are reasons why fifty-five hikers never returned from their day trips over the past fifteen years."

I fell silent, staring at Trinity. With a slow nod, I said, "Thank you, then, for agreeing to go with us."

Niles motioned for us to follow him. As we crossed the wide lawn, I looked around. The forest encroached on three sides. To the front, before a line of trees, the highway ran past. We were near the junction where Mt. Index Road turned off from the highway, right before a bridge crossed the South Fork Skykomish River.

"Just pull out onto the highway and turn right. Cross the bridge and a few moments later you'll come to the Chinook River Expeditions property. If you see their driveway, you've gone too far. Directly before you get to their land, there's a small access road that will lead you through the forest to a one-lane bridge over the North Fork Skykomish River. You'll come out on the Old Gold Bar–Index Road."

Herne was following on his GPS map. "Right, I see it."

"Turn left at the next turn. You'll approach the Lower Town Wall cliff, at which point you'll find another small access road to one side of the climbing wall. It will lead you to the top. From there, the access road bends northeast, toward Mount Bracken. Continue on. The drive should take about half an hour to reach a second access road—this one's marked Access Road 348. The going will be slow—the grade is steep and the road is full of potholes and rocks. The drive up the side of the mountain takes about thirty minutes. Be cautious. I chose a low-rise vehicle so you don't tip over from being top-heavy. If you forget my instructions, Trinity can lead you." Niles handed Herne the keys as we approached the SUV. It was a Subaru.

Herne motioned for Viktor to stow our gear, and we climbed in, with Kipa sitting between Morgana and Merlin, and Trinity and Viktor squeezing into the back. It would be a tight return with Raven, but I had the feeling Morgana could just blink herself back home if need be. We said our good-byes and headed out, across the bridge.

THE SKYKOMISH RIVER WAS POPULAR FOR RAFTING, AND kayakers abounded during the summer months when the water wasn't running high and dangerous. Salmon and trout filled the waterways, and fishermen lined the banks during fishing season.

There were two main forks to the river—the south and the north forks—and both had a number of tributaries branching off of them. Some of the stream names were evocative—like Troublesome Creek and Goblin Creek. The river was at the heart of an environmental controversy, with the local PUD wanting to build a hydroelectric project in the South Fork, and environmentalists and locals objecting that the project would destroy spawning grounds and disrupt the ecological balance of the area.

In the car, no one said much of anything, including Trinity. I glanced back, but all I could see was that he had taken out a tablet and was glued to something on it. I wanted to ask what he was doing, but decided to hold off.

We passed through the tall timber lining both sides of the river and sure enough, once over the bridge, it was only a short distance to the access road. Herne took a left, and we passed through a short patch of forest, coming out on the wide branch of the North Fork. There was a narrow one-lane bridge that led across a sand bar in the river to the Old Gold Bar–Index Road that ran parallel to a set of even older train tracks.

Crossing the tracks, we found the access road that led through the bare cliffsides that climbers referred to as the Lower Town Wall. The cliff face wasn't terribly high, but it was extremely steep and climbers came here to challenge themselves. We passed several of them who were crossing from the parking lot over to the base of the wall, roped up and ready to go.

The access road leading to the top, then past the Upper Town Wall—yet another more challenging bare cliff—wasn't well maintained, and as we chugged up the steep grade, I found myself grateful we weren't in Herne's Expedition. Any top-heavy vehicles could easily tip here, and roll down the embankment.

About three miles past the wall, we were headed up the back route to Mount Bracken, a jagged hill rising out from the treeline. I glanced up at the top. It was barren and bleak, with patches of snow left in places, and I realized it looked oddly familiar to me.

"I think…I've been here. The visions—we're nearing where they took place." I caught my breath, staring out of the window. "Why do you think Pandora brought her out here?"

Morgana looked up at Mount Bracken. "That would be a good place for—" She stopped, glancing back at Trinity.

"Say what you like," Trinity said, not even looking up from his tablet. "I'm not interested in much of what goes on outside my sphere."

Morgana paused, then shrugged. "It would be a good place for Typhon to settle when he comes in. Or for *other* dragons. I wonder…"

I felt an alarm go off in the pit of my stomach. "You think he's going to establish outposts?"

"It would make sense, wouldn't it?" Herne said. He paused, then said, "I'm going to just get something over with and out into the open. Trinity, heads up."

Trinity glanced up as I swiveled to see if he was paying attention.

"I brought you along for a reason other than to guide us," Herne said. "I'm going to fill the others in on who you are, so they don't feel like they're walking on eggshells. That is, unless you want to introduce yourself."

Trinity rolled his eyes and said, "Very well. I have no problem with telling you all. I'm Trinity, the Keeper of the Keys. I can unlock almost any lock, open almost any portal at will. Very little can keep me out—or in." He paused, then added, "Oh yes, I'm addicted to passion."

"He's a form of incubus," Herne said. "He feeds off sexual energy and creative energy, though if I remember right, you leave your victims alive."

With a snort, Trinity said, "My *victims*? Oh, they're *all* willing, trust me on that. They willingly give themselves to me and I leave them with no regrets."

"That depends on the person you're talking to," Herne said. "Anyway, Trinity's a valuable member of the team, and if we come to a locked door, chances are good he'll be able to open it for us. He's not going to give us away to the enemy."

"I work for myself and only myself," Trinity said. "I won't be used by a pack of flying lizards."

"That's what I thought," Herne said. "Anyway, continuing with our earlier discussion. My mother is correct. Typhon's children are returning even now. The vortex is slowly opening because he's waking, and so his children are able to return any time they like. There will be those who join with their father, and others who simply want to establish their own holds. The world will never be the same again. Pandora's most likely scouting for a stronghold, even while she tries to destroy those who could be an enemy against the forces of the dead."

The final push up to the summit reminded me of Hurricane Ridge when we'd rescued Rafé. One side of the road was tree lined, with straggly timber. The other side overlooked a steep drop off into the valley below.

The treeline ended at around forty-five hundred feet. Scrub took over from there, sparsely scattered around the massive batholith. The entire mountain looked like it had been the core of an ancient volcano, left standing when the sides fell away. More likely, it had been lifted out of the collision between the heaving tectonic plates that had birthed the Cascades. Whatever the geology, it was barren and stark and beautiful.

We parked. There was one other car in the parking lot, a sleek, black Jeep.

Morgana crossed to the car. She held out her hands

and closed her eyes. A moment later, she turned to us, her lips set in a grim expression. "Pandora's signature. And Raven's."

"We need to move. I doubt she knows we're coming, but you never know. If she does know, I wouldn't put it past her to kill Raven out of spite, to prevent us from finding her alive." I shouldered Serafina and my quiver, then fastened my sword, Brighid's Flame, to my belt. The sword was almost too long, but I had adjusted the sheath to slant backward rather than straight down, and as a result, I could carry the sword easily while walking.

Viktor slung on his own pack and mine as well—he carried my gear when we went out—and handed Herne and Kipa theirs. We all made sure of our weapons. Morgana and Merlin held out their hands and their staves appeared. Which reminded me...I fished around in the back and found my walking stick. Since I always ended up looking for one, anyway, I'd asked Herne to fashion me one that I could take with me each time. He had carved and polished a diamond willow bough that was five feet in length. Lightweight and sturdy, it did the trick.

We headed out onto the trailhead that would lead us to the summit. While there were some trees around, they were scattered quite a distance apart, but the scrub brush and wildflowers grew thickly among the long-bladed grass.

Herne and I took the lead, with Trinity by our side. Morgana and Merlin came behind us, and Viktor and Kipa followed behind them. We kept to the trail, which was compacted dirt, as we wound up the mountain. Kipa's wolves reappeared, and they kept pace, two to each side of our party.

The birds that inhabited the sub-alpine zone echoed their song as the afternoon faded into evening. I estimated the time to be around five. Up here, when the darkness fell it would be cold and lonely. I glanced around, trying to pinpoint anything that might look familiar from my dreams, but I couldn't pinpoint anything.

"Are there rattlesnakes up here?" I asked, glancing at Trinity.

"No," he said. "But there have been rumors of black widows, and the night hawks have been known to hang around here, come down from the Cascades."

"Night hawks?" Herne asked.

"They're similar to shadow people, caught between spirit and form. They're said to have faces like hawks, bodies of men, and their fingernails are the talons of the hawk. They prey on the unwary, and feed off warm-blooded creatures. Their favorite prey tends to be human, though Fae, Ante-Fae, and shifters will do in a pinch. They're powerful and ruthless. If you encounter them, don't let down your guard. To fight back, flood the area with light." Trinity glanced around, pointing out a patch of boulders nearby. "They hide in the shadows until dusk falls, and then they come out. A grouping of stones like that would be the ideal place for them to hide, so I suggest we move along."

Great. Black widows, spirits, and astral creatures hunting on the physical plane. Just what we needed. I turned back to the trail, focusing on the ever-steepening grade. The walking stick steadied my footing as I stretched my legs over a particularly wide break in the trail. The overhang I was scrambling onto was a good four feet off the ground. Trinity hopped right up as though it was nothing more than a street curb. He turned around and silently held out his hand.

I placed my fingers in his and instantly felt the pull of his magic. It was like a snake wrapping around my arm. He eyed me coolly as he began to pull me up. Behind me, Herne gave my butt a quick shove and I lunged forward, almost falling into Trinity's arms. He caught me, then let go as I steadied myself. Without a word, he turned and began striding up the trail. I quickly followed, trying not to let myself get unnerved as I glanced over my shoulder.

Behind me, Herne adeptly leapt up on the overhang, and Morgana seemed to just float up in the air and land on it. Merlin seemed to have no problem, either. I knew that neither Viktor nor Kipa would have difficulties and turned around to follow Trinity up the rocky path.

We were nearing the summit of Mount Bracken now, and I thought that maybe we'd luck out and avoid any unwanted interference, but the next moment Trinity paused, holding out his hand to stop us. He was listening to something, I could tell by the tilt of his head. After a moment, he quickly turned around, inching back down the steep slope. I leaned on my staff.

"What's up ahead?" I whispered.

"I don't know," he said, shaking his head. "I'm not sure, but I can sense something up there. Wait here while I—"

The next moment, a loud shriek came from behind one of the rocks to our left. A shadow flew out, hovering in the sky overhead. The sun was rapidly disappearing over the edge of the mountain, and the last rays of it caught the shadow, illuminating a fiercesome creature.

A *night hawk*. Bipedal, it had a head, but that's where

the resemblance to a person ended. The head was pointed at the chin, and its skull was rounded, the dome covered by the same leathery skin that seemed to cover the rest of its body. With arms as long as its feet, it hunched forward, the hump on its back rounded and knobby. Each of its hands had four fingers—two sets of two separated by a thick webbing of skin, with long, curved talons.

"Night hawk," Trinity whispered, backing up, raising his hands as his eyes began to glow with a golden light. "It can only be attacked when it's latched itself onto a person."

"Oh fuck, what are we supposed to do? Walk past it and give it a chance to attack us?" I cautiously edged my way back toward the edge of the trail. The rocks to the side, across the cliff face, were slick and even steeper than the trail, and there were a number of loose patches that could send an avalanche tumbling down the slope.

Herne pushed his way in front of me. "Let him attach to me. I'm a god, he can't harm me…much." He lunged at the night hawk, and the creature reared up, waving its arms, and then met his attack. They grappled, and then Herne let out a gasp.

"He's fastened onto me. Fuck, he hurts—I didn't realize…"

I had a sudden premonition that whatever this creature was, it was having more of an effect on Herne than he had thought it would. "Somebody help him!"

Kipa sprang forward, his wolves at his heels as we fell back. He landed on the night hawk's back and grabbed it by the scruff of the neck, trying to pull it off.

"It's sunk its teeth into his shoulder!" Kipa shot a glance at Trinity. "What can kill it besides brute force?"

"Blinding light will send it running, and fire can harm it." Trinity edged back, looking wary.

"Close your eyes," Merlin shouted.

I shut my eyes, turning away.

"Begone!"

The word thundered around us, as though Merlin had suddenly manifested a bullhorn. I could hear rockfall nearby, but I kept my eyes shut. I was glad I had because a second later, the feeling of brilliant warmth engulfed me, and even through my closed eyes, it was as though the sun had suddenly flared to life mere inches away. My skin felt hot and I realized I was instantly sunburned.

"There, that takes care of that," Merlin said.

Shaking, I opened my eyes and immediately looked for Herne. He was standing there, blood flowing from his neck, looking slightly dazed. Morgana moved to his side and placed her hands against the wound, whispering. A sparkle of light emanated from her fingers and Herne let out a sigh of relief as she backed away. The wound was still there, but it had partially healed. I had never seen Herne hurt in any significant way before, and the thought that there were creatures out there who could injure the gods themselves scared the hell out of me.

"I'm all right," he whispered as I threw my arms around him, looking up for reassurance. "I'll be okay. But if that thing returns, get out of the way. It would kill you and Viktor immediately."

He turned to Kipa, clapping him on the shoulder. "Thank you. You distracted it long enough for Grandfather to chase it away."

"Chase it away, my ass," Merlin said, arching his eyes. "I sizzled it to a crisp. But we must hurry. We don't want to attract any others. I don't have an inexhaustible supply of energy."

And so, we began the final climb to the summit of the mountain. As I followed Trinity, I wondered about him. Where had Herne met him, and was he planning on bringing him into the agency? Trinity seemed less than enthusiastic so I had my doubts about the latter, but I had learned to avoid assuming anything. Right now, though, all I wanted to do was rescue Raven. *If Pandora hasn't been working her over yet,* a voice whispered inside me.

"Please, no," I whispered, struggling over a patch of loose rock. But at that moment, Trinity motioned for me to join him as he stepped to the side. As I did, I found myself staring down into a crater-like valley. *The same valley I had seen in my visions.* As I realized that I was really here, I saw an opening to one side in the rock, far below, and I knew that we were about to go up against a goddess. And who knew what kind of protection she had with her?

CHAPTER TWENTY

I wanted to run down there, to barrel into that cave to find Raven, but I knew better than to act without thinking. I turned to Herne. "What now? I'm assuming she's down in that cave, since we saw the car in the parking lot and it had her signature on it."

"You're probably right." Herne glanced at his mother. "What do we do? You and Grandfather are our only defense against Pandora."

Morgana glanced up at the sky. "Pandora prefers to work in the darkness. Father?" She looked at Merlin. "Can you…?"

"I can, but it will drain me a great deal and I must prepare. You'll have to take over the assault." He raised his staff. "Are you ready?"

She nodded. "I am. Wait till I give the signal." She glanced at the rest of us. "Kipa, stay up here and keep an eye out until we call you. And don't argue. You're too emotionally involved in this. The rest of you come with me." She slowly rose up into the air, about a foot above the steep rocky slope leading down into the valley, and began to glide toward the center of it.

Herne turned into his stag form and I clambered up on his back. He began to race down the slope, following his mother, hooves barely meeting the ground. Viktor followed, nimble on his feet for his size, but the half-ogre was born and bred to wander the mountains and was right at home in this element. Trinity was making his way down the slope, and finally, Merlin followed his daughter's lead and levitated down to the valley.

As we neared the bottom of the valley, there was a movement by the pile of rocks that half-cloaked the cave entrance. I prepared myself, wondering what Pandora was going to send at us.

But instead of a golden-haired woman, two men stepped out from behind the rock piles. They were both pale as the moon, almost albino, with long white hair and glowing silver eyes. Taller than even the Fomorian giants, they were lean, and their hair swirled around them like capes. They were dressed in silver cloaks over ice blue trousers and shirts, and they looked like twins. One held a long spear, the other a wickedly sharp sword.

"Halt." The one with the sword pointed it directly at us. "Leave this place and we will spare you, but leave now."

I stared at them, trying to place what I was feeling. They were gorgeous, but there was a poisonous feel to them, as though anything that came in contact with them would corrode away. I slid off Herne's back and he turned back into himself. Viktor joined him and Morgana, while Trinity, Merlin, and I stood behind them.

"Send out your mistress while you can," Morgana said, her voice echoing through the barren meadow.

The men just stared at her, their expressions impassive. "She's not here. Leave. Now."

"We aren't going to leave," Herne said, stepping forward. "Your mistress is holding one of our friends. We want her back safely." His hand was on his sword.

"When Pandora returns, you'll wish you would have listened to us. Consider yourself duly warned," said the one with the spear. He raised his weapon, spear tip to the sky, and called out in a loud voice. A swirl of wind surrounded him and he rose up on it, one hand out toward us. Something was emerging from his palm. At first it was difficult to see what it was, but then, as it sailed toward us, I realized it was a twister. A vortex of wind, it spiraled our way, picking up loose rocks as it skittered across the floor of the barren valley.

"Cripes, it's a tornado!" As I yelled, Herne grabbed me and threw me to one side, sprawling over me. I couldn't see what was going on, but the vortex turned and it was bearing down on us.

"Hail prevail!" Morgana's voice cut through the evening as a band of hail, so harsh that it could cut our skin, sailed over our heads to pelt our enemies.

I peeked out from beneath Herne's shelter just in time to see the vortex of wind and the band of hail collide. There were sputters as both attacks died out. Herne jumped up, grabbing my hand and pulling me to my feet. He dragged me to one side. We were near the opening now.

"I'm going in there to find Raven," I said.

Herne shook his head. "Pandora—"

"Pandora's not here—you heard them. Will you be all right fighting them?"

"I hope so," he said, holding tight to my shoulders. "You know what they are, don't you?" He nodded back to the two men.

I shook my head. "No, I have no clue."

"White dragons. Vicious brutes who control the wind. Make no mistake, they will kill you if they catch you. So avoid them. And if something happens while you're inside, if for some reason—" He paused, the look on his face bleak.

"Don't say it," I whispered. "I'll find Raven and everything will be all right."

"If something happens, do whatever you need to in order to escape. I love you." He kissed me briefly then pushed me toward the opening.

I ducked behind the rocks, peeking out to see that Morgana was engaged in a battle with the dragons—wind versus water. I couldn't tell who was winning. I wondered why Merlin wasn't doing anything, but then remembered, he had said he needed to save his strength. Kipa was racing down the mountain, his wolves at his heels, and Herne and Viktor headed over to help Morgana as I ducked into the opening.

I TRIED TO CONTROL MY BREATHING AS MY EYES ADJUSTED to the darkness. I couldn't see a thing, not even the floor, and outside, they were fighting with the dragons. Nobody was going to come to my rescue. But the next moment, someone cupped my elbow.

I almost shrieked, but managed to stop myself. Freezing in place, I slowly exhaled, trying to place the scent. Then I knew who it was.

"Trinity? Is that you?" I kept my voice as low as I could.

"Yes, I'm here to help you. Herne sent me. I can see in the dark." He roughly grabbed my wrist. "Let me lead."

I had no choice. If it were just me, I'd have to either turn on my flashlight or turn back. I said nothing as he dragged me along, hissing a warning when we came to a rough patch in the tunnel, or when I needed to sidestep a hole.

As we hurried along to—well, I didn't know where we were going—I thought about the dragons that Herne and his mother were fighting. They looked as ruthless as Herne had described them. And then it occurred to me that we might find bigger, scarier dragons down here.

"Focus, damn it," Trinity whispered as I stumbled over a rock. "You may not be able to see, but I need you to pay attention." He squeezed my arm, shaking me out of my thoughts.

"Sorry," I muttered. I couldn't argue with him—I had been lost in my thoughts and I had slowed down.

We continued on. We were headed down a slope, deep into the earth. I tried not to think about how much rock-fall and dirt were piling up over our heads, but instead focused on Raven, keeping her firmly in my thoughts. We had to find her. I concentrated on putting my feet firmly one in front of the other as Trinity dragged me down the sloping incline.

A few moments later, he slowed, then squeezed my arm for me to stop. I could almost make him out now. My eyes had adapted to the dark, and I was also seeing his aura. It was brilliant green, like the green of leaves under the afternoon sun. I closed my eyes, trying to see if I could sense Raven's presence.

And there it was…I felt a shriek race past. Filled with pain and rage, it crackled with fire. *Raven's fire.* Feeling sick to my stomach, I tapped Trinity on the arm and whispered to him.

"I can feel her near."

"Look for light. Pandora works in the darkness, but she can't see to… She needs light to do what she does to her victims." Trinity paused, then said, "There, up ahead. My vision is blurring and it only does that in the dark, when light begins to cloud it."

We crept along until Trinity stopped me. "You're *still* making too much noise," he whispered. "If she's near, she'll hear you." Then, before I could say a word, he knelt. "Get on my back. I'll carry you. I can move far more silently than you can."

I didn't argue. I climbed on his back. He wrapped his arms under my legs as I held tight to his shoulders. I knew better than wrap my arms around his neck. I didn't want to choke him.

He started off again, as silent as a shadow. My thoughts drifted back to the surface, and I wondered how they were faring with the two dragons. But before I could get lost down that road, I forced my attention back to the present, to the darkness and Trinity, and to Raven who was somewhere down here, fighting for her life.

We must have gone another quarter mile when Trinity stopped. I blinked, realized that I was seeing a faint light from an opening to the side up ahead. I could see Trinity's silhouette now, so I leaned as close as I could to whisper to him.

"What do we do?"

He knelt again, letting me climb off his back. "You stay here while I sneak ahead and have a look." He began to creep forward. I leaned against the rock wall, snapping open the binding on my sword. With one hand on the hilt of Brighid's Flame, I waited, trying not to hold my breath.

As Trinity drew farther away, I could feel a shift. His energy had kept some of the darkness at bay, but now I could feel creatures swirling around me. They weren't corporeal. I didn't even know if they were *astral*, but I felt as though I had fallen into a field of writhing snakes. The air around me churned and I had to force myself to breathe. Whatever they were, the creatures felt as though they were suffocating me. I prayed they wouldn't notice me, because even at this point, I could tell they were dangerous and chaotic.

Trinity crept along the wall of the tunnel, and I realized that the grade had evened out. We were no longer sloping downward. I could barely see his silhouette, but his aura shone brightly. So, he was the Keeper of Keys. I wondered just what else he could do. All of the Ante-Fae were unique, all incredibly powerful even when they were young. Raven hadn't even begun to come into her powers yet and she could throw fire, as well as a number of other tricks. I wondered what she would be like when she was fully grown.

As Trinity stiffened, I felt a shift. I slowly withdrew my sword, waiting.

Another moment, and Trinity let out a shout as the tunnel lit up. Then, as the light dimmed, a tall woman with golden hair, wearing a PVC jumpsuit, swung around the corner. Her eyes were blazing with a crimson light, and she held out one hand, palm facing us, and laughed.

Trinity flew through the air, slamming into the opposite wall of the tunnel. The invisible force then found me, smashing me back against the wall and holding me tight. I struggled, trying to free myself, but I couldn't. The next moment, another wave came rippling through the air, and this time, everything went dark.

WHEN I CAME TO, I WAS CHAINED TO THE WALL OF A largish cavern. I was hurting—or at least my wrists were. They burned, feeling raw. I realized there was iron in the shackles. I winced, adjusting my arms so that they were in the middle of the shackles, barely touching the metal. If I moved in the slightest, my wrists would hit the metal rings and I'd get another jolt of pain.

I looked around, trying to figure out what the hell had happened. The walls were lit by globes of light, but they weren't overly bright—like forty-watt incandescent bulbs. I shook my head, trying to clear the cobwebs. A glance to my right showed me Trinity, also chained to the wall. He was alert and when he saw me staring at him, he gave me a solemn nod.

I glanced around the cavern. Mostly, there were just piles of rocks, and on the other side, I saw the exit back into the tunnel. There was another exit to my right, and if I gauged my distances right, it led out to the back side of Mount Bracken.

In the center of the chamber was a large metal table. I

caught my breath as I realized that Raven was lying on it, her legs and arms spread wide by shackles. There were pools of blood around the table, mostly near her face and hands, and her jaw was swollen and bruised. She was staring at the ceiling, moaning softly.

My stomach knotted. I wanted to talk to her, to ask how she was, but that might bring Pandora back in here.

I thought of tugging at the shackles, but I didn't want my wrists burnt, and right now they were already blistering. But soon my arms would get tired and the minute they started to drop, they would hit the sides of the shackles and burn even more.

I looked back at Trinity. The Ante-Fae weren't as hard-hit by iron, and he was wearing long sleeves, so he had some protection from the manacles. He caught my gaze and tentatively smiled. Grateful for the gesture, I felt like crying. I hated being helpless. When all control was stripped away, I had to face my vulnerability. Raven was obviously hurt, I could tell from the blood. And before long, I'd be burned too badly to do anything.

My sword, I thought. *Where's my sword?*

A glance around the cave told me that it was over against the other wall on a stone outcropping, along with my bow, and some other things that I assumed were Trinity's.

Drip. Drip. Drip.

The sound caught my attention. I looked around, trying to pinpoint it. There, against the other wall, near my weapons—a small trickle of water was slowly running down the rockface, pooling at the bottom. *Or was it?*

It was water all right, but as I squinted, I could see that

it wasn't pooling at the bottom, but rather flowing into a hole on the floor.

Frowning, I glanced at my wrists. I needed to go into trance, to try to see if there were any water elementals here, but that would require me to let go of my rigid stance. My arms would fester up once they rested against the iron. I tried to wiggle the sleeves of my jacket so they weren't pushed back by the shackles, but could protect my arms, but couldn't quite manage it.

I looked over to see Trinity watching me, a curious look on his face. I pointed to my wrist with my other hand and mouthed, "Need protection."

"Ah," he mouthed back, narrowing his brow. His gaze was focused on my hands, and before I realized what was happening, the sleeves of the jacket began to inch down my arms, folding themselves to fit through the shackles just enough so I could rest my arms without being too burnt. The pain was still there, but lessened and—for the immediate moment—I wouldn't be getting burned.

"Thank you," I mouthed.

I closed my eyes, relaxing my arms and pulling my focus inside. The sound of the dripping water seemed to grow louder, amplifying as I dropped further into trance. I narrowed my focus, homing in on the sound of the drip, the steady cadence as it dropped from the wall to the floor and slid through the hole. The rest of the world began to fall away as the sound reverberated in my mind. There was only the water, only the steady drip, only the liquid percussion.

Hello? I reached out, merging my consciousness with the essence of the water. *Is anyone there?* I listened, slowing my breath.

Then, slowly, echoing from someplace that felt so very far away, and yet so near, an answer came rushing past me.

I am here. We are here. Sister of the Water, what do you want?

I immediately realized that I wasn't dealing with a water elemental—the energy was different.

I'm trapped, my friends and I are being held captive. Where are you? Can you help?

A pause, and I thought for a moment I had lost contact. Then...

I am not yet fully in your realm. I am breaking through and will do what I can to help you, Sister of the Water. Hold tight.

Frowning, I waited, holding myself deep in trance. I imagined a light, a flowing blue light to guide the way. I wasn't sure who had been talking to me, or where they were, but the energy was friendly and I had to trust it. I knew that Herne would eventually show up, but would it be soon enough? Opening my eyes, I shifted focus so that everything was a soft blur as I waited.

A pale blue mist began to form on the wall near the water. I caught sight of it and poured all my focus into the energy guiding the mist as it began to grow and take shape. Whoever I had been talking to was there, coming through into our realm.

As the mist grew larger, taking the shape of a tall woman encased in swirling streams of turquoise and teal, there was a sound over by the entrance into the tunnels. I tried to hold focus, tried to keep my attention on the mist, but at that moment, Pandora stepped through into the cavern, a wicked grin on her face.

"Well, my pretties, you're awake. Time to play, children. Time to see what Pandora has in her toy box," she said, sliding the bag off from over her shoulder.

My stomach knotting, I jerked my attention back to the mist and the woman. She was growing stronger every moment, and Pandora hadn't noticed her. I wanted to give her time so I took a deep breath.

"You may be coming to play, but when I play, I never lose. What about a game, Pandora? Winner gives all?"

"Brave words for someone chained to my wall," Pandora said, smirking. She began to walk around the table toward me. I was shaking but the woman across the chamber was almost fully manifest. I had no clue who she was, but I knew she needed a little more time.

Trinity must have sensed the same thing because he hurked up a mouthful of phlegm and spit hard as Pandora walked by, the spittle landing on her chest.

"Got the money shot," he said, laughing gleefully. "How about it, doll? You and me? Next time it won't be my spit on your boobs!"

Pandora grew livid. "You insolent creature, how dare you? I'll teach you exactly what you get for that kind of insult!" But instead of reaching for Trinity, she grabbed my arm instead. She yanked me so roughly that the manacles pulled out from the wall.

I screamed as I felt something pop, and the next moment, found myself sailing across the room to land against a pile of rocks. Something gave in my hip as I landed, whether bone or a muscle, I didn't know. As the blinding pain hit, I tried to stand. The iron of the manacles was rubbing against my skin now, and I could feel welts beginning to rise up. I stumbled forward, landing near my sword and bow. I managed to get Brighid's Flame out of the sheath, all the while the iron searing my wrists with pain.

I crawled toward the table where Raven was lying, and Pandora turned, her eyes narrowing. As she held out her hand, a bolt of energy came shooting my way. I groaned, shifting, and managed to swing Brighid's Flame at just the perfect angle to deflect the attack. The bolt blasted the rock next to me. If it hadn't been for my blade, I'd be a splat on the floor. As I slumped near the edge of the table, Pandora snorted as she turned her attention to Trinity.

And then...everything shifted.

The woman stepped out of the mist, carrying a massive sword made of crystal. She raised it and her voice reverberated through the room.

"Before you take another step, Pandora, you must first go through me. I somehow expect you haven't fought a dragon before."

As Pandora turned around, her face paled and she backed up a step. At that moment, there was a noise at the door and Morgana, Herne, and Merlin rushed through, followed by Kipa. Kipa made a beeline for Raven as Merlin lifted his staff and brought it crashing to the ground.

"Shield!" Morgana screamed. I fell to the ground, hiding my face as Merlin's staff hit the ground.

"*Grian!*" he shouted, and a blinding flash filled the cavern. Pandora screamed long and hard, as everything else seemed to fall away.

CHAPTER TWENTY-ONE

*T*he world was spinning. My wrists were burning and one felt broken. I couldn't see. My hip throbbed and I felt adrift, floating on an endless sea of pain. I could hear, far away, the sounds of chanting and then another shriek racing through the wind, though this time I had no idea whether it was Raven or Pandora, or even me.

The ocean crashed, tossing me on the rocks, and I moaned, wanting the ride to be over. I kept looking for the way out, but all around me, the waves were rolling wild, washing the searing pain from my wrists all the way through my body.

I reached out, searching for help. Then, as I was about to give into the pain, a hand reached through the fog. The energy around it felt soothing and safe, so I took it, and instantly the pain began to subside. I exhaled softly, embracing the cool chill. As the waves of comfort folded around me like a blanket, I felt like I was surfacing, and the next moment, I opened my eyes.

I FOUND MYSELF STARING UP INTO THE FACE OF THE WOMAN I had seen forming in the mists. She was massive—as tall as Viktor, but lean and slinky, and her skin was pale, almost on the bluish side. Her hair was the color of the spring sky at morning, and she wore a silver circlet around her forehead. She was dressed in a dress that flowed out from her body, the color of ice with streaks of pale blue and plum running through it.

"Sister of the Water, you are alive." She reached out to stroke my cheek. "Your friend removed the instruments of torture from around your wrists." She reached out and placed a hand behind my back, steadying me as I slowly sat up.

I glanced around the cavern. Trinity was kneeling beside her, a set of keys in his hand. My manacles were on the ground, as were his.

"Raven? Is she all right?"

"Raven is hurt, my love. We're taking her back to Annwn so Ferosyn can help her," Herne said, coming up beside the woman and kneeling next to her. "Morgana and Kipa have taken her there. Trinity freed you from your shackles." He looked stricken. "I should have thought. I shouldn't have sent you down here alone."

"We thought Pandora was out. And you had to take care of those…" I paused, glancing up at the woman as I remembered that she had identified herself as a dragon.

"*Dragons*? Yes, Pandora has enlisted several white dragons to act as her servants. You may call me Ashera," the woman said. "I'm a water dragon—a blue dragon." She glanced at Herne. "Lord of the Forest, if you would allow me, I can move her to safety easier than you can, and with less pain to her."

Herne bit his lip, but he nodded. "Can you travel to Annwn?"

"Yes, and I promise you by my wings and tail, I will not harm your lady." Ashera held out her hand and Herne took it.

After a moment, he nodded. "Very well. How will you know where to go?"

"Trust me, I know my way into Annwn. You are headed to your father's palace?"

Again, Herne nodded. "Yes."

"We will meet you there. Tarry not. Merlin may have driven Pandora off for now, but she'll be back. And so will her guards." Ashera bundled me up in her arms and I was surprised by how the pain seemed to muffle when she touched me.

I started to ask her something, but she shushed me, and I found myself growing drowsy. I rested my head against her shoulder and the next thing I knew, I was falling back into the gentle fog that rolled in off the oceans.

I NEXT AWOKE IN A BED. I WAS IN A ROOM THAT WAS unfamiliar, but I knew where I was. I was in Cernunnos's palace. The feeling was unmistakable. I had a splint on one wrist, over bandages swaddling the burns, and more bandages on the other wrist. My hip ached, but I was able to ease myself up to a sitting position.

An Elfin woman was sitting near my bed, reading a

book. She glanced up as I shifted. The Elves never failed to daunt me. They were ancient and reserved, and it was impossible to read what was going on in their heads.

"You're awake," she said, moving quickly to my side. "Don't try to move too much—you have a lot of bruises and they're covered in salve. You don't want to wipe it off."

I cleared my throat. It was sore too, I realized. "My throat?"

"According to Lord Herne, you were screaming when he found you. Your throat will heal. I'll bring you some lemon and hibiscus tea with honey. Are you hungry?"

I blinked, trying to figure out exactly how I felt. "Yeah, I guess I am."

"I'll bring you some toast, as well. And I'll let Lord Ferosyn know you're awake." She bustled out of the room and a moment later, before I'd even had a chance to really look around, Ferosyn came in. Cernunnos's senior healer, the Elf was far older than just about anybody I knew—including Talia—but he looked young enough to be a Doogie Howser.

"Well, how's my favorite patient?" he said, giving me a jovial smile. Unlike most of the Elves, Ferosyn had a winning bedside manner. He flipped through my chart. "You have a nasty set of bruises on your hips, you have a sprained knee, which I've wrapped up, your arm was dislocated, and I put that back into place but you're going to be sore for a while. Your wrists have second-degree burns on them, and your right wrist is fractured. All in all, looks like a typical day's work for you."

I groaned, leaning my head back against the pillow.

"Raven? How's Raven?" I held my breath, praying she was still alive. I couldn't face it if she was dead.

"She lives. She'll heal up, but…" He paused. "Pandora tortured her. I'm pretty sure you know that. She'll need therapy. I hope she accepts it."

I closed my eyes, trying to breathe softly. "What did Pandora do to her?"

Ferosyn's expression darkened. "The Ante-Fae are strong, but Ravven is still young. And she's more sensitive than others of her kind. Pandora pulled out two of her teeth—molars. Needless to say, without any anesthetic. She also tore off five of Raven's fingernails. Those will grow back, but the pain must have been horrendous." He paused, looking queasy.

"What else?" I knew there was more.

"I'm not sure if it was Pandora who did it, or if she had someone else do it, but Raven has bite marks all over her body. Deep, painful, bite wounds. She's missing a bit of flesh from her left thigh, and another chunk from her stomach. I disinfected the wounds and packed them to encourage drainage. Both of her shoulders had been dislocated, and she has cigarette wounds all over her back. I've seen worse, but this was pretty bad. And it was done with thought as to how to make it hurt the most. That seems to be it. I've set her shoulders—they're back into place, but they'll hurt like hell. And I've cleaned all wounds and done my best to see that they don't leave scars."

"Not all scars are visible," I murmured, shutting my eyes, trying to block out the images that flooded my mind. "Is she awake?"

"Yes, she's awake. She hasn't said much. Kipa is with her right now."

"Good," I said, though it crossed my mind that Kipa might not have the best bedside manner. Though, when it came to Raven, he probably was in there doting over her. "I'd like to see her as soon as I can."

"That will be a few days. I want both of you to rest up here. Angel sends her love. Herne let her and the rest of your office know what happened. He's outside, waiting to talk to you, along with Ashera and Morgana."

I glanced down. I was in a white eyelet nightgown, which made me feel distinctly out of place, but I was decent. "All right. I'm ready."

"I'll show them in." He paused. "Do you need to talk to our counselor? You took some pretty rough damage there and generally, when Pandora hurts somebody, they're scarred both emotionally and physically."

I thought about it for a moment. I didn't feel scarred, so much as angry. Pandora had made herself an enemy, and while I had no idea what—if anything—I could do about it, I wanted revenge. For myself, for her victims, and mostly, for Raven.

"Nope," I said, shaking my head. "I'm fine."

Whether he believed me or not, I couldn't tell, but Ferosyn nodded and left the room. A moment later, the door opened again, and Herne, Morgana, and Ashera entered.

Herne was first to my side, and he gently sat on the bed, leaning in to give me a long, searching kiss. "My love. I'm so sorry, I'm so…" He choked on the words, tears in his eyes. "I should have known better than to let you go in there. I was such a fool."

I raised my left hand, wincing as the motion made the burns hurt like hell. But I reached out and stroked his face. "Herne, it wasn't your fault. The dragons said Pandora was out. We needed to find Raven, and you had to fight them. We did what we had to do, based on what we thought we knew. What happened to the dragons, by the way? Did you kill them?"

"They took some damage, but finally Mother called up a massive storm and chased them away with lightning bolts." He glanced at his mother. "She saved our asses. Dragons are a good match for the gods and while they can't kill us, they can do a lot of damage."

"The minute they left, we came after you," Morgana said. "We arrived just in time to see her attacking Trinity. Merlin chased her out with his blast of sunlight. Pandora works her best magic during the twilight or dusk. Bright light sends her scuttling for shelter, but it must be a light so brilliant that it would burn her."

"How is Trinity?" I said.

"He took a beating, but he's up and walking around. He came out better than you did." Morgana paused. "You're lucky you managed to contact Ashera."

I glanced over at the blue dragon lady. "I have no idea how that happened. How did you hear me?"

Ashera regarded me solemnly. "I felt your energy when I was spying on Pandora and Aso and Variance—the white dragons. They're twins, you know. A deadly pair who managed to slip through without us realizing it."

I blinked. "*Us*? Us...*who*?"

Herne pulled up a chair and sat down by my bedside. "It's rather complicated. Apparently, the core of the Dragonni—the dragon folk—are splintered in their opinions of what to do when Typhon returns. Ashera belongs to the Star Dragonni...she can explain it better than I can."

Ashera turned to me. "There are three factions among the Dragonni. First, the Star Dragonni are descended from the Celestial Wanderers. We are the blue dragons of the waters, the silver dragons of the stars, and the golden dragons of the sun. We do not believe in meddling in human affairs—and that goes for shifters, Fae, and the like. We almost always side with the Earth Dragonni, who are descended from the Mountain Dreamers. They're the green dragons of the earth and the black dragons from the deep caverns and high mountain crags. But...there are those who don't share our views."

"Let me guess," I said. "Fire dragons? Air dragons?"

She gave me a succinct nod. "Yes, actually. The red dragons of fire, the white dragons of the winds, and the shadowed dragons of the underworld are descended from the Luminous Warriors. They are born to conquer, and they thirst for power. They're willing to wage war to get what they want, where the Earth Dragonni and the Star Dragonni seek out realms and places that are free and open for holding. We're not pacifists, but neither do we believe in forcing others from their lands."

I struggled to take in everything she was saying. "So, the three factions—the Celestial Wanderers, the Mountain Dreamers, and the Luminous Warriors—all of you are descended from Typhon?"

"Yes, Typhon and Echidna—his wife. She vanished long ago and we've been looking for her ever since. Both Typhon and Echidna were born from the union of Tartarus and Gaia. But the Celestial Wanderers and the

Mountain Dreamers favor our ancient mother, while the Luminous Warriors stand by Typhon."

"Let me guess," I said, wincing at how sore my throat was. "Now that Typhon is returning, the Luminous Warriors are rising to stand by his side?"

"Yes. I am in an elite group of the Dragonni who are working against our more volatile kin. We cannot prevent them from entering your world, but we will be establishing lairs and working to prevent them from destroying the civilizations you have built up over the years. Now that I know they are already infiltrating, I can contact my superiors and we'll discuss ways in order to help you the best we can. I'll call on two of my Star Sisters to join me—one's a silver dragon, the other a gold."

I frowned. "How does water connect with the stars and sun? I'd think that your kind would be more akin to the... What are they? Mountain Dreamers?"

She smiled and her eyes spun like a kaleidoscope. "Oh, child, no. Water is controlled by the moon—the tides follow the moon's pull. The blue dragons are not only connected to the water, but to the Moon's influence."

"Well, we know one thing. We must figure out a way to repel Pandora for the long term. My grandfather's magic hurt her, but she'll be back. We can't kill her, but we have to put her out of commission for a long time," Herne said.

Morgana turned to him. "I know of one way, or at least my father does. Trapping her in stasis. If we can trap her in the Crystal Cavern in Annwn, we can keep her hidden and out of action for centuries. But that will take a great deal of planning."

"Not to mention, she's only one of the emissaries Typhon is sending. I'm afraid," Herne said, "that the world will never be the same. The tipping point will come soon. And there are more dangerous agents beyond Pandora. I fear what we'll see next."

Ashera sighed. "Well, you have the help of the Star Dragonni and the Earth Dragonni. And we are not lacking for power."

With that, they fell silent. Herne reached out and laid a hand on my arm, a worried look on his face. I wanted to cry. Everything around was changing so fast, and I was afraid he was right—it was going to get far worse before it got better. We needed all the allies we could get in this war.

Two Weeks Later: Walpurgisnacht—the Night Before Beltane...

Raven was home, and so was I. We had both stayed in Cernunnos's palace for over a week before Ferosyn let us leave. Now, we sat on the sofa in my living room with Herne and Kipa, and Angel and Rafé. Mr. Rumblebutt wouldn't leave me alone. I snuggled him tight, but I was still hurting, and my sprained wrist was still splinted. Ferosyn had put me on light activity only, and warned me that if I wasn't careful, I could develop a subdermal hematoma in my leg. Meaning, no rousing bed sports.

Raven's teeth were growing back in—the Ante-Fae had the ability to regrow teeth, and her hands were still bandaged until the nails grew back. Ante-Fae and Fae healed much faster than humans, so it wouldn't be long, but she had confided in me that she was sure to have a number of lingering scars, especially on her back.

Right now, though, we were all eating hot dogs and beans, thanks to Angel, and there was a cheesecake for dessert, and none of us wanted to talk about Pandora or the killings. All necromancers and mediums in the area had been warned to be on their guard, and they were flocking to the magical guilds, who had been ordered to allow them membership.

While Pandora hadn't shown up again, she would be back, we knew, and she would probably bring rein-forcements.

Kipa joined me in the kitchen when I went to replenish my soda. Ferosyn had forbade alcohol for either Raven or me until we were better, and so it was a dry Beltane. I didn't feel like drinking booze, anyway, and though we were all laughing and joking, there was an undercurrent of tension running through the room.

"Ember, can I talk to you about something?" Kipa asked.

I glanced up at him. "Of course. What's going on?"

"It's about Raven. I'm worried."

I nodded. "I know, but I doubt Pandora will target her again. She'll be gunning for all of us, especially Merlin, since he's the one who blew her socks off back on the mountain. And unlike Morgana, he's capable of being killed."

"That's not what's worrying me," Kipa said. "It's... She's *different*. She says she's fine, but I know she's not. She gets angry at me when I tell her to take it easy. She lashes out when I'm just trying to help her. I know I can be obtuse at times, but I'm *not* doing anything wrong. I'm trying not to hover, but I'm getting paranoid." He leaned against the counter.

"Ferosyn was afraid this might happen," I said. "He offered her a chance to meet with a therapist, but she refused. I think it's due to the lack of control she had in the situation. And also, Pandora hooked her in. Raven didn't have a clue she was talking to Pandora, and I think she's angry at herself. I think she blames herself for putting us all in danger." I paused. "Have you thought of talking to her mother? Phasmoria is pretty imposing. She might be able to take Raven in hand and help her."

"I'm afraid if I did that, Raven would never speak to me again. But it may be a chance I'll have to take. I know that I have to do something, because she's starting to act out. She didn't come home until four A.M. the other morning and when I asked her where she was, she wouldn't tell me. I know she's been hanging out with Trinity, and regardless of the fact that he helped us out, I just don't like the guy."

I could hear the catch in his voice. I rested my hand on his arm. "I know, Kipa. I know. I don't care for him myself. Give Raven some time. I'll talk to her and see if it helps."

As we rejoined the others, I couldn't help but wonder, though, how much Pandora had changed us all. Because I knew I had changed. And I knew without Raven telling me that she was desperate to regain control of her life, and Pandora's torture loomed like a gaping reminder that almost all control was merely an illusion to help us make it through the days.

I STARTED TO HELP ANGEL CLEAR UP AFTER KIPA AND

Raven went home, but Rafé took the stack of dishes from me and shooed me out of the kitchen. Herne swept me up in his arms and carried me up to the bedroom, with Mr. Rumblebutt racing along behind us.

As I curled up on my bed, I asked Herne to prop open the window. The warm evening breeze sailed through, but I could feel the promise of rain in the air, and I welcomed the prospect of wet streets and cloud-swept spring skies.

"Tomorrow's Beltane," I said.

"My birthday," Herne answered, lying back with his hands beneath his head. "I got a call from Viktor. Sheila's out of the hospital but she's scared to go back to work. She's moving in with him. I think it's a good thing. Oh, and Rafé has agreed to join the Wild Hunt as a clerk." He yawned and reached out to take my hand, carefully avoiding my wrists.

I took Herne's fingers, bringing them to my lips and kissing them. I wanted him, wanted all of him, but I wasn't sure if it was because I was horny or because I wanted some sort of desperate reassurance that things would be all right. He scooched up against the headboard and I rested my head on his shoulder.

"It's been a year since Angel and I came to work for the Wild Hunt," I said. "I've decided to get another tattoo. I have an appointment for tomorrow morning. What better time to get it than on Beltane?"

Herne glanced at me. "Really? What are you getting?"

"A crow, with outstretched wings. Your mother was right. I have to give in to my Leannan Sidhe blood. It's so much easier to accept my father's lineage. So I'm going to honor my mother and that side of myself with the tattoo, because it binds me to Morgana and to the sea. I feel I've earned it."

"You have," he said. "You're so much stronger than you were when I first met you, and I'm not talking about your body. That, too, but your courage and your strength. You put yourself on the lines for those you love. You ran toward that cave, not knowing what you'd find, in order to save Raven."

I nodded. "I have family now, and Raven's part of it. Angel, Talia, Viktor, Yutani, even Charlie. You're *all* my family. And I would fight to save any of you." I stared at my hands. "I know Kipa's worried about Trinity, but I think… I think Trinity can help Raven, even though he seems wildly chaotic."

"You might be right." Herne fell silent, his arm around my shoulders. He played with my hair, lightly toying with a strand of it.

The evening deepened, and outside, we could hear the frogs croaking. We had encouraged the critters to make their home in our garden, along with the dragonflies and bees, and birds. I closed my eyes as a light breeze hastened through.

Ashera had taken up residence on Bainbridge Island, a short ferry ride away, and she made it clear we were to keep touch with her regarding anything to do with Typhon or his emissaries. In fact, we were to meet with her come Monday to discuss the matter.

I let out a soft breath. "I love you, Herne. All I could think about when Pandora had me locked up was whether Raven was alive, and whether I'd see you again." I blushed. "I've decided to embrace my wild side. As soon as I'm healed up, I need to let my Leannan Sidhe side out where it's safe. With you."

"So you shall, love, so you shall. Your fierceness in love play won't hurt me. I look forward to it. I love it when you stroke me gently, and I'll love it when you thrash me around in the bedroom. I'm a good match for your temptress."

Then he lifted my chin and kissed me fully, his tongue lingering in my mouth, his hands firmly holding me to him. "There's one more thing," he whispered, sounding so serious that it made me sit up.

"What's that? Is something wrong?" I gave him a wary look.

"No, but it's Beltane, and I need to clarify something." Herne slipped off the bed and turned to face me where I was sitting cross-legged. He slid his hand in his pocket, then withdrew it, cupping something I couldn't see. Before I could speak, he knelt in front of me, on one knee.

"Ember Sabina Kearney, at the Winter Solstice, I gave you a promise ring carved from my own tine. Now, I want to make our promise a reality. My beloved, will you do me the honor of becoming my wife? Will you marry me?" He held out his hand, a ring box in his palm.

I stared as he slowly opened it. There, in the box, was a platinum ring with a square-cut sapphire in the center, and to each side were diamond and amethyst baguettes.

"Before you answer, remember this," he said. "If you marry me, it will be for life. You will become a goddess, like my mother did. I promise that I will never stray, never take a mistress, never deceive or lie to you. But you will forever be bound to me and my world."

"I…" I wasn't sure what to say. My heart screamed for

me to say yes, but my head warned me to think carefully before answering. "I *want* to say yes. I just…"

"You need time to think it over, and that time I give you. I'm in no rush, as much as I want you to wear my ring." He gently closed the box and placed it in my hand. "When you decide, either come to me wearing the ring, or come to me to give it back. You must be absolutely sure of your answer. And should you choose to say no, then we'll continue as we are."

And with that, he kissed me on the forehead and crawled back in bed. I stared at the ring case in my hand. It would be so simple to put on the ring now, so very simple. But Herne was right—it was a massive decision. And as much as I loved him, I wasn't quite ready to stand at that crossroad. I tucked the ring in my nightstand, and then we went back to cuddling.

Outside, the stars began to appear, and from some-where down the street, I could hear someone was having a party. Memories of Pandora kept flashing back in my head, but I did my best to chase them away. We were facing dark days, and even darker forces were coming against us. My friends and I were already caught in the vortex that Typhon was brewing.

But for now, we had a chance to heal and breathe. I squeezed my eyes shut tight and leaned into Herne's embrace. He began to sing, softly under his breath, and his voice chased away the shadows and pain, and staved off my fear that we'd lose our war against the coming onslaught.

If you enjoyed this book and haven't read the first ten books of The Wild Hunt, check out THE SILVER STAG, OAK & THORNS, IRON BONES, A SHADOW OF CROWS, THE HALLOWED HUNT, THE SILVER MIST, WITCHING HOUR, WITCHING BONES, A SACRED MAGIC, and THE ETERNAL RETURN. Book 12—WITCHING MOON—and Book 13—AUTUMN'S BANE—are available for preorder now. There will be more to come after that.

Return with me to Whisper Hollow, where spirits walk among the living, and the lake never gives up her dead. I've re-released AUTUMN THORNS and SHADOW SILENCE, as well as a new—the third—Whisper Hollow Book, THE PHANTOM QUEEN! Come join the darkly seductive world of Kerris Fellwater, a spirit shaman in the small lakeside community of Whisper Hollow.

I invite you to visit Fury's world. Bound to Hecate, Fury is a minor goddess, taking care of the Abominations who come off the World Tree. Books 1-5 are available now in the Fury Unbound Series : FURY RISING, FURY'S MAGIC, FURY AWAKENED, FURY CALLING, and FURY'S MANTLE.

If you prefer a lighter-hearted paranormal romance, meet the wild and magical residents of Bedlam in my Bewitching Bedlam Series. Fun-loving witch Maddy Gallowglass, her smoking-hot vampire lover Aegis, and their crazed cjinn Bubba (part djinn, all cat) rock it out in Bedlam, a magical town on a mystical island. BEWITCHING BEDLAM, MAUDLIN'S MAYHEM, SIREN'S SONG, WITCHES WILD, CASTING CURSES, DEMON'S DELIGHT, BEDLAM CALLING: A

BEWITCHING BEDLAM ANTHOLOGY, BLOOD MUSIC, BLOOD VENGEANCE, TIGER TAILS, and Bubba's origin story—THE WISH FACTOR—are available.

For a dark, gritty, steamy series, try my world of The Indigo Court, where the long winter has come, and the Vampiric Fae are on the rise. The series is complete with NIGHT MYST, NIGHT VEIL, NIGHT SEEKER, NIGHT VISION, NIGHT'S END, and NIGHT SHIVERS.

If you like cozies with teeth, try my Chintz 'n China paranormal mysteries. The series is complete with: GHOST OF A CHANCE, LEGEND OF THE JADE DRAGON, MURDER UNDER A MYSTIC MOON, A HARVEST OF BONES, ONE HEX OF A WEDDING, and a wrap-up novella: HOLIDAY SPIRITS.

For all of my work, both published and upcoming releases, see the Biography at the end of this book, or check out my website at Galenorn.com and be sure and sign up for my newsletter to receive news about all my new releases.

CAST OF CHARACTERS

The Wild Hunt & Family:

- **Angel Jackson:** Ember's best friend, a human empath, Angel is the newest member of the Wild Hunt. A whiz in both the office and the kitchen, and loyal to the core, Angel is an integral part of Ember's life, and a vital member of the team.
- **Charlie Darren:** A vampire who was turned at 19. Math major, baker, and all-around gofer.
- **Ember Kearney:** Caught between the world of Light and Dark Fae, and pledged to Morgana, goddess of the Fae and the Sea, Ember Kearney was born with the mark of the Silver Stag. Rejected by both her bloodlines, she now works for the Wild Hunt as an investigator.
- **Herne the Hunter:** Herne is the son of the Lord of the Hunt, Cernunnos, and Morgana, goddess of the Fae and the Sea. A demigod—given his

mother's mortal beginnings—he's a lusty, protective god and one hell of a good boss. Owner of the Wild Hunt Agency, he helps keep the squabbles between the world of Light and Dark Fae from spilling over into the mortal realms.

- **Talia:** A harpy who long ago lost her powers, Talia is a top-notch researcher for the agency, and a longtime friend of Herne's.
- **Viktor:** Viktor is half-ogre, half-human. Rejected by his father's people (the ogres), he came to work for Herne some decades back.
- **Yutani:** A coyote shifter who is dogged by the Great Coyote, Yutani was driven out of his village over two hundred years before. He walks in the shadow of the trickster, and is the IT specialist for the company.

Ember's Friends, Family, & Enemies:

- **Aoife:** A priestess of Morgana who guards the Seattle portal to the goddess's realm.
- **Celia:** Yutani's aunt.
- **Danielle:** Herne's daughter, born to an Amazon named Myrna.
- **DJ Jackson:** Angel's little half-brother, DJ is half Wulfine—wolf shifter. He now lives with a foster family for his own protection.
- **Erica:** A Dark Fae police officer, friend of Viktor's.
- **Elatha:** Fomorian King; enemy of the Fae race.

- **George Shipman:** Puma shifter. Member of the White Peak Puma Pride.
- **Ginty McClintlock:** A dwarf. Owner of Ginty's Waystation Bar & Grill.
- **Louhia:** Witch of Pohjola.
- **Marilee:** A priestess of Morgana, Ember's mentor. Possibly human—unknown.
- **Meadow O'Ceallaigh:** Member of the magic-born; member of LOCK. Twin sister of Trefoil.
- **Myrna:** An Amazon who had a fling with Herne many years back, which resulted in their daughter Danielle.
- **Rafé Forrester:** Brother to Ulstair, Raven's late fiancé; Angel's boyfriend. Actor/fast-food worker. Dark Fae.
- **Sheila:** Viktor's girlfriend. A kitchen witch; one of the magic-born. Geology teacher who volunteers at the Chapel Hill Homeless Shelter.
- **Trefoil O'Ceallaigh:** Member of the magic-born; member of LOCK. Twin brother of Meadow.
- **Unkai:** Leader of the Orhanakai clan in the forest of Y'Bain. Dark Fae—Autumn's Bane.

Raven & the Ante-Fae:

The Ante-Fae are creatures predating the Fae. They are the wellspring from which all Fae descended, unique beings who rule their own realms. All Ante-Fae are dangerous, but some are more deadly than others.

- **Apollo:** The Golden Boy. Vixen's boy toy. Weaver of Wings. Dancer.

- **Arachana:** The Spider Queen. She has almost transformed into one of the Luo'henkah.
- **Blackthorn, the King of Thorns:** Ruler of the blackthorn trees and all thorn-bearing plants. Cunning and wily, he feeds on pain and desire.
- **Curikan, the Black Dog of Hanging Hills:** Raven's father, one of the infamous black dogs. The first time someone meets him, they find good fortune. If they should ever see him again, they meet with tragedy.
- **Phasmoria:** Queen of the Bean Sidhe. Raven's mother.
- **Raven, the Daughter of Bones:** (also: Raven BoneTalker) A bone witch, Raven is young, as far as the Ante-Fae go, and she works with the dead. She's also a fortune teller, and a necromancer.
- **Straff:** Blackthorn's son, who suffers from a wasting disease requiring him to feed off others' life energies and blood.
- **Trinity:** The Keeper of Keys. One of the Ante-Fae. Mysterious and unknown agent of chaos.
- **Vixen:** The Mistress/Master of Mayhem. Gender-fluid Ante-Fae who owns the Burlesque A Go-Go nightclub.
- **The Vulture Sisters:** Triplet sisters, predatory.

Raven's Friends:

- **Elise, Gordon, and Templeton:** Raven's ferret-bound spirit friends she rescued years ago and now protects until she can find out the secret to breaking the curse on them.

- **Gunnar:** One of Kipa's SuVahta Elitvartijat—elite guards.
- **Jordan Roberts:** Tiger shifter. Llewellyn's husband. Owns A Taste of Latte coffee shop.
- **Llewellyn Roberts:** one of the magic-born, owns the Sun & Moon Apothecary.
- **Moira Ness:** Human. One of Raven's regular clients for readings.
- **Neil Johansson:** One of the magic-born. A priest of Thor.
- **Raj:** Gargoyle companion of Raven. Wing-clipped, he's been with Raven for a number of years.
- **Wager Chance:** Half–Dark Fae, half-human PI. Owns a PI firm found in the Catacombs. Has connections with the vampires.
- **Wendy Fierce-Womyn:** An Amazon who works at Ginty's Waystation Bar & Grill.

The Gods, the Luo'henkah, the Elemental Spirits, & Their Courts:

- **Arawn:** Lord of the Dead. Lord of the Underworld.
- **Brighid:** Goddess of Healing, Inspiration, and Smithery. The Lady of the Fiery Arrows, "Exalted One."
- **The Cailleach:** One of the Luo'henkah, the heart and spirit of winter.

- **Cerridwen:** Goddess of the Cauldron of Rebirth. Dark harvest mother goddess.
- **Cernunnos:** Lord of the Hunt, god of the Forest and King Stag of the Woods. Together with Morgana, Cernunnos originated the Wild Hunt and negotiated the covenant treaty with both the Light and the Dark Fae. Herne's father.
- **Corra:** Ancient Scottish serpent goddess. Oracle to the gods.
- **Coyote, also: Great Coyote:** Native American trickster spirit/god.
- **Danu:** Mother of the Pantheon. Leader of the Tuatha de Dannan.
- **Ferosyn:** Chief healer in Cernunnos's Court.
- **Herne:** (see The Wild Hunt)
- **Isella:** One of the Luo'henkah. The Daughter of Ice (daughter of the Cailleach).
- **Kuippana (also: Kipa):** Lord of the Wolves. Elemental forest spirit; Herne's distant cousin. Trickster. Leader of the SuVahta, a group of divine elemental wolf shifters.
- **Lugh the Long Handed:** Celtic Lord of the Sun.
- **Mielikki:** Lady of Tapiola. Finnish Goddess of the Hunt and the Fae. Mother of the Bear, Mother of Bees, Queen of the Forest.
- **Morgana:** Goddess of the Fae and the Sea, she was originally human but Cernunnos lifted her to deityhood. She agreed to watch over the Fae who did not return across the Great Sea. Torn by her loyalty to her people and her loyalty to Cernunnos, she at times finds herself conflicted about the Wild Hunt. Herne's mother.

- **The Morrígan:** Goddess of Death and Phantoms. Goddess of the battlefield.
- **Pandora:** Daughter of Zeus, Emissary of Typhon, the Father of Dragons.
- **Tapio:** Lord of Tapiola. Mielikki's Consort. Lord of the Woodlands. Master of Game.

The Fae Courts:

- **Navane:** The court of the Light Fae, both across the Great Sea and on the eastside of Seattle, the latter ruled by **Névé**.
- **TirNaNog:** The court of the Dark Fae, both across the Great Sea and on the eastside of Seattle, the latter ruled by **Saílle**.

The Force Majeure:
A group of legendary magicians, sorcerers, and witches. They are not human, but magic-born. There are twenty-one at any given time and the only way into the group is to be hand chosen, and the only exit from the group is death.

- **Merlin, The:** Morgana's father. Magician of ancient Celtic fame.
- **Taliesin:** The first Celtic bard. Son of Cerridwen, originally a servant who underwent magical transformation and finally was reborn through Cerridwen as the first bard.
- **Ranna:** Powerful sorceress. Elatha's mistress.
- **Rasputin:** The Russian sorcerer and mystic.
- **Väinämöinen:** The most famous Finnish bard.

The Dragonni:

- **Typhon:** The Father of Dragons (born of the Titans Gaia and Tartarus)
- **Echidna:** The Mother of Dragons (born of the Titans Gaia and Tartarus)

The Celestial Wanders (Blue, Silver, and Gold Dragons):

- **Ashera:** A blue dragon.

The Mountain Dreamers (Green and Black Dragons):
The Luminous Warriors (White, Red, and Shadow Dragons):

- **Aso:** White Dragon, bound to Pandora, twin of Variance.
- **Variance:** White Dragon, bound to Pandora, twin of Aso.

TIMELINE OF SERIES

Year 1:

- May/Beltane: **The Silver Stag** (Ember)
- June/Litha: **Oak & Thorns** (Ember)
- August/Lughnasadh: **Iron Bones** (Ember)
- September/Mabon: **A Shadow of Crows** (Ember)
- Mid-October: **Witching Hour** (Raven)
- Late October/Samhain: **The Hallowed Hunt** (Ember)
- December/Yule: **The Silver Mist** (Ember)

Year 2:

- January: **Witching Bones** (Raven)
- Late January–February/Imbolc: **A Sacred Magic** (Ember)
- March/Ostara: **The Eternal Return** (Ember)
- May/Beltane: **Sun Broken** (Ember)

PLAYLIST

I often write to music, and SUN BROKEN was no exception. Here's the playlist I used for this book. You'll notice I've taken a definite turn in my listening for writing.

- **Air:** Moon Fever; Playground Love; Napalm Love
- **Airstream:** Electra (Religion Cut)
- **Band of Skulls:** I Know What I Am
- **Ben Howard:** Esmerelda; Oats in the Water; To Be Alone; Burgh Island
- **The Black Angels:** Currency; Hunt Me Down; Death March; Indigo Meadow; Don't Play With Guns; Always Maybe; Black isn't Black
- **Black Mountain:** Queens Will Play; Buried by the Blues
- **Brandon & Derek Fiechter:** Night Fairies; Toll Bridge; Will-O'-Wisps; Black Wolf's Inn; Naiad River; Mushroom Woods
- **The Bravery:** Believe

- **Broken Bells:** The Ghost Inside
- **Camouflage Nights:** (It Could Be) Love
- **Colin Foulke:** emergency
- **Crazy Town:** Butterfly
- **Danny Cudd:** Double D; Remind; Once Again; Timelessly Free; To The Mirage
- **David Bowie:** Golden Years; I'm Afraid of Americas; Let's Dance; Sister Midnight
- **Death Cab For Cutie:** I Will Possess Your Heart
- **Dizzi:** Dizzi Jig; Dance of the Unicorns; Galloping Horse
- **DJ Shah:** Mellomaniac
- **Don Henley:** Dirty Laundry; Sunset Grill; The Garden of Allah; Everybody Knows
- **Eastern Sun:** Beautiful Being
- **Eels:** Love of the Loveless; Souljacker Part 1
- **Eminem:** I'm Back
- **Faun:** Hymn to Pan; Punagra; Sieben
- **FC Kahuna:** Hayling
- **The Feeling:** Sewn
- **Flora Cash:** You're Somebody Else
- **Fluke:** Absurd
- **Foo Fighters:** The Pretender; Come Alive; All My Life
- **Foster The People:** Pumped Up Kicks
- **Garbage:** Queer; Only Happy When It Rains; #1Crush; Push It; I Think I'm Paranoid
- **Gary Numan:** Dominion Day; Prophecy; Dead Heaven; Hybrid; Cars; Soul Protection; Confession; My World Storm; Dream Killer; Petals; Ghost Nation; My Name Is Ruin; Pray For The Pain You Serve; I Am Dust

- **Godsmack:** Voodoo
- **The Gospel Whisky Runners:** Muddy Waters
- **The Hang Drum Project:** Shaken Oak; St. Chartier
- **Hang Massive:** Omat Odat; Released Upon Inception; Thingless Things; Boat Ride; Transition to Dreams: End of Sky; Warmth of the Sun's Rays; Luminous Emptiness
- **Hedningarna:** Ukkonen
- **The Hu:** The Gereg; Wolf Totem
- **Imagine Dragons:** Natural
- **In Strict Confidence:** Snow White; Tiefer
- **J Rokka:** Marine Migration
- **Jessica Bates:** The Hanging Tree
- **Lorde:** Yellow Flicker Beat; Royals
- **Low:** Witches; Nightingale; After Hours; Plastic Cup; Half-Light
- **Many Rivers Ensemble:** Blood Moon; Oasis; Upwelling; Emergence
- **Marconi Union:** First Light; Alone Together; Flying (In Crimson Skies); Always Numb; Time Lapse; On Reflection; Broken Colours; We Travel; Weightless; Weightless Pt. 2; Weightless Pt. 3; Weightless Pt. 4; Weightless Pt. 5; Weightless Pt. 6
- **Matt Corby:** Breathe
- **Nirvana:** Lithium; About A Girl; Come As You Are; Lake of Fire; You Know You're Right
- **Orgy:** Social Enemies; Orgy
- **Pati Yang:** All That is Thirst
- **Red Venom:** Let's Get It On

- **Rue du Soleil:** We Can Fly; Le Francaise; Wake Up Brother; Blues Du Soleil
- **Screaming Trees:** Where The Twain Shall Meet; All I know
- **Shriekback:** The Shining Path; Underwater Boys; Over the Wire; This Big Hush; Agony Box; Bollo Rex; Putting All The Lights Out; The Fire Has Brought Us Together; Shovelheads; And the Rain; Wiggle & Drone; Now These Days Are Gone; The King in the Tree
- **Spiderbait:** Shazam!
- **Tamaryn:** While You're Sleeping, I'm Dreaming; Violet's In A Pool
- **Thomas Newman:** Dead Already
- **Tom Petty:** Mary Jane's Last Dance
- **Trills:** Speak Loud
- **Tuatha Dea:** Tuatha De Danaan
- **The Verve:** Bitter Sweet Symphony
- **Vive la Void:** Devil
- **Wendy Rule:** Let the Wind Blow
- **Yoshi Flower:** Brown Paper Bag

BIOGRAPHY

New York Times, Publishers Weekly, and USA Today
bestselling author Yasmine Galenorn writes urban fantasy
and paranormal romance, and is the author of more than
sixty-five books, including the Wild Hunt Series, the Fury
Unbound Series, the Bewitching Bedlam Series, the
Indigo Court Series, and the Otherworld Series, among
others. She's also written nonfiction metaphysical books.
She is the 2011 Career Achievement Award Winner in
Urban Fantasy, given by RT Magazine.

Yasmine has been in the Craft since 1980, is a
shamanic witch and High Priestess. She describes her life
as a blend of teacups and tattoos. She lives in Kirkland,
WA, with her husband Samwise and their cats. Yasmine
can be reached via her website at Galenorn.com.

Indie Releases Currently Available:

The Wild Hunt Series:
The Silver Stag

Oak & Thorns
Iron Bones
A Shadow of Crows
The Hallowed Hunt
The Silver Mist
Witching Hour
Witching Bones
A Sacred Magic
The Eternal Return
Sun Broken
Witching Moon
Autumn's Bane

Whisper Hollow Series:

Autumn Thorns
Shadow Silence
The Phantom Queen

Bewitching Bedlam Series:

Bewitching Bedlam
Maudlin's Mayhem
Siren's Song
Witches Wild
Casting Curses
Demon's Delight
Bedlam Calling: A Bewitching Bedlam Anthology
The Wish Factor (a prequel short story)
Blood Music (a prequel novella)
Blood Vengeance (a Bewitching Bedlam novella)
Tiger Tails (a Bewitching Bedlam novella)

Fury Unbound Series:

Fury Rising
Fury's Magic
Fury Awakened
Fury Calling
Fury's Mantle

Indigo Court Series:

Night Myst
Night Veil
Night Seeker
Night Vision
Night's End
Night Shivers
Indigo Court Books, 1-3: Night Myst, Night Veil, Night Seeker (Boxed Set)
Indigo Court Books, 4-6: Night Vision, Night's End, Night Shivers (Boxed Set)

Otherworld Series:

Moon Shimmers
Harvest Song
Blood Bonds
Otherworld Tales: Volume 1
Otherworld Tales: Volume 2
For the rest of the Otherworld Series, see website at Galenorn.com.

Chintz 'n China Series:

Ghost of a Chance
Legend of the Jade Dragon
Murder Under a Mystic Moon
A Harvest of Bones

One Hex of a Wedding
Holiday Spirits
Chintz 'n China Books, 1 – 3: Ghost of a Chance,
Legend of the Jade Dragon, Murder Under A
Mystic Moon
Chintz 'n China Books, 4-6: A Harvest of Bones, One
Hex of a Wedding, Holiday Spirits

Bath and Body Series (originally under the name India Ink):
Scent to Her Grave
A Blush With Death
Glossed and Found

Misc. Short Stories/Anthologies:
Once Upon a Kiss (short story: Princess Charming)
Once Upon a Curse (short story: Bones)

Magickal Nonfiction:
Embracing the Moon
Tarot Journeys